Accepting All Comers

SMALL TOWN SWINGERS CLUB
BOOK 2

Accepting All Comers

DIXON AHL-KNIGHT

4 Horsemen
Publications, Inc.

Dedication

To Erika L. and Erika F., the Erikas
who tolerate my dirty books and prod
me to do even more! I couldn't do
it without your support!

Contents

Chapter 1

What a stroke of luck! I had just decided to rent rooms in my house when I saw Rachel's post on social media. Rachel Mortenson was a fellow teacher at Waterton High School and the varsity girls basketball coach. She was a good friend, and she and her wife were instrumental in making sure my life didn't collapse around me after the accident. It also helped that Rachel knew basketball so well. We could bond over that. We were both former Division III players and total basketball geeks. So, I immediately reached out to her when I saw her social media post about a friend who needed a rental house. Rachel called me back almost immediately.

"Matt, I'm so glad you reached out. I didn't even think how perfect this might be, but Monica Richardson and her husband are divorcing, and she is looking for a rental. Your house might be perfect for her. You are close to where she lives now, and although her kids are in college, you have room for them if they visit."

I was amazed. I had discussed my plan for renting out my four-bedroom house with Rachel, but I meant it as an income property. I intended to move out of it first. She seemed to think I wanted roommates. That possibility hadn't occurred to me, but now that I thought about it, it might be a good change. However, I didn't know Monica well at all. There was a joke at school about how we had Monica and Rachel as coaches; now, all we needed was Ross and Chandler to join. Monica wasn't a teacher, so I didn't know much about her, except for two things. She was the varsity volleyball coach at our school and was the only woman to get my heart racing and my dick hard since I lost my wife. I had only seen her a few times, but every time, I was blown away by her. And I couldn't tell you why, exactly. I mean, yes, I could tell you that she was unbelievably pretty, with eyes so blue the sky was jealous, and that her long blonde hair flowed down her back in a way that demanded you follow it and admire the volleyball player's body she hadn't lost over the last 20 years.

But it was more than all of that. She was kind and nurturing, but serious, which makes sense for a coach. She also had this "I'm no big deal, just a mom and wife in small-town Iowa" kind of humility. She seemed gorgeous and mysterious but very down-to-earth at the same time.

And, of course, married.

I had asked Rachel about Monica after seeing the two of them talking in the school office, thinking she was a new teacher.

Rachel laughed at me and said, "Matt, that's Monica Richardson. Our volleyball coach. She's been here for three years. Both of her kids graduated in the last couple of years. She and her husband have been friends of mine for a while now. You need to get out more."

When I heard she had a husband, the punch to my gut was very foreign. I was surprised that it upset me. I hadn't thought about being with any woman in months, and now, all of a sudden, some woman I saw for ten seconds had me feeling jealous and all sorts of other emotions.

Now, on the phone, hearing that Monica was getting divorced, I tried to hide my emotions and play it cool with Rachel.

"Jeez, Rachel, I have never considered renting to just one person. But if she needs a place, I have a lot of room. After the renovations, I now have five bedrooms, and four are empty. So, give her my number, and she can call or text me about it."

I had renovated my four-story house after the accident. The upper level had four bedrooms, the main level had a kitchen and living room, the lower level had a large den area, and the basement was large and finished. So, I had a lot of room. I had intended to sell it, but after I turned the den area into a huge main suite, I couldn't bring myself to do it. I converted the basement into a mancave with a wet bar, so now the house had five bedrooms and two generous living areas. I felt that if I needed to, I could rent the upper level out to a family or four separate people and make a killing in rent money. Hell, I wasn't going to turn down the income!

I sure as hell never considered sharing the house with the one woman I had a massive crush on, however. Sharing my house with strangers sounded awkward; sharing it with Monica might elevate the awkwardness about 20 levels. But this was putting the cart before the horse. Monica might not be interested in renting from me, and maybe already had a place. I would play it by ear and didn't expect to hear from Monica for some time.

My phone *immediately* vibrated with an incoming text. I had only hung up with Rachel three minutes before! I swear that when you think nothing will come of a dilemma, something happens immediately. Monica must have texted me as soon as Rachel texted her my number!

Her text was a simple message saying she was interested and would like to meet and see the house.

I told her I was around through Friday, and she said she could come over immediately. I gave her the address, and she said she would be right over.

And just like that, I would meet Monica and see if she wanted to live with me. I couldn't believe it. A part of me hoped that this meeting might cure my crush on her. Maybe she wouldn't look gorgeous, have a terrible sense of humor, or decide to pass after not liking the house and me. Then it would all be over.

Nope.

She showed up, looked gorgeous, and was easy to talk with. She loved the old main bedroom, how close the house was to her ex-husband for her kids' sake, and my renovations. She was all business but still fun and friendly. I was … in love!

I'm kidding.

Kind of.

I hadn't lost my head completely. But, hell, I couldn't believe how I felt around her. And, how tight my pants seemed to fit with her around! I worried that she could see the lump in my pants.

"So, how much?" she asked.

"What?" I asked, completely lost in my erect thoughts.

"How much do you want for monthly rent?"

"Oh, I hadn't considered a single person renting. I thought $1,200-$1,500 monthly for a whole family to rent the house. What are you thinking? I certainly want to make this easy for you through this transition."

"I appreciate that. How about we say $400 a month for me and then work out something more if the kids are ever here long term? They are away at college and might stay at my ex's house if they visit. My daughter, Ashlynn, is a freshman at Pitt, and my son, Nick, is a sophomore at Notre Dame, but we haven't discussed what happens when they come home yet."

She paused.

"Sorry, I'm babbling. Suffice it to say, it will just be you and me."

This was a fair bargain, and the "you and me" comment was unfair to my throbbing erection.

She added, "And let's go month to month because I don't know how long I'll be here."

"Of course," I said. "Besides, a woman as attractive as you will have plenty of better men to stay with."

I immediately regretted what I had said. Talk about a non sequitur! I tried to be funny, but it was a stupid and somewhat insensitive line. I was more nervous and caught up in my attraction to Monica than I thought. Before anything else was said, I quickly apologized.

"Sorry. That was a bad joke; it didn't come out right."

"So, you don't think I'm attractive?" she asked.

"No. Not that part. I think you are super attractive. I mean, I think you would be a catch for anyone lucky enough … shit, I'm just digging a deeper hole here. Back to talking about the rent! Yes, to the $400, and you can move in whenever. We can pro-rate this month, and then I can pay you a penalty anytime I say awkward things, like just now!"

She laughed and put out her hand. "Deal."

Then, she half whispered, "It was cute to see you squirm like that."

I think I blushed. I felt like I had a neon sign above me proclaiming, "I like you! I really, really like you!!"

Ugh.

She smiled and said, "Great. I'll start moving in on Saturday, if that works?"

"Yeah, if it is in the afternoon. I'm gone Saturday morning."

"Sounds good. I am running a volleyball camp on Saturday morning. 1:00?"

"Sounds great. I can't wait," I answered.

With that, she thanked me and left.

What had just happened? I had decided this morning to rent out my house. Now, an hour later, I had a roommate—an extremely gorgeous roommate who made sensible conversation difficult for me. This was going to make the school year very interesting.

Chapter 2

I'm an avid biker and love to pedal throughout the summer break. After Monica left, I put in 20 miles, hoping to get my mind off things. My road bike, with a carbon fiber frame, is my baby, and the urge to distract myself powered me on my 20-mile loop around the town. Well, at a distance around the town. A loop directly around this town would only be about six miles. I add some county roads, get some hills in, and usually feel great afterward.

Today, I returned sweaty and feeling well-exercised. I jumped into the shower and felt good as the water hit my tired muscles. I stood in the stream, letting it hit my back, and thoughts of Monica crept back into my head. I absent-mindedly started to touch my penis. It immediately got hard, and the thoughts of Monica consumed me.

"Matt, I'm here to move in. However, I was thinking of just sleeping with you every night instead. Show me to that bedroom, please. Oh, this is nice but a little warm. It would be cooler if we took our clothes off. That's better. Oh, you seem to have quite an impressive erection! I sure haven't seen that in a long time. My ex-husband's small cock couldn't get hard without medical help. And trust me, it never lasted four hours. Let me see if I can help you get rid of this. Oh, you are incredibly hard in my hand. Is it

okay that I am stroking it like this? Yes? Here, let me get a closer look by getting on my knees. Oh, that's better. And I may need both hands for this length. Very impressive. But I wonder what it tastes like. Do you mind if I put my mouth around it? No? Umm, that tastes great. Your big head fits perfectly. Let me spend some time with it and see if I can get it down my throat. Wow, that was fantastic, but you still haven't come yet! Maybe it needs to be down my throat while I play with your balls. Here goes."

And there I went. I exploded with a grunt in the shower. I sprayed rope after rope of my semen on the back wall. My worn-out legs buckled, and I lost my balance for a second. I stood in the shower gasping for air and trying to come down after one of the most powerful orgasms I had ever given myself.

Jeez, what the hell would I be like when Monica was here in two days?

Honestly, these kinds of feelings were foreign to me. I dated off and on in high school, met Robyn at age 18, and then got married at 21. I hadn't felt this way, except with Robyn, 16 years ago. I didn't know how on earth to do any of this!

Should I hide my feelings or declare them?

No, telling Monica about my feelings now seemed the wrong time and place. She was coming off a fresh divorce. Hell, she may not be officially divorced yet. Having not reacted to a woman like this in a long time, there was so much I was unsure of, which told me to play the role of gracious host. I decided to go for the slow game.

Slow game! That made me laugh. I had no "game" to speak of! I had been a widower for a year and married for almost 20 years before that. I didn't even know what the dating game was anymore.

Plus, there was another problem: small and gossipy Waterton, Iowa. The whole town would know if one person knew I was interested in Monica. The news she was renting a room from me was only a couple of hours old and was probably already going around town as gossip. People might already think we were an item. I couldn't wait for all of the questions over the next month. People would think I was a homewrecker. They would think Monica ran away from her husband because of her passionate love for me. And I would have to tell them that not only was that all wrong, but I had only met the woman when she needed a room. I would have to tell them I had only known her for two weeks.

So now, I only had to let Monica into my home while making sure not to admit my feelings for her, all while trying to keep the small-town gossip from spreading like wildfire. I am glad Waterton is so safe and clean, but I could do without the gossip and questions. Keeping my romantic feelings for Monica a secret would be challenging if my neighbors were constantly asking me if I had them. Ugh. This may not be a good idea. This could be one big backfire for both of us.

I was starting to feel anxious.

But then, I thought about this whole thing from a parent's perspective. Monica was surely struggling with many things right now as her life changed. One of the biggest would be how her kids would be affected by the divorce and changes. As I thought about how I would have done anything for my kids, I realized that this closeness to her ex might alleviate some parenting worries. Plus, she had the same path to work, so her daily commute (a hilarious term to use for Waterton) would not change. That might be helpful.

Plus, I was reacting as if she had signed a hard two-year lease with me. Our deal was informal, and she might only be here for a few weeks.

I had no clue what the town thought of this divorce. Maybe they wouldn't even care that much. Hell, maybe I didn't need to care that much about what they thought. I sure didn't after the accident. Some wanted me to start dating again, and some seemed to want me to be in perpetual mourning. No one, except Rachel and my closest friends scattered around the country, told me to take it at my own pace and do what was good for me. I even remembered a conversation with a fellow teacher at the high school, Deborah Valentine, about how you need to be on the same page as your partner, especially as a working adult far along in your career. Deborah and her husband, Lane, seemed very much on the same page as we talked.

I don't know why that conversation with Deborah popped into my head—maybe because Deborah and Rachel were friends—but here, a few weeks later, it seemed as if it had foreshadowed a big change in my life!

So, two days later, on a beautiful August Saturday afternoon, Monica showed up at my door with an SUV full of stuff parked in my driveway. She didn't have as many things as I thought she would, and I told her as much. She laughed and told me this was load number one—the important stuff for everyday living. For now, much of her stuff was going into a storage unit.

"I'm just so unsure; I don't want to move everything now and then decide I'm living somewhere else in six weeks."

"Makes sense," I said.

"Oh, I forgot to ask; I saw a bed and furniture in that room when I was over the other day. May I use it?"

"Yes," I said. "Every room had a queen bed and dresser, so I left them all and bought a new bed and furniture for the new main suite. So, you and your kids don't have to worry about that."

"Thank you so much. I don't know how to express how much I appreciate this. All of this feels so deadening. I'm just treating everything like logistics at this point. I know I haven't allowed myself to feel through my emotions, but this eases the load a lot," she said.

"I know exactly what you mean. I assume you know why I am in this big house by myself?"

"Not really. Rachel told me that you would tell me if you wanted to," Monica said a little sheepishly.

"Oh, she did, huh?" I asked and laughed. "Well, if you are going to live here, you deserve to know."

I hoped to keep this short but didn't know if I could.

"The last 13 months of my life have been traumatic and taxing. It started in July of last year. My father, who had been fighting cancer for months, finally lost his fight. This left me without any immediate family, save my wife and kids. I was an only child who had lost both parents to cancer before I had turned 40 years old. The one saving grace about my dad's death was that we had time. Time to plan, time to get his affairs in order, and time to say goodbye. I mention this because there was also a large inheritance coming my way, and Robyn, my wife, and I decided to put that away and use it for our kids when they were older. This was the only silver lining in the situation with my dad. Especially with my family history, now my wife and kids would be taken care of forever, even if something happened to me."

Monica looked at me with a very concerned and attentive face but said nothing. I hoped she would say something to break up my story, but it didn't happen.

I continued, "Unfortunately, it wasn't me that something happened to. We never could have anticipated what would happen just 32 days after my dad died."

Now Monica looked at me with curiosity and sadness, and I couldn't quite take it. I hurriedly continued with my story, hoping to make it to the finish line without losing it.

"I'm a high school science teacher, and Robyn and the kids would traditionally take a trip without me at the end of the summer as I prepared for the start of school. It was a combination of staycation for me and time to work. We had done it for years because I spent so much time with the kids during the summer, and my wife didn't. This year, my wife was taking them to Wisconsin Dells for waterpark fun, cheese curds, and crappy souvenirs. My kids would have fun, and my wife would love that one-on-one time with them. Plus, I would love the solitude to prepare for the school year. It was supposed to be great."

Monica still looked at me, never taking her eyes off mine. She seemed so caring, so invested in me, in this moment, and I couldn't begin to figure out why. We instantly connected as if we had been friends for years, but we had only just met. Suddenly, I felt about five different emotions at once. I felt sadness, grief, strength, and warmth with Monica, and guilt about how deep my feelings of lust for her were. I didn't know what was going on with me. I had never felt so conflicted.

Tears in my eyes, I looked at Monica and continued with the hardest line, "Unfortunately, they never made it to their destination."

Now Monica had tears in her eyes.

"Robyn took the kids to Madison to see the city first and then drove North to the Dells. On I-90, north of Madison, a deer ran out in front of a car, and the driver slammed on the brakes. Unfortunately, the semi behind the car couldn't stop in time and slammed into the back of it. My wife and kids never had a chance. They slammed into the back of the semi at a very high speed. Only the truck driver lived."

Monica moved to speak, but I looked down at the floor and continued speaking before she could say anything.

"I don't know why, but I always say it like that. I don't mention my wife and kids. I say that the truck driver lived. I've gone through therapy, and it has helped a lot, but I still say it that way. The reality is that I had lost everyone in my family in about a month."

Monica said, "Matt," and I looked up at her. "I'm so sorry. I can't believe the pain you have gone through."

"Thanks," I said. "The subsequent months have been difficult. Grief would overcome me out of nowhere. I struggled to get good sleep. I couldn't bear the sight of happy families. Plus, I live in a small town. Everyone knew. I could see the pity in their eyes every time I was out. It made it very hard for me to leave my house at all. I knew I wasn't in a good place, but I also had the school year to prepare for. I tried to get the school year off on a good note, and yes, the school worked with me as much as possible. They had a long-term substitute teacher stay with my classes full time as I worked on and off to get the year started in that first month, but you don't get 30 days of bereavement on a teacher contract. I needed to get back to school and move on with my life. At first, I thought that just being around the kids and the work was a good distraction, but then it all hit me two weeks into the year. Thankfully, I have good friends and an excellent school nurse who finally sat me down and gave me the number of a therapist. The nurse insisted that I call, and I did. Thanks to the nurse and the therapist, things are much better now. The school year was the most difficult time of my life, but I made it through with a lot of help. I am in a better place now. I can't say that I was a new man, but I was now comfortable where I was, physically, emotionally, and mentally. I even renovated the house, but haven't been brave enough to make other life changes. I finally decided that another change would be good and rented the house out. And now, here we are!"

I finished what felt like an outpouring of everything I still had inside and just looked at Monica. She wiped tears away from her eyes, and I handed her a Kleenex from the entry table. I had to chuckle at the fact that I hadn't even let Monica into the house yet. Talk about a very strange greeting.

"Sorry," I said. "I haven't even invited you in yet, and I am babbling my life story. That was not what I intended. Thanks for listening. Do you still want the room, or will you run away from this crazy guy?" I asked and laughed.

Monica didn't laugh. She just looked at me, not with pity, but with sympathy and almost pride.

"No, I am more impressed with my new landlord now. The strength you show in coming through all of that is impressive. And, for someone who just experienced the end of an almost 20-year marriage, I find it inspiring. I am just so sorry for your loss."

"Thanks. I appreciate that, but I have to be honest; on the other side of my grief and recovery, I realized that, in some ways, I did have a completely new start. Or maybe, 'reset' is a better term. Oddly, as much as it hurts, it became a second chance. I know you have an ex you still need to work with and kids you are still raising and loving, but you may find your second chance. I hope that doesn't sound cliché. Just know that I am here to help you through this. With this place to live and anything else you need."

She looked at me, and I thought she would cry again. I hadn't intended that, but what I said was honest and from the heart. Our losses were different, but losses were losses, just the same. I decided to change the subject before she had a chance to break down.

"Come on then, let's move you in and get you comfortable in your new place. I hear the landlord is a real asshole!"

"I am starting to think he is really sweet," Monica said.

"Maybe, but don't tell anyone. I want it to be our little secret." I laughed.

She laughed, and we went to her SUV. The majority of her belongings were clothes and bedding. She had some other things for work and some pictures, but mostly, she was living with bare bones for now. It only took us about two hours to get everything settled.

"Home, sweet home, for now," I said as we stood back and looked over the room.

She turned to me, nodded, and looked like she wanted to speak, but no words came out. She just started sobbing. I felt for her. I knew these moments well and had no shoulder to cry on when this happened to me. I put my arm around her, and she surprised me by falling into my arms. Falling into my arms sounds romantic, but it wasn't like that. She was clinging to me and sobbing into my shoulder. I could hear her muttering, "How did you do it?"

I gently put my fingers on her chin, raised her head, and looked into her eyes.

"I don't know. I had help from friends and therapists, but I'm not sure if I did 'do it,' if you get my meaning. I am in a good spot right now, but that could change. I don't know if I am fully there. It takes time. That's the best I can give you."

She kept her wet, red eyes focused on mine for a second longer, then buried her face into my shoulder.

"You are sweet, you know," she said.

I said nothing but just kept holding her. I felt her pain. I knew how important it was to have a shoulder to cry on. I also knew having Monica in my arms was amazing; nothing had felt so good in the last year.

When Monica stopped crying, she pulled her head back to look at me again but didn't move from my hold. She started apologizing for her outburst, but I told her there was no reason.

I said, "Monica, listen, this might be good for both of us. We seem to both have some things to work out, and it might be nice to do it together. I'm not saying we need to go to therapy together, we barely know each other, but we can be here for each other as we work through things. And that will be a good way to get to know each other!"

She had a different plan to do that. She responded by pressing her lips to mine!

Chapter 3

This kiss was sweet and loving. It was a kiss that caught me by surprise, and I didn't give an immediate response. This kiss initially felt comforting, not passionate. It also should have felt foreign and perhaps even wrong, but it didn't. It felt routine, like I should have kissed those lips my whole life. Perhaps her kiss was meant to last a second, but after that initial connection, it was like a switch flipped in both of us. That sweet kiss disappeared, and we attacked each other's mouths. Our lips pressed together in an animalistic need for each other. Our tongues opened each other's mouths, and our teeth crashed together. We explored and tasted like we had no bigger desire in the world. Right then, I *didn't* have any bigger desire in the world. Monica tasted so unbelievably good, and the only sensation I could take inventory of was my cock straining at my pants.

I kept my lips locked on hers until I could take no more. I finally moved down her neck and kissed every inch of flesh I could find as I listened to her moan in ecstasy. I am afraid that I left multiple hickies as I kissed, sucked, and nibbled on her neck. I don't know what possessed me, but I even bit gently on her earlobe, and she cried out like she had orgasmed. I kept doing that until I needed her mouth again. Our tongues tangled, and the taste of her, the warmth of her, made me even more excited and horny.

I lifted her shirt over her head and arms and leaned down to kiss her chest. She wore a basic sports bra, not some sexy date night lingerie, and I didn't care. She came over to move things in, not turn me on. As it turned out, it didn't matter. Yoga pants, sports bra, and T-shirt didn't make this woman any less sexy. I stopped kissing her for a second to get her yoga pants off, and as I did, she took her bra off quickly. I gawked at the sight of her amazing breasts. They were incredibly firm and pert, and her amazing nipples, already hard as a rock, drove me crazy.

Completely distracted, I moved my mouth to her left breast and took it in my mouth, sucking on it like I was trying to inhale it all! She gave a soft moan and finished my job of removing her pants. I then pulled back and sucked only on that left nipple. I could tell she liked this better. I swirled my tongue around the nipple while sucking it. I then thought about her ear lobe cry and applied the same nibbling to her nipple. She cried out and threw her head back. I kept at this, alternating between nibbling and sucking until I felt her right nipple was feeling lonely.

I then gave it the same action and slowly moved my right hand down into her panties. These were basic cotton panties; for some reason, these clothes made this feel much more exciting and spontaneous.

Her V of pubic hair was trimmed nicely and felt amazing on my hand as I slid it down between her folds. Her soaking-wet folds, to be precise.

Now, I would like to regale you with tales of hours of foreplay and Kama Sutra positions, but that didn't happen. In a move best described as awkward, I pushed Monica back on the bed, slid her panties off, practically ripped my clothes off, and slipped inside her. Again, tales of being very much in control would sound better, but that didn't happen.

As I slipped into her, her moan was lost in the volume of mine. She felt wet and tight and, well, fucking amazing! I hadn't been inside a woman in over a year, and as I sank as deep into her as I could, I stayed there, kissed her, thought about slow lovemaking, and then suddenly forgot all of that as I raised and started pumping in and out of her. I would normally have been nervous about how I was doing, but this felt so good, so in rhythm, so … right. It felt like we were an experienced couple of lovers, not almost strangers. This felt so perfect. I guess Monica felt good, too, because she had a body-shaking orgasm, which I thought might mean I should slow down, but that was not correct. I could tell she didn't want me to stop. I kept pumping away, feeling her tightness around me until I felt my orgasm build. As my body tightened, I cried out and felt her pussy clench around me. As I exploded deep inside her with a roar, ejaculating rope after rope of my orgasm inside her, I heard her cry and felt her body shake. I collapsed on top of her, and she clung to me. I clung to her, too. As her hold on me released, I rolled off next to her, and we lay there in silence, catching our respective breaths.

We hadn't spoken at all. Just moans and cries. What was she thinking? What would she say? Did she want this to happen? Would she regret it? Would she tell me she had been thinking of me this way? Would she tell me feelings that I would be forced to admit I reciprocated?

I waited. I sensed she was going to say something.

She caught her breath, and I knew it was coming. I braced for this deep conversation of feelings and emotions—about what had just happened and how seriously we needed to discuss this. I worried she might tell me this was a one-off thing and could never happen again. I didn't want to have that conversation. I wanted this to happen again—many times again. I braced myself for the return to maturity and seriousness.

"You know, you're a lot bigger than my husband," she said.

I burst out laughing. I wasn't expecting that, but I was very flattered.

"And way better in bed," she said.

"Good," I said. "You make it very easy."

I kissed her cheek and rolled onto my side to hold her close.

"Oh shit!" I said. "It has been so long for me. I didn't even think of condoms. I am snipped, so we don't have to worry about that, but I am sorry. I'm sadly so out of practice. Do we need them?"

Monica looked at me and smiled. She said, "No, we are good there. And if you think you are out of practice, I cannot wait to get more repetitions in with you!"

I breathed a sigh of relief and pulled her close again. I was surprised by how snuggly we seemed to be. Perhaps we would move on from this quickie, get dressed, and have a few awkward moments figuring out what the rest of the day held. Instead, Monica first surprised me by snuggling up to me, then second, gently pushing me onto my back. She ran her hand down my stomach and straight into stroking my now soft cock. It took one and a half strokes to get me back to rock hard.

I couldn't believe what was happening or how good it felt. I had never expected anything like this. I was worried about building a relationship, hiding my feelings to spare her discomfort, and maybe telling her in a few weeks that I was interested in her. Instead, moving-in activities excluded, having mind-blowing sex was how we were starting this relationship. Now, she was stroking me at a wonderful pace. The lubrication on my cock from our quickie gave the perfect lubrication as this hand job felt almost like a massage. It was like she was keeping me at the point of pure pleasure, not allowing me to build to orgasm and finish. It was amazing.

However, not as amazing as when she mounted me, resumed that perfect friction with her vaginal muscles, and continued the pace.

Now, a few things had happened here that had blown my mind. My wife and I had not done this position much at all. My wife didn't like it; I think it went against her prudish nature. Also, I do not wish to say anything against her memory, but it never did much for me, either. But Monica, I don't know if it was her pelvic structure, vaginal muscle control, or just the angle, but she felt so tight and wet around me. It was like her hand massaging me (but way better), keeping me locked in pure pleasure, making it last forever.

Additionally, and I had never experienced this, she orgasmed on top of me out of nowhere. It surprised me, and I was afraid this might end, but she didn't miss a beat. She came with a cry, kept riding me like that, and went on like nothing happened. It so confounded me that I think it helped my stamina. She ended up having multiple orgasms until I finally felt my orgasm coming.

"Oh my god, yes," I cried. "I'm going to come. You are so amazing. Come again with me!"

And she did. She started pumping on top of me faster, and when I couldn't take anymore, I bucked up into her thrusts, coming deep inside her. I screamed out as my orgasm twisted through my balls and into my stomach, making my legs go numb. My cock seemed to spasm and twitch inside her for the longest time until I dumped her off me onto the bed and rolled on top of her. I slipped my not-softening cock back into her and made very slow love to her as I kissed her so passionately that I wasn't sure I would ever let her out of this bed.

Eventually, after we each reached another climax, I rolled over and snuggled in next to her.

"Yep, so much better than my ex," she said. "And you even hold me afterward. That prick just rolled over and went to sleep."

"Well, you are too gorgeous and wonderful not to be good for. That was amazing. My stomach hurts in a good way. I've never felt an orgasm in my stomach. Holy shit, that was amazing!" I repeated.

"Well, you did mention getting to know each other. This was a fun start," she said.

"Yes, it was."

"Okay," Monica said, "let's tell each other one thing about ourselves that we think no one else knows."

"Oh. Okay," I said.

"I'll go first. Let's see, oh, here's one. I'm not a fan of the conservative Christian nature of this small town. My husband and his family were very religious, and we always went to church. I fucking hate going to church, and that is one of the many good things about leaving him behind. It always felt like a sham for me to go, anyway. It was all about belief, and I didn't believe in it. I was more interested in going home and watching football!"

I laughed. "Oh, you would get along very well with me and my family, but not my deceased wife. She was super Christian. I begrudgingly went along to church. I get what you are saying."

"Okay, it's your turn to tell me something about you that nobody knows," Monica said.

"I *really* like having sex with you and then talking in bed while you are in my arms! Does that count?" I asked.

"No! But I love hearing that."

"Okay. Here goes. This is in your wheelhouse, anyway. You might know Rachel and I are good friends through basketball because we both played in college, but I have never told anyone, even Rachel, that I so regret not getting into coaching. You may understand since you coach, but I didn't get into it right away, and then, with marriage and kids, I didn't feel I had time for it. I've been playing with the idea of getting into it now."

I had been mulling this whole coaching thing over recently, and it felt surprisingly good to share it with someone. This was especially surprising since I was sharing secrets with this woman I met only a few days ago. Talking with someone, hell, snuggling with a gorgeous, naked woman, made me realize that maybe I had been lonelier than I originally thought. Yes, it felt weird, but again, it felt so right, especially with Monica.

There was a slight pause, and I could tell she was thinking seriously about what I had said. The pause made me worry that I had said something wrong.

Monica finally spoke. "So, becoming an assistant coach as you get your coaching license would be easy, right? That would let you see how much you like it. Rachel and I could always use the help. Think about that."

"No, I never really thought of that. I *will* think about it. And just so you know, since we are talking seriously, I love lying here with you, and incredibly, since we barely know each other, I like you a lot, but I am not putting any pressure on this. Us, I mean. I'm not calling you my girlfriend now, asking you to sleep in my bed every night, or saying we must be mutually exclusive and official on social media. I want to help you. If you are upstairs in your room one night and can't sleep, come snuggle in with me if you like."

I paused and then added, "Or, if you want to spend every night in my bed having mind-blowing sex, *please* feel free to pick that option!"

Monica laughed at this and turned and kissed me sweetly.

"Again, whatever you need to help you with this transition. I know this sounds super cliché, but I mean it. I'm here for you on whatever terms. Although, holy shit, the sex is amazing!" I said, and laughed.

She laughed, too, and once again told me I was sweet. She kissed me quickly, and we got up to finish getting her stuff ready at the house.

Chapter 4

That night, we made a quick spaghetti and salad dinner, and Monica left to meet Rachel and Deborah for drinks. This was the last girls night out before Rachel and Deborah went back to the grind of the teaching and coaching year.

I stayed in and was on my way to bed when Monica came home. She apologized for her lateness, but I told her this was her house, too. I was not here to make rules. She thanked me for that, and we went to bed—separately.

For now, that was fine. I wanted her in bed with me, but I knew this was not the time. I was sticking to my idea of the slow game, no matter how much I didn't want it to be slow. I wish it were a story of how Monica came to my bed that night for an all-night lovemaking session, and afterward, we got married, adopted many underprivileged children, and lived happily ever after.

But instead, the slow game turned into a nothing game. The next day, Monica had to spend the day getting more stuff and arranging things with her ex. I was busy finishing up a lot of summer tasks because the next day was the start of the back-to-school week for teachers. So, I was busy, and Monica was super busy working all day and coaching volleyball at night. I barely saw her on Sunday at all. We did eat breakfast together, and then I saw her for a few minutes that night to hear that her ex was an asshole, and she couldn't believe she had ever loved him. She was tired and pissed, and we both had to be up early the next day.

So, as that week went by, we were roommates, and roommates only. We barely saw each other. And if you think that was good for me, you would be wrong! They say absence makes the heart grow fonder, and that may be true, but it was also making me hornier and incapable of getting her out of my mind. I just kept imagining us doing, well, everything. Yes, I was having the dirtiest sexual fantasies about her, but I was also dreaming of talking, taking trips, coaching together, and a list of a million other things.

It made the teachers week difficult to concentrate on.

However, Friday was the worst. Well, it started okay. I was finally feeling prepared for Monday's start of school and keeping thoughts of Monica at bay. All that came crashing down when Rachel stopped in my classroom and said, "Hey, stud. Monica says I need to get you to tell me your secret!"

Holy shit. Had Monica told her about Saturday afternoon? That I had an orgasm so powerful it made my stomach hurt? Was Monica trying to figure out how I truly felt about her? I was panicking.

"What?" I asked and audibly gulped.

Rachel looked at me weirdly.

"Something about coaching basketball or something?" Rachel said, her voice showing some confusion at my guilty reaction.

"Oh, that. Yeah. I told Monica on Saturday that I had been regretting never getting into coaching, and now, since the accident, it has been on my mind."

"Okay. Two questions here: why didn't you ever bring this to me, and why exactly are you sharing secrets with Monica when you barely know her?" Rachel asked

"Well, umm, I guess it just came up."

"Bullshit. You are a terrible liar. Especially when you are blushing. Is there something I am missing here?" Rachel said.

I looked up, almost past Rachel. Like I was talking to an empty room. "Well, shit. Yeah. You are missing the fact that since Robyn and the kids died, I've had zero interest in women except one—Monica. I didn't know her, and she was married, and I didn't want to let myself go down that road again. Then, your message said she needed help, and I truly want to help her through this transition, but it is all kind of ... messy. At least in my head, it is."

"Okay." She paused. "Wow. But why the secrets?"

"Oh, I don't know. We were lying there, and she wanted to share something so we could get to know each other and—"

"Wait," Rachel interrupted. "Lying there?"

"Oh ... shit. Did I say that out loud?" I muttered loud enough that Rachel could hear.

"Oh, my god. Did you two sleep together on Saturday? Like, before she came out with Deborah and I? Like, on the day she moved in?" Rachel asked excitedly.

I just sat there, not saying anything and not looking at Rachel. I didn't want to get into this.

Rachel spoke before I could and said, "Oh my god. You did. I know you too well to need your answer. That's... that's ... amazing!"

I looked up at her.

"Amazing?" I asked.

"Yes. I love you both, and you would be great together. I had briefly considered trying to hook you two up but decided to wait to bring it up in a few weeks. I was going to see how the room rental went first."

There was a pause. I still hadn't said anything.

"Was it good?"

"Rachel, it was amazing. Mind-blowing. We felt instantly and perfectly compatible. But you CANNOT say anything to anyone. Shit, Rachel, her divorce isn't even final. She is hurting; she is trying to figure out her life while *living* her very busy life, I should add, and she doesn't need me telling her I'm crazy about her," I said, in a tone that I was hoping sounded in control but instead seemed to sound defeated.

We both paused again.

Finally, Rachel said, "Listen, I am not saying anything about this to anyone else, and I realize that this is happening at an inopportune time, but you both are too old for games. I know you, and I know your heart. You went through a terrible loss, but you don't have to shut yourself off. If you like her, give her some space during this, but also be honest with her."

She was right; we were too old for games, but that didn't mean we would solve this all in one conversation.

"Listen, you are right, but I don't want to push anything right now. I will see where this all goes."

"Okay," Rachel said. "Just don't wait around too long."

"Ha. I'll do my best,"

After staying late at school, I went home and fired up the grill. I made steaks and potatoes, which were ready just as Monica walked in the front door.

"My god, that smells good. I'm worn down and hungry. This was a long week," Monica said, defeated, falling into a chair at the kitchen table.

"How did practice go this afternoon?" I asked.

"Fine, but we need a lot more work next week to be competitive in our first game.

"When is that?"

"A week from tonight. Don't remind me." She laughed.

We ate, and drank beer, laughed, and relaxed. It was nice. Life was just so easy with her. We felt like old friends.

As we finished eating, I got up to clear the dishes, and Monica stretched her arms above her head and cracked her neck. I put the dishes in the sink and immediately went over and massaged her shoulders. She instantly melted into my touch and relaxed. I moved my hands to her neck and carefully rubbed circles into her sore muscles. Her whole body seemed to relax as I moved up and down her neck. Her body felt so good, and I found my hands couldn't stop touching her. Suddenly, I was a professional masseuse and an expert in human anatomy. My hands were magic, and I wanted this connection never to stop. Again, it was this instant compatibility we had. I moved my hands down to her shoulders and started massaging there, listening to her breathing slowly and hearing little moans of pleasure. Suddenly, she felt like way more than an old friend.

"Come down to my bedroom," I said.

She rose, and I led her, hands still on her shoulders, down to my bed.

"Take off your clothes and lay face down. Get comfy," I said.

She did exactly that, and I kept my eyes on her shoulders.

When she was settled, I took a bottle of massage lotion from my bedside table and squeezed some into my hands to warm it. I started massaging her shoulders again with long strokes of my hands down her back. When I felt her body relax, I squirted a generous amount of oil on her and started digging my thumbs into her shoulder muscles, working those areas from her lower neck and between her shoulder blades. I was listening to her body now and listening for the slightest moan of pleasure when I hit the right spot with the right pressure. I sensed the slightest muscle twitch and felt when the muscles I was working on relaxed.

I squirted more oil on her, and I moved my hands down her back, slowly moving down along her spine while I got closer and closer to her waist. I finally made it down to her hips and rubbed my full palms on the muscles there, creating a nice friction, almost like I was trying to warm my hands. I moved into her butt cheeks, using more oil and making sure to give those very important muscles the relaxation they deserved.

Her neck, back, and ass were slick with oil, and I finally allowed myself to take in the view of her ass. It was gorgeous! It had a nice tone but also a nice plumpness. You could tell this woman was a former athlete and still taking good care of herself. I could also tell that I wanted to spend a lot more time with it.

I squirted a bit more oil right above her butt crack and slowly moved it down with my index finger. Her gasp of pleasure surprised me with its loudness but pleased me. I repeated the action, but this time, I stopped at her back door and gently massaged it with my finger. I didn't insert my finger but just continued to rub her hole and then massage the whole crack. Each time I ended this motion, I would gently touch her pussy, realizing how wet she was there. Those muscles didn't need oil!

After making sure to give her a good massage, I spent more time teasing her ass, running my fingers all over it and up and down her crack. Then, I finally ended one of those trips down her spine and ass crack by slowly inserting my index finger into her pussy. She gasped and moaned and squirmed on my finger. I slowly moved it in and out, again in more of a massaging way than a sexual way. After a bit, I pulled out, squirted oil on her asshole, raised her to her knees, and carefully put my index finger into her ass as deep as it would go. I swirled it around, feeling her sphincter relax, and then started the same slow in and out I had been doing on her other hole. As she relaxed around me, I pulled out and returned with my index and middle finger, driving as deep as I could into her ass. I didn't move them around; I just stayed there deep inside her and let her adjust and moan and squirm some more. When I knew she was ready, I started moving in and out of her faster. As her moans picked up, so did my speed. I could hear her breathing harder, and I knew she wanted more. So I plunged both fingers deep and held them there while my left hand grabbed the oil and squirted it on the rest of my hand, not buried in her ass. When I was sufficiently lubed, I added my third and pinky fingers to her soaked pussy and completely discontinued slow and massaging. I pumped my fingers in and out of her holes and enjoyed her cries as I did. My lubed fingers glided in and out of her and I felt her orgasm quickly. I ignored this because I knew this was just the beginning. I continued to pump my hand inside her as she came down from her first orgasm and started building to another. She was screaming with pleasure now, and her holes tightened around me as her breath caught. Then her body exploded with a guttural roar as her second orgasm shook her body.

I stopped my hands because she had fallen forward on the bed. I slipped my fingers out of her, grabbed the oil, soaked my already weeping erection, and pulled her back up on her knees. She was trying to catch her breath and was working to stay there when I buried myself deep in her ass.

Monica shouting out "Oh fuck. Oh my god!" was music to my ears as my slippery and rock-hard cock slid balls deep into her ass.

I stayed there momentarily to ensure she was ready, and her body seemed to go into new gear. She pushed back against me, and I made three slow pumps in her ass. It was going to be more, but suddenly, I lost control, and this suddenly became animalistic and furious. I pounded into her with everything I had. I knew I wouldn't last long, and listening to her made me even more feral. There were no moans or cries anymore, just loud and deep shouts. We were in a different plane of consciousness, oblivious to the outside world. Suddenly, I sensed her breathing pause, but before I could think, her asshole clamped around me, and she shuddered out her third orgasm in what must have been only minutes. She cried out, and my balls, which hadn't seen any action in a week, emptied stream after stream of my orgasm as deep in her ass as possible. My cock took forever to stop twitching, and my body was completely numb. I couldn't feel my legs, and in a move that was both silly and athletic at the same time, I crashed us over to our sides with my dick still in her ass.

We stayed like that until I finally softened and pulled out of her. She gasped as I did so, and as I held her, she whispered, "Get on top of me and make love to me slowly."

This got me back to rock hard, and I did what she asked. I mounted her and just moved my hardness in and out of her pussy for what seemed like all night. I don't know how many more orgasms we had, but our bodies were one, and our lips were locked. It was unbelievably erotic, and I was the happiest guy in the world.

As we lay in bed, holding each other after, I wasn't sure this was playing the slow game, but this was exactly what I wanted.

Chapter 5

Any hope I had that holding each other in bed would become a regular event went out the window after Friday night. Monica woke early on Saturday morning and left to run a Saturday morning practice with her team. She was up and gone before I even woke up.

She didn't say anything to me before leaving.

I was enjoying a lazy morning and trying not to think about Monica or where we were in our relationship. This didn't prove easy because that made me think more about the fact that I wasn't sure what you even called our relationship. We seemed to be friends with benefits, but some might argue that we hadn't known each other long enough to be friends yet. We were roommates with benefits, and I wasn't sure if that was a good basis for a deeper relationship.

As I lounged around the house looking for motivation, Monica returned from her practice. I was walking past the front door when she walked in.

I stood there and waited for her to come in and close the door.

"Hey, I missed you this morning," I said.

Monica looked a little upset, and I instantly realized that must have sounded like I was calling her out for ditching me after spending the night. It wasn't what I meant at all. I meant that I hadn't seen her leave this morning.

I added, "I didn't even get to say hello or goodbye before you left for practice. What's up?"

Any awkwardness I thought I created wasn't there, or Monica just ignored it because she said, "Funny, you should mention practice."

"What happened?" I asked.

"Remember when I said assistant coaching would be good for you?"

"Yeah, you mean the after-amazing-sex, laying-naked-in-bed-together conversation we had about coaching? Yes, I remember that very well."

I could tell she wasn't having a good morning, and luckily, this comment got her smiling.

"Well, my assistant coach just found out that her dad has terminal cancer and is leaving town for an indefinite time to be with him."

"That's terrible. I know exactly what she is going through."

"I know. I thought of you. And you are right; it is terrible. I don't want to compare my suffering to hers because it isn't in the same realm, but it hurts me because I could use another coach to assist me. I have a new teacher and a former college player helping me, but one more assistant would be nice. Would you be interested?"

"Hmm, so I would get some coaching experience, and I would get to spend more time with you?"

Monica blushed and asked, "Is spending more time with me enticing or a deal breaker?"

"Oh, very enticing, actually," I said, and laughed. "I'm in. Even though I know nothing about volleyball, I will be your assistant coach."

"Oh, thank you. That takes a lot of worry off my mind," Monica said, and I could see her body relax.

"What else do you have going on today?"

"Well, I need to go into the office and catch up on some work. I usually work on Saturdays during the volleyball season because I lose so much time at the school for practices."

"I get that," I replied. "I remember how much time practices took as a player in college. I want to say I spent my weekends partying, but I spent a lot of time in the library."

"Well, you were a better student than I was, then! It took me a couple of years to figure out that I needed to slow down the partying and pay more attention to my classes. Let's leave it at that."

"You got it. I won't ask you anything about your crazy, drunken party orgies then," I said.

Monica blushed again, looked down, and said nothing.

"Oh, Jesus, I was making that up. Seriously? You have—" I stopped myself. "Sorry, I said I wouldn't ask!"

I laughed and moved out of the kitchen toward the bathroom. "Have a good day at the office. I won't be here until late tonight. I will be at a friend's house watching the Iowa game and then hanging out here tomorrow, watching the NFL games and getting ready for the week ahead. You know, I have a new gig coaching volleyball starting up on Monday."

"Yes, you do, and you had better take it seriously. That head volleyball coach can be a real dictator!" she yelled after me.

I laughed and disappeared into the bathroom. I didn't see Monica again until late Sunday. We watched some Sunday night NFL games and then went to bed. Separately.

I realized now how much I wished she would spend every night in my bed. Falling asleep with her in my arms on Friday night was wonderful. It felt so natural, somehow. But clearly, she wasn't ready for a sleeping-together-every-night relationship yet. And that was fine. I had already resigned myself to a slow game, and that was how I would play it. I fell asleep, wondering if I would be good at coaching high school girls volleyball.

So, on Monday, I reported to the gym after school and started helping the volleyball team with their practice. I felt so uncomfortable since it was the first time I had seen Monica since we left for work that morning, and I was always excited to see her. But even more than that, I wasn't confident in my volleyball knowledge or skills, and I had no idea if I would connect with the girls. Monica gave me a great introduction, and I detailed my basketball background and admitted that the only thing I could do was chase balls around the court. That garnered a laugh from the team, and even if it were a pity laugh, I'd take whatever I could get.

As practice moved on, though, I started to feel more comfortable. I was back in a gym working on athletic skills and was very comfortable with that. Then, as the practice continued, I started to see what I could do to help. Motivation is always crucial for young athletes, but Monica had so many fundamentals to go through and so many positions and strategies to teach that I found myself as the cheerleader on the sideline. I excel at being the motivator!

I also connected easily with Monica's assistant and former college player, Mercedes. She had just started teaching at Waterton's middle school and hoped to coach one day. Mercedes was the perfect stereotype of a former college volleyball player. She looked like a fitness model. She was tall and gorgeous, with a toned body and long braid locs that bounced behind her head with every move. She had endless energy and brought a passion to the court that was good for the team to see. Also, as one of the few Black women in Waterton, she brought diversity to our coaching staff. This was an unquestionable plus for our team.

As practice concluded, Monica asked me to lead the team cheer. With me saying, "Cougars on three! One, two, three!" and the girls screaming, "Cougars!" in response, my first volleyball practice was over.

"So, what did you think?" Monica asked.

"Well, I think I found my footing a bit. I still have no idea what a libero is, but I think I can already pick up on some things."

Monica and Mercedes laughed.

"You'll get there," Monica said. "I think you did great. I'm glad to have your help."

"I'm happy to help," I said to both of them, then turned to Monica. "See you at home."

"Wait, umm, are you two ... together?" Mercedes asked, confused by my comment.

Monica laughed, but I was glad to hear that it wasn't the type of laugh that signaled to Mercedes that her question was entirely off base. This was more of a quick noise from the back of her throat. More to comfort Mercedes and make sure she didn't feel stupid for asking. Maybe *I* was stupid, but there seemed to be some hope for a different answer.

For now, Monica told the truth. "Oh, no. Sorry, Mercedes. That is a long story. I'm renting a room at Matt's while I figure out everything about my divorce."

Her response was accurate and a wonderful synopsis. Strangely, it hurt to hear her not say yes. My heart wanted her to say yes. I wanted us to be together. I had *thought* that was what I wanted, but now I *knew*.

I said my goodbyes and drove home. I couldn't stop thinking about how I wanted to tell Monica how I felt, but I knew this was the wrong time. She was busy with a divorce, work, and especially, volleyball. Plus, now I was helping her with the team. That added another element of awkwardness if I brought up my feelings and found them unreciprocated. I decided that I would wait for a better moment.

As it turned out, it was a great decision. Monica didn't get to the house for another hour. She came into the house sobbing. I had just finished eating and could hear her sobs before the front door even closed. I moved to her, and before I could even reach her, she shouted, "Fucking bastard!"

"Me or someone else?" I questioned as I walked toward her.

Monica gave a half smile and calmed a bit. "My fucking piece of shit ex-husband," she said. "Never you. You are the sweetest and most helpful man I have ever met."

I took her in my arms. Not in a romantic way. I was letting her collapse into me. "What happened? Want to talk about it?"

"Fuck, there's nothing to talk about. Simply put, our plans of working out finances and other issues fairly and between ourselves are no longer on the table. An amicable divorce is a term that is now long gone. He and his lawyer are getting nasty and want to fight this in court. I fucking hate his backstabbing, lying, cheating ass. My lawyer just called me and told me all of this. I've been sitting in your driveway for 30 minutes talking to him and then crying."

She paused for a second to wipe tears from her face and eyes and added, "And, to make matters worse, I'm starving. I want a burger and a beer."

"Umm, I know you just complimented me on my helpfulness, so I'm not trying for any more points, but I grilled some burgers up just now, and I have a beer. So, your food and beverage wish could come true."

This made Monica smile. "Oh my god, you are the best. Lead me to the kitchen!"

After she ate, with me joining her at the kitchen table, she detailed some things in their divorce. The divorce came as she discovered a years-long relationship he was having with a woman in another town. Monica thought he was frequently away on business trips but now knew he was lying about those. He was going away to be with his girlfriend. Plus, she told me, the marriage had been fizzling out for a couple of years anyway.

"Probably because he was more in love with his girlfriend by that time," she said bitterly. "But the thing that gets me is that he was the one who was all about getting married and settling down and having kids. I was coming off a good collegiate volleyball career and wanted to pursue that for a few more years. But no, he wanted to be married with kids and the picket fence and shit. Now I hate myself for not seeing this all earlier."

"I don't want to pretend that I understand any of this, but I do want to throw in that this new legal fight might be coming from the girlfriend," I offered.

Monica looked at me with questioning eyes.

"A friend from college went through this. He and his wife had no kids, but my friend was loaded. He ran a very successful software company. Unfortunately, he was too married to the company, and his wife met another guy. They were going down the road of a very amicable divorce, but then the wife's boyfriend got money-hungry. He pressured the wife to take my friend for all he was worth. It got ugly because of the boyfriend, not the wife. And in a somewhat funny twist, they ended up with what they would have gotten just going down the path they were going. The boyfriend got pissed, he left my friend's now ex-wife, and she married another rich guy about a year later. So the boyfriend pushed for all of that shit and got nothing. The ex-wife doesn't talk to the old boyfriend, but she and my friend are still on speaking terms after all that went down. They probably get along better now."

Monica rolled her eyes at that, and I quickly added, "Not that you can't tell your husband to fuck off forever! However, he may be getting pressure from a third party."

"A third party. What a fucking way to describe the skank," Monica said.

"Oh, maybe not my best choice of words, but I thought 'the Fuckhole' might be a little harsh since I don't know her," I said.

Monica looked up at me and burst into laughter. She laughed for a while and wiped away the rest of her tears, both from sobbing and now laughing.

"Oh my god, it feels good to laugh. You make me feel good, you know that."

I rose from the table and offered her my hand. She took it and I gently pulled her up from her chair. I looked into her beautiful but now red eyes and said, "Let's go to my bed so I can continue to make you feel good."

Without hesitation, she led the way!

Chapter 6

Monica held my hand the whole way to my bedroom. I followed behind her until she reached the bed. I didn't let her turn around to face me, as my mouth was on her neck the second she stopped, smothering it in kisses. My lips traced a line, up and down behind her right ear, over the back of her neck, and then up and down behind her left ear. My tongue licked at her incredibly soft skin as my hands rubbed up and down the sides of her thighs. Her skin tasted so good and felt so tender on my lips.

We quickly fell into a nice pattern, with Monica letting her head fall to the opposite side of the one I was kissing. A move that gave me more room to make love to her neck but also an involuntary action as her body relaxed into the moment.

But suddenly, that was all done as Monica spun around and took my mouth with hers. Our lips crashed together. There was no frantic twisting of tongues and teeth mashing and ferocity. This was more passionate and sweeter. Horny desire had driven the other times we had been together. There was a primal need to satisfy an urge. This was not that. This was coming from a place of intimacy and closeness. This was not a "fuck me now, I need to get laid" moment. This was about memorizing every inch of each other, holding each other, and being as close as two people could. This was about lovemaking.

As we finally started breaking what seemed like a five-minute-long kiss, I unbuttoned the two buttons on Monica's shirt and lifted it. The form-fitting camisole she had on underneath showed off her beautiful body much better than the shirt did. I removed the camisole and left her in her bra while I went back to her neck. It wasn't supposed to mean I needed her to take it off, but she undid the clasp in the back faster than I could, and I stopped kissing for a second to slide her bra off her arms.

I quickly dropped my pants, took my shirt off, and in one of those bedroom moves that only works because it is almost involuntary, I used my arms to push Monica down onto the bed gently. As we moved to the bed together, I let gravity take my mouth off her neck and slid down to take as much of her left breast in my mouth as I could. I was never really a boob guy; I usually went for athletic, lean women. Monica was, I knew now, a 32C cup, and although a lot of guys in my college locker room would think that was small, I thought they were perfect! (Hell, I thought every part of her was perfect!) Her nipple, which my tongue was currently twirling around, became unbelievably hard. Her nipples were larger than I was used to, and I liked it. I slowly backed my mouth off her whole breast, letting it slip out until my lips were only on that hard nipple. I sucked and batted at it with my tongue, making sure to break off occasionally and circle my tongue around her incredibly smooth areola. Her moans let me know I was doing this correctly. It also helped that she frequently said, "Oh my god, Matt, that feels so good."

I took the positive reinforcement as my cue to switch to her other breast. This nipple hardened instantly as I suckled it, alternating flicks of my tongue and licking around the circumference of her areola on this side. I was taking my time, and Monica was in no rush. I could feel her whole body relax into the ecstasy of the moment, but I could also feel her body pulse with desire.

My mouth left her breast and slowly kissed up and down her chest and stomach. I then traced one line down her sternum and stomach with my tongue. Her abs were incredibly taut, making almost an oval around her belly button, which excited me more than I expected. Monica didn't have six-pack abs; we were both almost 40, but the amazing tone this woman had in her stomach just seemed to direct my tongue down that perfect V-shape of muscle from her belly button to her matching V of pubic hair. I kept my tongue going down through her trimmed pubic hair and ran my tongue through the lips of her pussy. Her breath caught in her throat as I ran my tongue slowly up and down her slit, getting her wetter and wetter.

Then, as I could hear both her moans and breathing accelerate, I pushed my tongue inside her. This second gasp made me lose some of my control, and my tongue picked up its pace, exploring her pussy and twirling inside her.

But suddenly, the pace I was going seemed too frantic. I knew right there that I had slipped out of patient and thoughtful lover mode and was in horny teenager mode. That wasn't right. This night was not about me. This was to make Monica feel good, and I would focus on that.

I pulled my tongue up to her clit, and very slowly twirled my tongue around her hard nub. I was purposely slowing down the tempo, but Monica's breaths didn't slow. They kept up their faster pace, but I could feel her body melt into the bed. I suddenly knew that this was exactly what she needed. Her mind was too full of everything going on to throw herself into an orgasm quickly. This was going to be a slow build and, oh, holy shit, was I going to be there for her!

I stayed right there with my tongue dancing around her clit as I worked to maintain this relaxed pace. My tongue continued its dance as we lay there on the bed. It was like two people lying around on a lazy Sunday afternoon. The only differences were a lack of clothes and the location of my head.

Now, I could hear Monica's moans pick up again. I could tell that the buildup to her orgasm was starting to happen. She wasn't there yet, but I could sense all of those other thoughts leaving her head, and her body was completely focused on her pleasure. I reached up and grabbed her right breast, pinching the nipple gently in between my fingers. Monica gave a loud moan at that, and I continued what I was doing while adding my right hand to her left breast. There I was, in this superman position, and feeling like I was invincible. I didn't want this to end. I wanted to be there all night. However, my shoulders did not share this feeling, and I soon had to find another place for my hands. That turned out to be no problem, as I slowly inserted my index and third finger deep inside Monica's wetness. And that is where they stayed. For quite a while. I massaged her clit with my tongue while gently rubbing her G-spot continually, never picking up speed and never rushing her along. And the results were wonderful.

Monica just moaned over and over in pleasure. At one point, I wondered if I should change things, but as if she could read my mind, she said, "Yes. Yes. Please don't stop. Just like that. Oh my god, please keep doing that."

I happily obliged!

I stayed right there, continuing to give her the most intimate massage of her life. And then, after a very long but glorious time, I felt her body start to stiffen a bit, and her moans picked up. After a bit longer, her body started pulsing with her building orgasm. Her moans became louder, and she started breathing hard.

"Oh my god. Oh my fucking god, that feels so good," she yelled out.

I had to use the most self-control ever to keep myself from frantically finger fucking her. I just had to stay here with this rhythm and this pressure. And I managed to do it as her moans became shouts and her hips started rising off the bed. But she wasn't there yet. Her hips bucked off the bed repeatedly like she thought her orgasm was coming, but her body was still building it. It was as if this orgasm was something unlike anything she had had before, and she didn't know how to control it. My mouth and hands followed her every movement up and down as if locked to her. There was no way I was stopping now. Her breaths and shouts were very quick and ragged, and her pussy was dripping wet.

And just like that, her hips bucked off the bed, her body froze in that back-arching state, she sucked in a huge breath, and she exploded in a body-shaking orgasm. Her breath exploded out of her in a shudder and a scream. Her pussy soaked my face and hand with warmth, and her hips collapsed back onto the bed. I would have stayed where I was for a little bit longer, but her body was trembling, so I quickly moved up to her shoulder and held her tight to my body. She clung to me and said nothing. Her trembling took a while to stop, and I could see tears in her eyes and knew that the hormonal rush of this orgasm had released more than a warm stream from her pussy.

"I'm here. Just hold on to me," I said.

She said nothing, but now her tears had turned into full-on crying. I knew she was feeling so much, so I needed to keep things going slow. That seemed to be a theme for us right now. She soon regained control over herself and wiped the tears off her face.

"I'm sorry," she said. "I don't even know what is going on with me. I have never, ever come like that. That was the most unbelievable thing I have ever experienced. You are unbelievable. Holy shit!"

"Hey, you have nothing to apologize for."

"But you didn't get any pleasure."

I laughed. "Oh my god, you don't think I got any pleasure out of making you have the best orgasm of your life? That was the hottest thing I've ever seen."

Monica smiled. "Well, it was that. Did I... well, did I—" she broke off.

"Did you what?" I asked.

"Did I... there's no other word for it. Did I squirt? That's never happened before," she said, slightly embarrassed.

"Oh yeah, all over my face, and I fucking loved it, so never be embarrassed about that. That was new for me, too. I wanted to make you feel good. I hope I succeeded!"

She smiled and held me even closer. "I've never felt better in my life," she said.

I smiled to myself and listened to Monica breathing right next to me. I wanted to hold her like that forever!

Chapter 7

As it turned out, I should have been careful what I wished for. We must have fallen asleep immediately because a few hours later, the pain woke me up still in that position. My back felt like it was broken. I got out of bed, went to the bathroom, and then came back to the side of the bed, where I stretched my back out a little. I must have disturbed Monica because she suddenly said in her sleepiest voice, "What are you doing? Come back to bed."

I said nothing but slipped right back in next to her. I was on my side just looking into her beautiful eyes when she said, in that sleepy voice, "Make love to me."

And I did. I slipped inside her and made love to her in that wonderful, half-asleep, middle-of-the-night love-making that is both intimate and quick. No foreplay, no hour-long stamina. Just passionate, make-each-other-come-and-fall-back-asleep-in-each-other's-arms-before-the-alarm-goes-off, lovemaking.

And the alarm went off way too early for both of us.

"Shit," I groaned." Time for work."

I jumped into the shower and took a quick one. I secretly hoped that Monica would join me, but she did not. And for good reason. When I returned to the bedroom, she was fast asleep in bed. I went over to kiss her on the cheek, and just as I did, her snooze alarm went off on her phone. I jumped at the sound and hit my knee on the bed. All of this startled the hell out of Monica, and after a moment's pause so we could both figure out what had just happened, we broke into a fit of giggles. I was on the bed rubbing my sore knee while my towel was falling off, and Monica was trying to hit the button on her phone to turn off the alarm. I stopped rubbing my knee and slinked up the bed to kiss her this time. She accepted it and kissed me back. Very passionately, to be exact. I broke the kiss off and said, "Oh, there's no way that can continue because we are never making it to work if you start kissing me like that!"

"Fine," she said in a fake pout and got out of bed.

She stood there saying something to me, but she was still completely naked, and I was struggling to focus on her words. She finally stopped talking, and I realized she was awaiting a response.

"I'm sorry, what?" I asked.

"Oh, are you a little distracted?"

"Very," I breathed out. "What did you say?"

Monica giggled and said, "I asked if you had any questions about our practice this week."

I thought about it for a second. "Oh no, I think our sex practice is going well. However, we need a lot more of it. Don't you agree?"

She laughed and turned to the bathroom. "I was talking about volleyball."

"Oh, *that* practice."

She didn't give me time to say anything else before she shut the bathroom door.

As we grabbed some breakfast and left for our respective jobs, I told her I would see her at practice tonight and to have a good day. She smiled and told me to behave myself at practice.

"So, no checking you out and pitching a tent in my pants, then?"

She rolled her eyes at me and got into her car. I got into mine and drove to school.

The thing about teaching is that no matter what mood you are in before the first bell, those kids demand your best, and your focus immediately turns to the task at hand. You have hundreds of lives, good and bad, that you have to deal with every day. It isn't necessarily difficult, but you had better be on your toes. So, my focus was taken up that day with chemistry and physics. The nice thing about my classes is that I tend to get college-track kids, so my students are fairly interested in what we are doing. I tell them, especially in chemistry, "We are here to learn, have some fun, and not blow anything up!"

As the final bell rang, I cleaned up my things and headed for the gym. The girls were starting to gather and get their stretching started. Mercedes and I got the net up and wheeled the ball cage over as the girls stretched. Monica then talked to the team about what today's practice would focus on. It seemed like the girls were getting into their heads that their first game was in a few days, and they seemed more focused. I thought the practice went well, and Mercedes and Monica agreed after the practice was over. We cleaned up the gym, and then Monica and I went home. Pulling into the driveway together in separate cars made us feel like roommates. I unlocked the front door and let her go in first. Food was the first thing on my mind as I closed the front door and asked Monica what she was hungry for.

"You," she said.

Her lips were on mine, and I fell slightly backward into the door. I bounced right back to her as I returned her kiss. Our mouths attacked each other, and our tongues wrestled as we did our best to maintain the kiss while we dumped our clothes right there by the door. It took us no time at all to be naked in the entryway, kissing, our hands gripping each other's backs, until Monica broke the kiss, her mouth left mine, and she sank to her knees. I didn't have time to register what was going on before her mouth clamped around the head of my ramrod-stiff cock. Her lips were so tight, her mouth so warm, and her tongue so amazing that I fell back against the door again. She then slid her mouth down my shaft and just bobbed up and down on me while my legs went numb, and I gasped.

"Oh my god, that feels amazing."

"Good," she said as she came up for air.

She sucked me off with absolutely perfect pressure, and I was afraid my legs wouldn't hold me up.

"You really are big," she said. "I like that a lot."

She didn't let me respond. She buried all of me down her throat and slowly moved her mouth up my shaft to my head, where her tongue went back to work.

"Oh my god, I am going to come," I said.

Monica continued to suck the head of my cock while her tongue madly went back and forth on the underside. I didn't last long before, with a tremble in my legs, I started coming into her mouth. She didn't take her mouth off me but instead stopped her bobbing motions and just stayed there, moving her tongue on my head while I continued to shoot into her mouth. When I was finished, and she had swallowed every drop, she licked me clean and still twirled her tongue around the head of my cock and licked up and down the shaft. I was trembling again as I was way too sensitive for this. I pulled her up to my mouth, but instead of kissing her, I backed her up into the kitchen. It was only about 20 steps back, and I hoisted her up so she sat on the kitchen island. I am not sure what she thought I was doing, maybe she thought I was going to reciprocate the oral sex she had just performed on me, but she certainly wasn't expecting me to bury my already hard again cock into her pussy. She gasped as I entered her and started pumping in and out of her at a high tempo. This was not like the slow massage of last night. This was a carnal desire. I wanted us to come together, and I told her so.

"I want to watch you come right here in the kitchen. Right on my cock," I said, staring into her eyes.

Her moaning and breathing hard was her only response. It seemed like we were lasting forever, the pleasure just endlessly building, until she suddenly pinched her eyes shut tight, and her vaginal muscles matched the tightness of her eyes. As her pussy spasmed around me with her orgasm, she screamed out one "Ohhh!" dragging it out for what seemed like seconds.

I was right there with her, coming deep inside her. But instead of letting this end, I remembered how she had just used her tongue on me after I came into her mouth. I was too sensitive for it, but would she be?

She wasn't.

I immediately went down on her. I could taste both her wetness and mine on her pussy, and it was even more of a turn-on than I thought. Her clit was rock hard, and my tongue was instantly driving her crazy. I kept my tongue on her clit at a good pace and continued to make love to her with my tongue. Unlike last night, her excitement drove me past my control. I slipped two fingers back inside her and started pumping away at her while licking her. It was awkward positioning as the kitchen island was high off the ground, but it didn't matter. My tongue, my fingers, and her body were pulsing in rhythm, and Monica was starting to buck her hips already. This was my cue that she was close, and I wouldn't stop. As her body rose, froze, and then shook with another orgasm, I slowed my tempo way down and let her body relax. As I sensed she was good, I pulled her back up to me and kissed her. She returned the kiss but pulled away and said, "I really like having sex with you and kissing you, but can I get off this hard counter now?"

I laughed and pulled her off the island into my arms. I held her, and she wrapped her legs around me. Her entire weight was in my arms, which was a tremendous feeling.

"We could have sex like this," she said.

"Yeah, until my back gives out," I said, and laughed.

I kissed her and put her down slowly and gently.

"We should get dressed and get some food," I said. "What sounds good?"

"You mean like going out?"

"Not necessarily," I said.

"Good, because I want to wear sweatpants and a T-shirt and relax," she said.

"How about I cook pasta, and we just have that?"

"Sounds like a plan."

I kissed her again and returned to the front door to get my clothes. Monica went up to her room to get into something comfy. I didn't like that she still had "her room." I didn't want her to have a separate room. I wanted her to share a room with me. I wanted her to sleep with me every night. Forever!

Whoa, what? Forever?

Did I honestly think that? I might be more head over heels for this woman than I thought. This had seemed like a fun little fling the past couple of days, but now, working in the kitchen to run water into a pot, everything was hitting me hard. She was going through a divorce. A new, messy divorce. I was coaching with her. I was helping her out with a place to stay. Through all this, I was supposed to be a friend, not fall in love with her after only a few days together. I mean, how the hell could I even approach the subject now? Her entering a relationship, hell, being *invited* to start a relationship, was the worst idea at the moment.

"Umm, yeah, Monica, I know it has been a few days, and you are still getting comfortable here, but I'm falling in love with you and wanted to know— Sorry, what's that? Yes, I am in love with you. Oh, I see you are completely freaking out and now feel uncomfortable here and hate me because you need to leave here and find a new place because I fucked this all up before it barely got started. Oops."

I could picture the whole conversation in my mind. I needed just to let this be whatever it was and relax. Besides, things were going well for a guy falling for a woman he just met. I couldn't complain about that. We were having amazing sex, yes, but we were also becoming friends. I felt so remarkably ... compatible with her. It's not a very romantic word, but we just worked well together. I was so happy to have her in my life, and I vowed not to make this weird for her.

"What are you thinking there?" Monica asked from behind me.

I must have been lost in my thoughts because I jumped and sent the silicone spoon in the pot of water flying across the stove.

"Easy there, jumpy," she said.

"Yeah, sorry. You surprised me." I turned to look at her and was even more surprised. "Jesus Christ, you say you want to get comfy, and you come back looking like that? I'm going to take you on the kitchen island again."

She was wearing black yoga pants and a pink cami. This did nothing to hide her tall and athletic body. She was not skinny, but she was lean and muscled. I imagined she had looked like this 20 years ago when she was a college volleyball player. She looked so good. I didn't catch myself staring until she said, "Hey, how's the pasta coming?"

"Not as well as I'm going to be coming after supper, I hope," I joked.

She laughed, gave me an eye roll, and approached the stove to help me with dinner.

Chapter 8

I woke up in Monica's arms. This was the second night in a row that she had spent with me, and it already felt like the most normal thing in the world. It made no sense, considering we barely knew each other. Honestly, we had never even gone out on a date. We skipped that step and just went straight to moving in together. This was under very different circumstances from most moving-in-together scenarios, but it still seemed surreal.

We both got ready for the day, and Monica told me that she wouldn't be home for dinner because she was going out with Rachel and Deborah. I had no idea if Rachel had told Deborah about knowing that we had slept together that first day, but I figured she had. What I didn't know was if that conversation had continued. Was Monica communicating with Rachel all about this thing we had going on, or was Monica keeping it between us? That started to niggle at the back of my mind. I didn't mind if Rachel knew about my secrets, but I realized she would probably know Monica's. That was something I hadn't considered. I was curious about what Monica had said to Rachel. I hoped it matched what I had told Rachel about my feelings.

The day at school helped take my mind off Monica a little, and I made it to practice. Again, Mercedes and I were there before Monica. I preferred it that way because I never had to greet Monica and possibly let the team and Mercedes see there was more between us than coaching. This way, I was busy with Mercedes, and Monica could arrive and start with the team. Then, we were all in practice mode by the time we joined to break the huddle to start.

Speaking of practice mode, Monica had told the girls that this was our last big practice before the first game on Friday. Tomorrow's practice would be more of a walk-through of what we wanted to do. Monica didn't want the girls tired for Friday. So, Monica needed everyone to be in serious practice mode, and she got exactly that. This was my third practice, and I saw this team operating way better than they did on Monday. I was impressed. I had no idea if this would translate to Friday night's match, but I was impressed with the team, especially Monica. I loved watching her in her element. She was encouraging and demanding, letting the girls know what they were doing well and what they needed to improve. She was very much the expert and teacher. Watching her lead was very sexy.

Not only were things clicking for the girls, but Monica also seemed very much in her element and more relaxed than in the previous practice. Considering that it had been before she got the news that her husband was going full asshole on the divorce proceedings, I was impressed that she seemed better tonight, even after that news. I hoped that maybe she was doing better because of me. I hoped my helping her coach, relax, and orgasm was what she needed. And I was most definitely willing to help. My thoughts last night were that maybe I was in love with Monica. Today, I wasn't exactly sure if I was in the middle of falling in love with her or if I had already completely gotten there. The excitement I felt watching her coach told me this was not a trivial emotion.

Plus, I was enjoying being around the team. Coaching was even more fun than I thought it would be. So far, the girls liked having me around. My ignorance of the game made them laugh, but my willingness to try to learn impressed them. Plus, as I have mentioned, I became the cheerleader in practice. I had no problem with that. I had always been that guy on the basketball teams I played for—the "glue guy" who brought the team together and brought out the best in his teammates.

Toward the end of practice, I noticed that Rachel and Deborah were watching. I waved to them both and continued to do whatever I could to help. Again, the specific fundamentals of volleyball were unknown to me, but I could help retrieve balls and throw balls at the girls in a simulation of balls being hit toward them. It worked well, and I liked this team. Whether luck or Monica had led them to this, they were unselfish and worked hard. They realized that hard work and teamwork would lead to success and that winning would be fun. I liked the attitude I was seeing from the team.

As practice ended, Mercedes and I cleaned up, and Monica huddled the team and ended the practice. I talked to Rachel and Deborah as Monica and Mercedes discussed things for tomorrow's practice.

"Hey, Coach," Rachel said.

"I don't know if I have earned that title yet. I barely know what I am doing," I said.

"Oh, I beg to disagree. I think you are doing a fine job out there," Rachel said.

"Thanks. You think so?"

"Yes. Totally. Well, maybe not when I catch you staring at the head coach, but that's pretty cute," Rachel said.

I rolled my eyes and said nothing. I just glared at Rachel and then pointed my eyes at Deborah.

"Oh, Deborah knows. But that's it. I had to tell Monica I knew, and then we couldn't exclude Deborah," Rachel said.

"So Monica knows, you know? Like you talked about it?" I asked.

"Yes, Matt. We have talked about it, and that's all I am saying. The rest is between us girlfriends. Besides, we are going out for dinner tonight, and I think we might discuss it more."

"Hey, you two. Are you ready to go?" Monica asked, coming up behind me.

It took everything I had to act like I was not freaking out about this, but I did desperately want to know what was said between them. I was like a 13 year old begging his crush's friend to tell him if the crush liked him. I suddenly felt silly, as well as curious.

"Fine," I said. "I know when I'm not wanted. If anybody needs me, I'll be at home watching volleyball fundamentals videos on YouTube."

I turned to walk away as Monica said, "I'll be back at the house pretty soon."

I turned back, took a dramatic step toward the trio, and said, "Well, now that I know everyone here knows what is going on, I'll just say that I can't wait!"

With that, I turned around and left. I might have heard some giggles behind me, but maybe I was still acting like a 13 year old.

When Monica got home, I greeted her with a hug, which she turned into a kiss. A lusty kiss!

"We talked a lot at dinner about what has been going on between us, and it made me want you so bad. Please take me to bed," Monica begged.

I'm not sure if it is possible to be utterly surprised and completely ready to act on someone's demand simultaneously, but in record time, we were naked and on my bed, me on top of her, kissing. I slid off her body and was perched next to her as my mouth hardened her nipples and my fingers went to her sex. I wanted to ensure she was ready, but that was a foregone conclusion. Her nipples were instantly hard as my tongue played around them, and she was already soaking wet when my fingers trailed down through her pubic hair to her pussy. What I was doing was unnecessary. Speaking of that, her tugging on my cock was also unnecessary. I pulled away from her hand, put my knees between her legs, and lost no time sinking myself into her as deep as I could.

Monica cried out, kicked her legs up, and pulled them back. Her feet were right by her head. I wasn't even sure she was aware of the fact she was doing it. It was as if she was opening herself up as much as possible for me. My cock seemed hard as a rock as I pumped furiously inside of her. Her vaginal muscles seemed to clinch around me constantly, and her warm wetness enveloped me. The pleasure I was feeling was unlike anything I had ever experienced. We were both so close to our climaxes, and just when I thought nothing could top this, Monica's head started bopping to the rhythm of my thrusts, and she started screaming in pleasure. Her hands let go of her legs, and they landed on my shoulders as she started convulsing with her orgasm. She curled them around my neck and pulled me closer to her like we were in a wrestling match.

I lost complete control.

"Oh my god, I'm gonna explode inside you!" I yelled as she was holding me with her legs.

And with that, my body simultaneously started convulsing and pumping in Monica's soaking wet, erection-clamping pussy. I shook. I mean, shaking like I had fever chills for multiple seconds as I pumped rope after rope of thick semen into her.

Monica's moans took a long time to die down as I lay, utterly spent, collapsed next to her.

"Oh, I added something to your bedside table. I hope you don't mind," Monica said.

I had no clue what she was talking about. She had been just screaming with an orgasm, and I was preparing for round two. Was she moving on to something else already?

I opened the drawer and pulled out a large dildo vibrator with a clit massager on it. I had never seen one in real life before. My wife had never been this broad-minded in the bedroom. I didn't mean to look confused, but Monica's next statement told me I looked very confused.

"It's a vibrator, and it goes here," Monica said as she plunged it into herself and started the motors.

I stared at her. My god, she was so attractive, masturbating for me. I continued to watch her pretty pussy vibrate as I jerked off, captivated.

"I came home for lunch today and was hungry for something different. So I came down here to your bed and had some fun with my vibrator. Do you like it?" she asked.

"Oh my god, yes," I breathed in a super husky voice.

"But here's the problem: I have this hole filled and nothing for you to do there. But ... I do have a solution," she whispered to me.

And with that, she flipped onto her knees and stuck her ass out toward me. It was an invitation that got my instant RSVP!

My tongue swirled around her beautiful, tight back door as I heard her moan loudly. I worked her open with my tongue and fingers as the constant buzz of the vibrator provided the soundtrack to this absolute bliss. When I felt she was taking my two fingers with relative ease, I returned to the bedside table and got a bottle of lube out of the drawer. I squirted a generous amount on her asshole and massaged it into the skin surrounding it. I tested her sphincter again with my now lubed fingers and was positive that she was ready. Another dollop of lube massaged onto my cock, and I slid into her ass effortlessly. Her cry of pleasure as I buried myself in her just added to the soundtrack of my ecstasy.

I stayed there, buried deep, just feeling her warmth, tightness, and the incredible vibrations coming from her pussy. Not only did I have the pleasure of being deep inside her, but the vibrator was giving me the same pleasure it was giving her.

Monica moaned wildly as she sped up the vibrator.

"Oh fuck, that feels amazing," I cried out, still not moving inside Monica.

I wanted her to feel filled up, and I wanted to make sure she was comfortable.

She was, on both counts, as she grunted, "Yes, oh my god, I've never felt anything like this."

As the double penetration continued to drive us both wild, I started slowly pulsing my cock inside her. I could hear her breathing get faster with each little movement I made. I could tell that she was going to come again, so I continued to make slight movements and took in the wonderful sensations that I was feeling. The vibrator speed was now at what I figured was maximum, and Monica's body started quivering. Her muscles contracted around me, and she shook. Her moans got louder, and then, with a large inhale of breath, she clamped around me as tight as she could and cried out with pleasure.

Other than her body shaking, I didn't move, and neither did she. Before she could completely recover from this orgasm, I started pumping in her ass. Slowly at first, but when her moans picked back up (in what seemed like record time), I started pumping much faster. I don't know if it was the vibrator, the orgasm she just had, or my imagination, but it seemed like Monica's whole body was now vibrating with pleasure. I could tell I wasn't going to last much longer.

As my pumps became faster and more ferocious, Monica's moans became screams.

"Oh, my god. Oh my god. Harder. As hard as you can!" she screamed.

I did exactly that. And after only a few seconds, we hit our orgasms at the same time. Monica clamped around me even tighter, as my back went ramrod stiff and my legs and abs tightened so much it almost felt painful in this moment of ecstasy. We cried out together as my seed filled her, and she lost control of the vibrator, and it slipped out of her pussy and fell to the bed, still vibrating. As I pulled out of her, I held her tight as we were both numb and quivering with pleasure. My left leg felt incredibly wet, and I figured out that Monica had another explosive orgasm. She said that squirting had never happened before, but with me, it was becoming a regular occurrence. I liked that a lot.

We rolled over on our sides; Monica turned off the vibrator, letting it sit in the wet spot on the bed, and just continued to stay in that same position, me spooning her as tight as I comfortably could.

Monica finally said, "That was so amazing."

I whispered, "Yes, it was."

"And a little kinky."

I whispered, "Yes, it was," again.

"I liked it," Monica said.

"So did I," I replied.

"Umm...would you be interested in other kinky things?" Monica asked.

I didn't know what on earth she was talking about. Was she talking about this hypothetically, or did she have something specific in mind? So I asked, "What did you have in mind? I assume, whatever it is, if it is with you, my answer will be yes."

She turned around in the bed to face me.

"Well, I found out tonight that Deborah and her husband have started hosting swinging parties, and she invited us to the next one on Saturday," Monica said, half excited and half sheepish.

"Oh, that could be fun."

I probably could have been more excited with my answer, but I didn't know how I felt. I was at a point where I had no interest in sex with other people. I was consumed with this woman lying next to me, and every sexual experience with her felt like a fantasy coming to life. Right then, I knew I had fallen for her completely and was now conflicted. I wanted to tell her how I felt and that I didn't want to share her with anybody. I also had no idea if she felt anything close to that about me. She seemed excited about this party, and maybe she should be. She was coming off a divorce and was having fun with me. We weren't dating. We were room-mates who were fucking each other. Oh, and coaching volleyball together.

This whole thing seemed to spiral out of control when I thought about it. That may be my problem. I hadn't been thinking about it. I hadn't thought that maybe Monica had no interest in me outside of the bedroom. But that didn't make sense, either. We had shared too much in this short time, and she had asked for my help with other aspects of her life. She was interested in me at some level, and I realized I needed to accept it, relax, and stop trying to make this more than it was.

"You know what," I said. "That party sounds like it could be fun. Let's do it."

Chapter 9

I had no idea if this party would be fun or not. I had never been a part of something like this. I knew Monica was no stranger to partying in high school and college. From her blushing the other day, I assumed some sex party experience was part of that. I certainly wasn't around many parties in my day, and none of them were sex parties, I can tell you that. My wife's prudish nature was not something that started in adulthood. We met and started dating our senior year of high school. She didn't want to have sex until she was married, and although we dated all through college, she didn't go to the same college as me until our third year. She transferred there, and we married the summer before our senior year. As it turned out, I discovered shortly after we were married and lost our virginity together that she wasn't that into sex, which probably made it easy for her to go that long being a virgin.

It was more difficult for me. I was tempted to be with other women but always remained faithful to Robyn. Hooking up was a part of the lives of the other guys on the basketball team, and I got plenty of ribbing in the locker room as the "married guy," even though Robyn and I were not officially married yet. So I was excited to start my life, and sex life, with Robyn. As it turned out, my life with Robyn was great. The sex was not. Sex was rare and not exhilarating or passionate when it happened. It felt like she had a "fine, let's get this over with" vibe. That is why sex with Monica was so mind-blowing. It was amazingly pleasurable, but it was also fun and experimental. Plus, it showed me that I was a good lover. I had always wondered if maybe I was doing things wrong with Robyn. I wanted to talk about it with her, but she wanted no part of a conversation about sex.

So, here I was, thinking about going to a sex party with my new … whatever Monica was. I wanted to say girlfriend, but I avoided that term like the plague. Asking someone to be an exclusive partner didn't seem to be the proper response to that person asking you to accompany them to a sex party. So, here I was, thinking even more about Monica and our future.

It was Thursday morning, and all these thoughts went through my head as I ate breakfast at the kitchen table. Monica walked into the kitchen, fresh from the shower and ready for the day. She grabbed a cup of coffee, and a question popped into my head.

"Wait, is Rachel invited to this sex party, too?"

Monica looked at me like I was missing something.

"No, Matt. Would you invite Rachel to an event where straight people were having sex?"

"Oh, good point. I was thinking that… Well, never mind. I guess I wasn't thinking straight, no pun intended."

"No worries, but seeing you a little nervous is cute. You've never done anything remotely naughty like this, have you?"

"Go to a sex party? No. And you are correct; I am nervous. What if I am no good? You better help me practice sex tonight and tomorrow night. It would only be fair," I replied with a devilish grin on my face.

"Oh, you don't need the practice, trust me. But if you need me to come all over your face again tonight, that can be arranged," she said, closing the door behind her.

Her words caught me totally off guard and left me with an open mouth and a rock-hard cock. This woman was too good to be true.

Teaching once again took my mind off Monica and the upcoming party. Well, partially, anyway. It wasn't until lunch that I ran into Deborah and Rachel.

"How was dinner last night?" I asked.

"Oh, wouldn't you like to know?" Rachel said.

Rachel was one of my best friends, and being teased by her was nothing new. But I didn't know Deborah very well. Our paths didn't cross much in school, as she was busy with the drama program. However, these truths got a little confused in my head as I stammered my reply.

"Hey, I am not looking for any details. I get it. Monica said I was discussed and told me about Deborah's party. We'll be there," I replied flippantly.

Maybe too flippantly. I hadn't thought about the fact that you probably shouldn't publicly accept someone's invitation to a party when it's a sex party. Oops.

We all paused, not knowing what to say.

Finally, Deborah said, "Good, I'll see you there."

Deborah and Rachel said goodbye and returned to their classes. I ate quickly and returned to my classroom, too.

It hadn't occurred to me at first that even though I wasn't saying anything out loud about the specifics of the sex party, I was telling Deborah that I would be with her on Saturday for sex. I tried to be nice and tell her I appreciated her party's invitation. It may sound unbelievable or naive, but I hadn't thought too much about having sex with people other than Monica. I had spent a whole year avoiding people, thinking I would be alone forever. The only person who ever got my blood pumping had been Monica. Now that I had met her and was having mind-blowing sex with her, I considered this the jackpot. My focus was all on her.

Besides, I didn't even know how a swinger party worked. I knew the basic premise of a swinger party, but the reality finally hit me that I would be having sex with other people. And to be honest, I wasn't sure how excited I was to have sex with other people. Deborah was a very attractive woman, but she was not Monica. I mean, no one was Monica! I couldn't get her out of my mind. I was crazy for her, and my time with her made me realize something. I was lonelier than I ever thought. I don't want to be sappy, but Monica had fixed another piece of my broken heart.

And I didn't know how to tell her.

Plus, Monica was excited for Saturday. I could tell she was much more comfortable with the idea than I was. She didn't have the same feelings about being exclusive with me. So, I decided to suck it up and keep these thoughts to myself. I'd try Saturday's party out, and maybe I would like it more than I thought. For now, I had classes to teach and a last practice before the opening match of the volleyball season!

At practice, I didn't do much. Monica and Mercedes ran the girls through everything they had practiced for the last few weeks. Monica's attitude was to talk it all through and then practice the fundamentals. I understood what Monica was doing. She was running practice backward from normal, starting with the more complex strategies, working on those on the court, and finishing with easy warm-up drills. She was trying to build confidence. When the girls left the gym, the last thing they remembered was confidently doing simple but fundamental things.

I just sat and listened for most of the time. However, I did serve as the "opponent" for much of the on-court work, throwing the ball over the net to different positions so the team could work on returns. I could do this easily, and seeing and feeling how locked in the team was was great fun. I also couldn't get over how much I admired Monica as a coach. She was all business around these girls but could also smile when needed. The girls seemed to respond to her perfectly. The girls understood the game but also felt respected by her. That was rare for a guy who spent years with basketball coaches who were one or the other. They either knew their Xs and Os and couldn't communicate anything else, or they were master motivators who knew little about teaching the game's nuances. I understood why Monica wanted my help. She saw that I could help the team dynamic and be that voice that supports and motivates while she handled the technical aspects with Mercedes. She was smart, thoughtful, and dedicated to these girls. It made me love her even more!

After practice was done, I could tell Monica was tense. I suggested that all three of us go out and eat something. This was met with overwhelming positivity. We were all hungry.

At Bonilla's, the Mexican restaurant in town, the food and margaritas were excellent to take the edge off. I stuck to a glass of water as Mercedes and Monica ordered their second. One margarita was fine, but more than that would have me up all night regretting the decision. There wasn't enough antacid in the world to help what might happen to me when I tried to lay down and sleep. As it turned out, maybe nobody should have had more than one because Monica and Mercedes ditched the small talk and got personal.

"So, I haven't even asked how you like teaching," Monica said.

"Oh, I love it. I was nervous, but I think my college program prepared me well," Mercedes answered.

"Do you have a significant other?" Monica asked.

This caught me off guard. I didn't think we would dive into the 22 year old's love life in my first week on the coaching staff. I wasn't entirely comfortable with this because these things can go around the table, and I don't like bringing the whole dead wife and kids into dinner conversation. I wouldn't say I like bringing it into any conversation.

"No, I don't. That's a long story. My college girlfriend and teammate surprised me right before graduation by telling me she wouldn't move with me after graduation. She was staying at the college because our head volleyball coach had offered her a coaching position. It was a surprise because I didn't think they got along well. Then, the next day, I got a text from my girlfriend that said she had 'talked to Mercedes and told her about the coaching position but couldn't wait for all the 'positions' they would be in tonight.' I instantly recognized that she thought she was texting the coach and she had been cheating on me with her. When I told her that I thought she had texted the wrong person and we had some things to talk about, she told me the truth. They had been seeing each other for months and playing it like they didn't get along to hide that they were getting along very well. I felt so betrayed and, well, stupid for not seeing it. So here I am, teaching, coaching, and single back in my hometown."

"Oh, that's terrible. It hits way too close to home for me. My husband informed me a few weeks ago that he would leave me for his longtime girlfriend. It sucks to be cheated on and left alone. That's why Matt has been such a life-saver for me."

Wow. I loved hearing that. I smiled at Monica from across the table.

"So, are you sure you guys aren't a couple?" Mercedes asked. "You sure seem good together," she added.

"Oh, no. Just roommates and coaches. But he is quickly becoming a great friend," Monica said.

Okay. I *didn't* love hearing that. I continued to smile at Monica, but now it seemed fake.

"And," Monica said, "we should connect you with my friend Rachel. Rachel knows every lesbian within a 40-mile radius. She would be a good person for you to know, anyway.

She teaches and is our head girls basketball coach. She and Matt have been good friends for a long time. She had the idea of me crashing at Matt's until I figured out what I would do with my life."

So, there it was. Monica, my *roommate*, crashed at my place and was my *friend*. That told me where she stood on the subject of our relationship. My feelings were very different, but at least, now, I could stop thinking I should tell her how I felt. I needed to go on being her *friend*, support her through this difficult time, and apparently, keep having mind-blowing sex with her.

I don't remember anything else about that dinner. I drove home with Monica right behind me. She had to go over things for work and her divorce, so I watched TV alone. Like the rest of dinner, I don't remember anything about that. I eventually went to bed, and later, Monica snuggled in and wrapped her arms around me. She thought I was asleep, but I wasn't. I was lying there, staring at the wall, nervous about the volleyball match the next day, confused about where Monica and I were in our relationship, and frustrated that I couldn't get those words from dinner out of my head.

Chapter 10

We won the volleyball match! It was a blowout, and the girls played great. I had told Monica I wanted to join the pregame and postgame talks but refused to go into the girls' locker room for obvious reasons. Monica solved this problem by doing pregame stuff on the court and postgame talks with me, standing by the locker room door and holding it open. I could hear them, but I couldn't see them. When Monica was done, I closed the door, and the team could shower and get ready to leave.

Tonight, everyone was ecstatic in the locker room as Monica gave a postgame speech praising the girls but reminding them that it was simply one match with many more to come. She wanted them to remember that it would be a long season and we needed to stay hungry. I congratulated the team as they entered the locker room and closed the door after Monica finished. It was a home match, so I left and went home.

Arriving home reminded me how lonely it felt again. Monica and I hadn't talked since dinner last night. Yes, there were a couple of lines of morning banter as she got her coffee, but she left for work soon after that. I stayed after school and got some grading done before the match. Since it was in our gym, I only needed to go home and grab a quick bite. When I did, Monica wasn't there.

So, I was on my couch, postgame, watching a college football game I didn't care about, when Monica walked in.

"Oh my god, does it feel good to get the first game over with," she said as she collapsed on the couch beside me.

"Well, the girls played great, but that's because they have a great coach," I said.

Suddenly, whatever negative feelings I had disappeared because Monica kissed me. I returned it like I couldn't live without her for an instant. She met my energy perfectly, and we were on each other instantly. Our mouths explored each other, our clothes came off, and it took my mouth only moments before it was busy between her legs. Monica sat back on the couch and opened herself for me. I don't know how long we stayed with that, her relaxing on the couch and me exploring every inch of her sex with my tongue, but it seemed like a glorious eternity. Her orgasm seemed to build and build endlessly, but when I felt she was close, I inserted my two fingers and repeated the G-spot massage I had done the other night. My tongue went straight to her hole, where my fingers were massaging, and licked right on the rim and up to her clit. Her pussy was soaking wet and had already made a puddle underneath her on the couch.

As it turned out, that was nothing.

As it turned out, her build to orgasm wasn't endless.

The orgasm came and shook her entire body as an explosion of warmth erupted out of her. This was not a squirt but more of a stream that showered my face.

I returned my tongue to her clit, but she flinched terribly and rolled up onto the couch in the fetal position.

She gasped out a whisper of "too sensitive" and said no more.

I snuck my body up between her and the back of the couch and spooned her, giving her time to recover for round two. But that never happened. I soon recognized the sounds of her sleeping hard! I got up, held her in my arms, and carried her to my bed. She barely made a sound as I tucked her in. I got in on my side of the bed and lay there thinking about how wonderful this woman was and how we were a few hours away from a sex party. So much for a normal and calm school year!

We both slept hard that night, and when we woke simultaneously, Monica barely knew where she was for a second.

"Umm, how did I even get here?" she asked.

"Like, in an existential way, or do you simply mean the bed?"

She laughed and said, "The bed, silly. The last thing I remember is being on the couch."

"Well, after what was another wonderful and powerful orgasm, you fell instantly asleep on the couch."

Her hand instantly moved to my cock, and she said, "Oh, can we go for another time?"

"What? You falling asleep on the couch?"

"No. The orgasm part," she said.

I was now very erect in her hand.

"I think if you keep jerking me off like that, I will be the only one to have an orgasm, and I would prefer it if we did it together."

I rolled over on top of her, teased her hole with my cock, realized she was ready for me, and slid inside her. We kissed as I moved slowly inside her, listening to her moan in pleasure and feeling her teeth bite onto my lower lip. This put an end to "slowly" as I pushed up off Monica so I could get a better thrusting position. With my arms locked straight and my hips pumping into Monica, she felt so tight. I continued to pump my hips until I finally felt my orgasm build. My legs went straight and tight like I was doing a plank. My hips started thrusting powerfully into her, and after a minute of this athletic move, I came. I didn't keep my plank position as I came back to Monica's mouth and went back to kissing her. I kept pumping in and out of her, and my cock stayed hard, and I still wanted her to come, which she hadn't yet.

I quickly pulled out of her and got on my back.

"Ride me," I gasped.

Monica got up and positioned herself atop me, but I stopped her.

"No, not facing me. Turn around. Reverse cowgirl," I begged.

"Oh, I see," she said.

Now, this is why I found this woman mind-blowing in bed. I feared she would have to re-position herself and lose the moment awkwardly. However, she didn't move except to lower herself down on my still rock-like member. Then, in what would be an impossible move for me, she almost spun a 180-degree turn while I was still buried inside her. Just that move had sent sensations shooting through my extremities and had me breathing hard.

"Oh my god, you are amazing," I said.

She said nothing. She put her feet on the bed and started moving up and down on me. Slowly, at first, letting us both build in our intensity and pleasure. But then, reminding me of myself when I was on top, she decided to say "fuck this" to going slowly, and she started bouncing up and down on me. Her speed, friction, tightness, and warmth drove me crazy.

"Oh fuck, I'm going to come again, Monica. You are going to make me come!"

My hips started bucking up to match her thrusts, and suddenly, she stopped bouncing. She impaled herself on me, sitting on top of me, clenching her vaginal walls, and coming hard on top of me. The clenching sensation drained all of my seed into her, and she toppled off me onto the bed. She locked onto my mouth, kissed me, and snuggled beside me.

After a moment, she giggled.

"What?" I asked.

"Well, we shouldn't be doing this today. We will be too spent for the party this afternoon."

"Oh, my god. There is no way I am ever regretting this!" I laughed. "You are so amazing."

I kissed her again.

"But, I was wondering if you wanted to go out for breakfast because I think if we stay here, we will spend the day wearing each other out," I said.

"That sounds good. I don't think I ate last night. I'm hungry."

"Well, let's shower, get dressed, and head down to the Main Street Cafe."

"Sounds good," she said. "I'll head upstairs to my bathroom."

"No way. This morning, we need to conserve water," I said, with a twinkle in my eye. "I insist you share my shower with me."

"Oh, well then. I can't resist that. Are you sure you can come a third time so soon?"

"Oh, yeah. No problem when I am with you. I know we should be saving our energy for this afternoon, but one more time in the shower can't hurt."

It ended up being twice!

Chapter 11

Monica and I drove over to Deborah's house. She and her husband Lane were hosting, and, from what Monica said, they had done this before. I was glad someone had because I was sure a newbie to this.

I didn't know what to think about it all. I knew I loved having sex with Monica, but I had no clue if I would enjoy the others. I was feeling a mix of different emotions. I was nervous and excited and felt like maybe I wasn't really into this. As we pulled onto Deborah and Lane's street, I figured it was too late to turn back. Plus, I knew Monica was excited about this. Perhaps she was more excited about this party than I wanted her to be. I wanted her to want me exclusively, but that is not where she was. I had to accept it for now.

Deborah was wearing a green kimono with orange flowers as she greeted us at the door. It showed off her body perfectly, and I felt a response in my pants. Now, excitement outweighed trepidation. I was suddenly way more excited than nervous.

Deborah greeted us and invited us into the living room. They had an open floor plan house, where you walked straight in the front door and into their kitchen. Beyond that was the living room with what I assumed were bedrooms off to the left. The kitchen had plenty of liquor on the counter, and the living room had plenty of sex toys on the coffee table. I think if you had told me I was going to walk into a room of sex toys, I would have been a little turned off but seeing them all there really turned me on.

Lane, Deborah's husband, was talking to Rob and Kasey McHenry in the kitchen. Anna and Ethan Webster were pouring themselves drinks at the kitchen island. I knew all these people, as you tended to in Waterton, but not very well. Then Deborah opened the front door again, and another couple I didn't know walked in. Living in a small town, I figured I knew everyone, so this surprised me. Deborah brought the new couple into the living room and introduced them as Sarah and Logan West. They were not from Waterton but were friends of Deborah's.

"Okay, now that everyone is here, we can get started," Deborah said, ushering us into the living room.

Lane got up, went to the kitchen, and poured a drink for everyone who didn't have one. I am not much of a drinker, but a gin and tonic seemed a good idea to help with any nerves I felt. Lane joined us again once everyone had been served, and Deborah resumed talking.

"To make this more fun and to help with mixing part-ners, we will randomize things today. First, partners. The men will draw names out of a hat for their starting partner. Then, I will draw an activity out of the hat, and we will start there. Is everyone ready?"

We all nodded tentatively, but Lane put the five female names in a hat and came to me first. I reached in and pulled out Deborah's name. She smiled and came over to me. Rob pulled Monica's name next, and I felt jealous. Ethan pulled Kasey's name, and Logan pulled Anna's name. That left Lane with Sarah.

"Now that everyone has a partner they didn't arrive with, I will pick an activity. This will be fun!" said Deborah.

I didn't know what she meant by activity. Did she mean a non-sexual activity to get the party started gradually? Something like an icebreaker?

Lane put the pieces of paper with activities written on them into the hat and shook them up. Deborah reached in and pulled out a piece of paper.

"Blowjob line," she said. "Men, line up next to each other."

Nope. No icebreaker. We were jumping right in!

Four of us, minus Lane, immediately did as we were told. The women just giggled at us. Before we could ask what was funny, Deborah said, "Gentlemen, you may want to follow Lane's lead here. It will help you enjoy the blowjob line."

We turned around and found Lane removing his clothes.

"Oh, yeah," I cracked. "That would probably help."

We all got naked and stood next to each other in a line. The giggles had stopped. I looked around and felt all eyes on me. I was more "up" for the party than I had thought. The other men were not hard yet; my cock was rock hard and at attention.

"Okay, ladies. It's our turn to get rid of our clothes and then on our knees in front of our partner. I will call out when we are done, and we will switch to the next cock," Deborah said.

The next few moments kind of blurred together. Deborah dropped her kimono and took my erection in her mouth in what seemed like one motion. I barely even got a look at her incredible body, and now all I could see was her face and my hard cock disappearing in her mouth. Her warmth, tightness, tongue skills, throat skills, and eye contact were unbelievably hot. I suddenly could tell why this woman was hosting sex parties. I tried my best to maintain eye contact with her, but I tended to roll my eyes back in my head with ecstasy. Deborah's deep-throating, ball-sucking, and shaft-licking was at a perfect tempo, and I was in heaven.

But suddenly, Deborah pulled off me, wiped her mouth, and called out, "Okay, ladies, time to switch one person to your left. Continue until I call out the next switch."

Now Anna's lips were around my head, and her tongue was licking up and down my length. Anna was not giving me the eye contact or deep-throating that Deborah had before, but she was bobbing her head up and down on me, which felt incredible. She then pulled off me, twirled a long bit of saliva around the head of my cock, and slid her tight lips back down on my cock. She came back up, running her tongue up to my head, where she flicked at my opening with her tongue, making sure to clean the pre-cum there before devouring me one more time. I was close to coming, but Deborah called out another switch.

My mind was going numb with the pleasure coming from the different mouths. Every new mouth was like a trip down another road of pleasure. This time, I had Kasey devouring me, and I was amazed. This seemingly professional and demure woman had my entire scrotum in her mouth while her hand jerked me off. She had no idea how close I was to coming because she had just gotten to me. She had no signals other than the one giant moan I uttered as her mouth came up from my sack to my cock. Unfortunately, she didn't get her mouth on me in time, as a long rope of cum exploded out of my cock and splashed right between her eyes and forehead. She recoiled from the spray, but not far enough as my second ejaculation sprayed onto her nose. My third and final launch did not have as much force and dropped down on her small but firm tits.

"Oh, fuck. Sorry," I said.

But Kasey was unfazed.

"Not my first facial there, stud," she said.

And with that, she rubbed my semen into her skin like a lotion and licked the head of my cock clean while her hand massaged my balls. She didn't let me soften and had her lips around me instantly. She gently sucked me, knowing I was super sensitive, but Lane, who was standing next to me with his cock buried in Monica's mouth, had watched me blow my load on Kasey's face, and that sent him over the edge. He yelled out and exploded in Monica's mouth. I hadn't looked over at her, and it was now, watching her swallow Lane's seed without pausing her mouth on his cock, that I realized how much I missed her. No offense to the other three women, but they weren't Monica.

This thought was interrupted by Deborah calling for the next switch. Monica moved over to me and swallowed me. I mean, nose touching my pubic hair and throat muscles constricting around me like some machine made for pleasure. I cried out, and my legs felt numb. I was so unbelievably hard, and already I felt another orgasm coming on. I think I had orgasmed during oral sex about twice in my life before meeting Monica. I was about to do it twice in just a few minutes.

Her left hand moved to massage my balls as she came up for breath, sucked on her second and third fingers on her right hand, and then my cock disappeared down her throat again. I gave a quick thought to why on earth she sucked her fingers, but the thought was quickly eliminated by her throat attempting to try to milk every drop of cum she could out of me. I knew this had to be the ultimate pleasure, but I was wrong. I quickly realized that those fingers had been sucked to lubricate them. They played at my asshole and slipped inside me without much trouble at all. I gasped and shuddered with pleasure. Monica was now massaging my prostate with her fingers and massaging my cock with her throat.

I came. Really, really, hard.

I don't know how much reward I had left for Monica to swallow, but I couldn't feel anything in my body to know anything was happening. The room spun for a second, and

I involuntarily pulled my now hypersensitive penis out of her mouth. She came back to me and licked me clean while pulling her fingers out of my ass. Feeling my sphincter spread as she pulled out gave me another sensation beyond anything I had ever had, and the room spun again. I awkwardly half-sat, half-collapsed on the floor.

I tried saying something to Monica but couldn't form words. And besides, Deborah called out the last switch. Sarah found me there on the floor and told me to lie back on the floor. She straddled her pussy over my face and then leaned forward to take my now soft member in her mouth. I wasn't sure we were supposed to improvise off the blowjob line, but I wasn't sure there were strict rules here. Besides, the smell and taste of Sarah's pussy blocked out any rational thoughts other than eating her wonderfully wet pussy out.

I have no idea how I could recover so fast, but Sarah's moans, muffled by my now, again, rock-hard cock, told me our improvisation was working fine. I found that my mouth was positioned perfectly to get my tongue both inside her and on her clit. Those moans got louder, and just as Deborah called out an end to this blowjob line, Sarah pulled up off my cock, screamed out, and planted her pussy down on my face, rubbing her clit hard on my chin while my tongue was buried deep inside her. With a shudder that suffocated me, she came hard all over my face and then collapsed off me. We both lay there on the floor while the group came over and looked at us.

Deborah smiled at us and said, "That wasn't fair, you guys. I never said the woman could receive oral. She was just supposed to give."

I looked up, wiped my wet face, and said, "Well, I didn't see anything in the rules against it!"

The group laughed at this, and Deborah told us we would take a drink break in the kitchen.

"Join us there, cheaters," Deborah said to Sarah and I, and we got up and followed.

Once in the kitchen, with a drink in hand, Deborah announced she needed to tally the score.

"What score?" Logan asked.

"The orgasm score, of course," Deborah replied.

"Matt?" Deborah asked.

"Two," I said.

"Logan?"

"One," Logan said.

"Lane?"

"Two," Lane said.

"Ethan?"

"Jesus, Logan. Only once? That was the hottest thing that has ever happened to me! You have the stamina, I guess. I came three times," Ethan said.

This elicited a cheer from the ladies.

"Rob?" Deborah asked.

"Two, as well," Rob said.

"Okay, and I assume Sarah is the only one on the ladies' board with a point?" Deborah asked.

All the ladies nodded and teased Sarah for "breaking" the rules.

"What's next?" asked Lane.

"Well, back to drawing out of the hat," Deborah said with a smile.

Chapter 12

"Butt plugs," Deborah said.

That was the first piece of paper pulled out of the hat.

"But for whom?" asked Rob.

"Be patient," Deborah said. "We'll get there."

"I take it we are drawing partners again?" Lane asked.

"Exactly," Deborah answered.

This time, the papers in the hat partnered Monica with Rob, Sarah with Ethan, Kasey with Lane, Deborah with Logan, and Anna with me.

"Now that we have that settled, let's find out who gets the plugs. I will flip a coin. Heads will be men, and tails will be women."

She flipped the coin, and it landed on the floor.

"Heads," she said. "The men take the plugs."

"Do we pick one?" Lane asked.

"No, your partner will decide and insert it. After that, you can do what you want as a couple," Deborah replied.

Anna took my hand and led me over to the table.

"Which one do you want?" she asked.

"Surprise me," I said and got down on my hands and knees in the living room, facing away from the sex toy table. As I did my best downward dog yoga pose, waiting with my ass in the air, I finally felt the sensation of Anna spreading lube all over my ass. I surprised myself with how calm I was about this *very* new experience, but I loved the sensation of Anna's hands massaging the lubricant over my ass cheeks, and my body spasmed with pleasure when her fingers ran up and down my ass crack. I'm afraid my moans gave away how turned on I was by this action. Anna then stopped, and I heard the sound of the lube bottle opening and closing.

Before I knew it, I felt something slowly run up and down my crack, which was not Anna's fingers. I was enjoying the teasing as Anna ran the toy up and down my ass crack, but I wanted the real action. I wanted her to...

"Oh, fuck," I screamed out as Anna interrupted my thoughts by plunging the small plug inside me.

"Oh, you like that, don't you?" Anna teased.

"Yes. Oh my god, yes," I breathed out.

"Good," Anna said. "But you took that very easily. Let's try something bigger."

Anna left the small plug in while she grabbed and lubed a different toy. I stayed in my ass-up, head-down position, enjoying not knowing what was coming next.

I felt a tug on the plug inside me, and it slipped out, gloriously stretching my sphincter. But that was nothing compared to what replaced it. This plug was much bigger, and Anna slowly inserted it, stretching me further and further.

"Yes. Fuck yes. Oh my god, that's so good," I said in a husky voice.

I couldn't wait for the plug to pass my surprisingly elastic sphincter and anchor deep inside me, but it didn't happen. Anna pulled it out to the tip and slowly stretched me again. She did this over and over.

"Fuck. You're teasing me. Please do it," I begged.

I wasn't even touching myself and thought I might come right then and there! Anna refused to give me what I wanted, though. She was still slowly going back and forth, stretching me to the widest point of the plug. And then, right when my body adjusted, when my asshole relaxed, when my breathing calmed, Anna buried the plug inside me. It hit my prostate perfectly, and my whole body spasmed with this orgasmic, full feeling.

I lost my mind.

I spun around, grabbed Anna, bent her forward over the couch, and started eating her gorgeous ass. I had no "slow" or "romantic" or "gentle" in my vocabulary right now, only an animalistic urge to pound this woman's asshole into oblivion.

As Anna moaned, my tongue fucked her asshole and soaked her ass crack with my saliva. I got the lube, dropped a dollop on her puckered hole, stroked some onto my rock-hard cock, and entered Anna. I went slow so she could adjust to my insertion, but I did not stop until I was as deep as I could be. I stayed there for a moment, pulsing my cock, and making sure she was ready. It was all I could do not to start pumping wildly inside her. But I waited, then pulled out of her quickly, loved hearing her gasp as I left her, and then plunged back inside her. This time, her cry of pleasure was too much. I lost all control and started pumping in and out of her. This was not sexy, and I had no thought process. My mind was numb, and all I could focus on was this almost athletic performance I was engaged in. It felt like one of my endurance bike rides. Shut off the brain and go.

I realized Anna was clamped around me, screaming and coming. Her fingers worked her clit as she exploded.

I didn't care.

I kept pumping and pumping, just focused on how amazing this felt.

After a moment, my focus shifted to the table of sex toys, and I glanced at a big pink dildo. I grabbed it, stopped pumping for a second, and slid it to Anna's wet pussy. Anna grabbed it and started pistoning it inside her pussy as I resumed pumping her ass.

Anna soon started crying out again, and I knew she would come. I didn't change anything I was doing; I was keeping that steady, almost frantic rhythm. As her ass clamped around me again, she shuddered with her orgasm, let go of the dildo, which practically shot out of her onto the floor, and gasped for breath.

I pulled out of her, flipped her over onto her back, pulled her legs apart and into the air, and pushed back into her ass. I fucked her ass vigorously while holding on to her ankles and looking into her eyes. The sensation of the large plug in my ass, mixed with the sensation of my cock plugging Anna's, built to an incredible tightness in my balls. When I finally cried out with my orgasm, my ass clenching around the plug and my hips spasming with each shot of my cum into Anna's ass, Anna came with me, shuddering as well.

I pulled out of her and sat down on the couch next to her.

"Holy shit," she said.

"Yeah, you can say that again," I replied. "You just kept coming and coming. That was almost as fucking hot as your ass is."

Anna laughed and thanked me.

"You know, that cock of yours is pretty amazing, too. Did you like the plug?"

"Yes. I guess I am still technically enjoying it."

"I love having my ass plugged. I come so hard every time," Anna offered.

"Well, you seemed to come hard when I was plugging your ass!" I laughed.

"Definitely," she said.

"I still have a drink to finish. Want to join me?" I asked.

Just as she was going to respond, Lane called over.

"Anna, get over here; I need to eat you out while Kasey rides my dick."

Anna looked at me like I might be upset if she refused my drink offer.

"Hey, how can you resist an invitation like that?" I laughed.

Anna smiled, got up, and quickly started riding Lane's face as Kasey bounced on his manhood. I decided I could finish that drink alone and returned to the kitchen. I watched Kasey and Anna with Lane while Ethan fucked Sarah in a classic missionary position on the floor. Logan was pounding Deborah in doggy-style anal on the couch while she held a wand-like vibrator on her clit. All of this was fun to watch and hot, but that quickly dissipated as I noticed Monica and Rob weren't there in the living room. I wasn't sure what that was about, but I suddenly got protective. No, that wasn't the correct word. Jealous would be a better description. I decided a trip to the bathroom would be a good way to check out what was going on with Monica and probably a good time to remove the plug in my ass.

As I walked through the living room area, awkwardly close to Anna, who was still riding Lane's face, and returned to the bathroom, I peeked in the first bedroom. There she was, riding Rob. Monica was facing me, eyes closed in pleasure, and bouncing on top of Rob. I couldn't tell if he was in her ass or her pussy, but she was enjoying it. I could tell that.

Jealousy now pumped through me. I was surprised. I figured she would look amazing riding some other guy (and she did), but I had heard that some guys get off on watching their partner with another guy. This was very much *not* the case for me. I wanted her off him and with me. I wanted to leave this house, take her home, and spend the rest of the day having sex with her.

I suddenly realized that her eyes were open, and she was looking at me and staring at me. She gave me a wicked smile, and I... Well, I think I gave a smile back. I felt so confused in my emotions. I had been enjoying this party way more than I thought I would, but now, I wasn't so sure. At this moment,

I realized that I knew exactly what I wanted. Scratch that. I now knew exactly *who* I wanted. I know I had just had mind-blowing sex with another woman, but there was no connection there outside of a great fuck. But watching Monica, I could tell she connected to this party more than me. She was enjoying not only having sex with other men, but she seemed to be enjoying *being* with other men. That wicked smile told me that being exclusive to one partner was not on her radar.

Monica motioned me in before I could think or move on to the bathroom. I moved, almost robotically, and stood there beside the bed.

"Do you still have your ass plugged?" she breathed out as she continued to bounce on Rob.

"I do," I said.

"Not fair because I want my ass plugged. Get around here and give me a DP," she said.

Even in my confused emotional state, this gorgeous woman was almost magically able to excite me instantly. My still-lubed cock got hard again as she leaned forward, showing off her gorgeous back door. I stood up on the bed and squatted down, rubbing the tip of my cock on Monica's asshole. This awkward position made me glad my knees weren't damaged from years of basketball. I had my feet right next to Rob's thighs and my legs spread and bent, leaning over Monica's back so I could slip inside her. However, "slip" is not the right word. Because of the positioning and Monica already having one cock inside her, it took some doing to finally penetrate her tightest of holes. I adjusted my feet for balance as I sunk deep inside her, feeling Rob's thrusts through her inner walls. Her gasp, as I bottomed out inside her, erased all rational thought, and I resumed my role as a human butt plug. Rob and I finally found some rhythm together, but this didn't last long as Monica and

Rob exploded together in an orgasm. I didn't. I pulled out of Monica and walked back out to the hallway.

"Where are you going?" Monica asked.

"To the bathroom."

I got in there, closed the door, removed the plug, and stared at myself in the mirror, lost in thought. I knew I wasn't going to orgasm there with Monica and Rob. I was too spent. I also knew that was only part of the excuse. I wasn't exactly sure who I was at that moment, but I wasn't excited about the guy staring back at me in the mirror. This didn't seem like me. Was I now a dirty sex guy? I couldn't get past the fact that I wanted Monica to be with me and only me, but that didn't seem remotely like what she wanted.

I was confused as I continued to stare at myself in the mirror.

I stayed like that for a while.

Chapter 13

When I left the bathroom, I felt spent. I knew why I felt physically spent, but now I was emotionally spent, as well. This experience was fun at first, but now I realized I didn't want to be with anyone else. I also realized that Monica was still having fun, she was busy fucking Lane when I walked back into the living room, and she *did* want to be with other people. Exclusivity was not on her mind. We had never discussed it, but now the proof was before me.

Sarah and Logan also seemed to be exhausted from the party activities. They were sitting at the kitchen island, drinking and talking. I joined them but didn't get to say a word before Deborah called out to me.

"Matt, get over here and join in. I've got plenty of holes that need filling!"

Suddenly, I felt almost disgusted. This dirty talk seemed so cheap and insincere. I wasn't interested in "filling holes." I had spent a lonely year working to put my heart back together, and this "stick it in whomever" attitude was not where I was at.

"Oh, you have way more stamina than I, Deborah!" I laughed. Not very convincingly, I suspected.

I collected my clothes, and Sarah and Logan did the same. They had to go to another engagement, so they dressed and left. So it was left to me to sit at the kitchen island and wait for my date, the woman I was falling for, to get done having sex so we could leave. It would have probably been funny if I didn't feel so miserable.

I watched as Deborah, Anna, Kasey, and Monica all lined up on their knees and took cumshot after cumshot on their chests. Monica and everybody seemed to be in heaven, which didn't help my mood.

Once everybody else cleaned up and got dressed, they all came to the kitchen and joined me. Deborah commented that the orgasm count got lost a long time ago and declared everyone winners of the event. Everybody cheered this while I sat there, not exactly playing along. I just wanted to go.

I had to drive home with an ecstatic Monica and hear all about her experience. When she finally stopped gushing about it all and how well she had been fucked by these other guys, she finally turned to me.

"Did you love it, too?" she asked.

"Yeah, it was okay."

"Okay?"

"Yeah, it was okay, but sex with you is way better. I wish we had just stayed home and spent the day in bed."

Monica laughed.

"Well, thanks for that, but you have to like the diversity of partners and getting new experiences, right?"

"Not really. My experiences with you make me not want any other partner," I said.

I probably shouldn't have said it. It was too much of an acknowledgment, or confession, of how I felt about her.

There was silence in the car.

Finally, Monica broke that silence.

"What do you mean?" she asked.

"Honestly, I don't quite know."

She said nothing in response. I took her silence to mean that I should say more.

"I have liked what these past couple of weeks have been. I love being with you. Whether in the gym at practice, eating dinner, or being in the bedroom together. I have a lot of fun with you. We connect well. I didn't feel that with anyone else today."

This was met with more silence.

"I guess," I continued, "that the party wasn't my scene. Call me a serial monogamist or whatever."

"But we aren't in a relationship," Monica said.

That hurt like hell, but she was right. We weren't in a serious relationship. I knew that. But it didn't take away from me wanting one.

"True. But I am just telling you the party wasn't my scene. That's it."

Still more silence.

"I'm sorry," Monica said in a quiet voice.

"For what?"

"Making you go to the party."

I sensed there was more to this apology. She was sensing the truth about how I felt about her and saying sorry for leading me to this place, but I was having none of it.

"Oh my god, don't apologize for anything. I am so glad you did bring me along. I had never been part of anything like that before. I like my new experiences with you and don't regret going. I didn't hate it. I would just much rather spend my time making you come instead of those other women."

This got me a genuine laugh, and that made me feel better. I was hoping to avoid something close to a fight, something where Monica would scream that she couldn't handle trying to get into a relationship with her divorce still going on and tell me she didn't want to see me again. Luckily, it seemed like we had avoided that.

As I pulled into my driveway, Monica asked what I wanted to do for supper. I looked at her and bit my lower lip.

"Can we do something we have never done?" I asked.

"What did you have in mind?" she asked with a devilish twinkle in her eye.

"Can I take you out for a nice dinner?" I asked sheepishly.

Monica laughed. I mean, laughed hard and long. Once she calmed down, she said, "You are the cutest guy. You know that, right?"

I said nothing.

She laughed again and said, "Yes, I would love that. It sounds like a great idea."

It almost wasn't.

Chapter 14

I rarely went to Patrick's in downtown Waterton. My wife never liked it; I always thought it was pretentious. It always felt like it was trying too hard to be big-city chic and felt out of place in little Waterton. However, people loved it, and it was seemingly one of the most successful restaurants in town. Of course, it wasn't like this town had many successful restaurants. Taking Monica here would leave Ryan's Pizza Pit and House of Dragon as the only two remaining places to take her in town for dinner. Patrick's seemed the most obvious spot for our first date, and I told her as much.

By the time we got there, all seemed well. A weird, albeit fun, afternoon had melted into a very comfortable evening. It always felt really good to be with Monica. That was what I couldn't get over. I had not been in good spirits at the end of the party. It solidified my thoughts about where I was and where Monica was. To her, I was convinced, this was only a fling. For me, it was way more than that. I wasn't sure, but today, seeing her with other guys and me being with other women solidified that she was the only one I wanted to be with. But, as we drove to the restaurant, I reconsidered my bad mood. It occurred to me that I hadn't said anything about how I felt. I hadn't suggested we try dating or taking our relationship to more serious levels. She wanted to fuck, and coach volleyball, and I hadn't argued with her at all. So, I realized I couldn't expect her to instantly fall for me, especially with what she had been going through. So, this was my new plan. Take her out to dinner and do this the traditional way. I suddenly found myself excited!

We were seated in the restaurant's back corner, which didn't offer a great view of the other people. Seclusion was desirable since Monica and I discussed the party and our first-date vibe. The conversation was relaxed, the wine was magnificent, and we connected wonderfully, as always. It erased my bad mood. Any time alone with Monica was now my happy place, and seeing her so happy today made me even more so.

"Oh, so this is our first date?" she asked.

"Well … yeah," I said. "I'd like to think so."

"Yeah, but it isn't quite the same thing since you know I will be going home with you no matter how well this goes!" She laughed.

"Okay, okay. You got me there, but still, it helps my linear thinking mind to think of us having a first date, no matter how well it goes, as you say."

She looked at me and smiled.

"Trust me, I think it will go well enough for you to take me to bed tonight."

"Wait, do you have any stamina left after today?" I asked as I shook my head at the sexy way she nodded at me.

She was just magical, and once again, I felt like we were meant to be together. I hate to say this, but it felt even more comfortable than my time with Robyn. Nothing could bring this moment down.

And then a voice came from behind me.

"Well, you certainly look cozy," the man said.

I saw Monica's face register recognition and then clinch tight. I knew immediately that it was her ex.

"John," Monica said

"Hello, Monica. I guess you didn't waste any time finding someone new."

Right then, I realized I didn't even know his name until now. Monica had never said it before. He was her "ex-husband" in all of our conversations. And trust me, Monica didn't speak of him often. And if she did, it wasn't complimentary.

Right now, I could tell Monica was uncomfortable, but I wasn't expecting the response she gave.

"Oh, Jesus, John. It isn't that at all," Monica seethed. "Matt has not only offered me a place to live after my husband dumped me for his longtime side piece, but he also is helping me with the volleyball team. He is kind, thoughtful, interesting, and doesn't stab me in the back. It is a refreshing departure from you. So, please, leave me alone so I can have dinner with my friend."

"Fine, Monica. You enjoy your *friend*," John spat and left.

There was silence as Monica stared at the table, visibly trembling. I let her have a moment, and she finally looked up at me, tears in her eyes.

"I'm sorry about that," she said.

"What? Your ex being a fucking asshole, or the way I got put in the friend zone?" I said with a big smile.

Monica laughed a little at that.

"Well, maybe both. I meant my ex being an asshole, but I did put you in the friend zone there."

I laughed. "Monica, five minutes ago, we talked about going home to bed together. We are only a couple of hours removed from a sex party. We have had an incredible time since you moved in. I have no idea what 'zone' we are in, but I am not worried about it. I am very glad to be your friend. If we decide to be something more than friends, we can take that as it comes."

"Pun intended?" Monica asked.

"Always!" I responded.

This made her laugh, and she reached across the table and took my hand.

"Thank you for being so, well, incredible. I meant those things I said to John, and I don't know what I would have done without you these past few weeks."

The tears that had welled up in her eyes started to run down her face. She wiped them quickly and tried to compose herself.

"Yeah, I get it. That volleyball team wouldn't be anything without my expert knowledge. I am glad I could lead that team to success," I joked.

"Oh, shut up. You still don't even understand the libero, do you?"

"Nope. Not one bit." I smiled.

This had us both laughing until we were interrupted by our dinner arriving. The rest of dinner was immediately back to our usual magical connection. Except now, it felt like we were even more on the same page. I don't want to exaggerate an awkward five minutes with an ex, but it felt like we had experienced a traumatic event and triumphed over it together. It felt like we were some team that had emerged triumphant over hardship and were now even more closely knit. I was no longer falling for this woman because I was now firmly in love with her. I also felt like maybe she was starting to have the same feelings for me.

After dinner, Monica and I drove home. Monica's hand was on my leg the whole time. She wasn't doing anything with it, but it rested comfortably there. What could have been a disaster at dinner had seemingly brought us closer together. I drove home feeling very good about things. I wanted to get home and get Monica to bed with me. Whatever that meant. If we just held each other, that would be fine. After the day we had, I wasn't sure more sex was on the agenda.

Monica looked over at me. "What are you thinking there, silent one?"

"Just about what you said at dinner. About us. I'm just happy to have you here and so happy that you have included me in your team. I emailed Eastern Iowa Technical College, and their coaching program is all online, so I could complete the course in a few days if I wanted. I'm looking forward to coaching, and I thank you for it. Like I said, I'm just happy you are here."

Monica didn't say anything, and I looked over at her. Tears were back in her eyes.

"Hey, what's wrong?" I asked.

"I just haven't ever had someone be so nice to me. I don't want to get weird here, but you are more like a husband to me than John. He's always felt more like a roommate. After we got married, I swear to God he fucked me twice to get me pregnant and then a few more times when he thought he must. He was never complimentary and never was kind. He never gave my coaching much time or credit. I honestly think he married me because he thought I was the sensible choice, like buying shoes. I am not sure he ever loved me very much. And I was so faithful and raised his kids so that he could go out and get his dick wet whenever he wanted."

Monica was being so honest and was pouring her heart out, but "get his dick wet" cracked me up.

"Get his dick wet!" I laughed. "Hilarious if it wasn't so pathetic. His treatment of you is disgusting. You are attractive, dedicated, intelligent, thoughtful, funny, and so good in bed! He doesn't know what he is missing. Shit, he doesn't know what he missed."

"Do you mean all that?" she asked.

We had just pulled up in the driveway, and I parked the car. I turned off the car and turned to her.

"Every word," I said.

She kissed me softly at first and then with a fierce passion. We stayed there for a few minutes until she broke off and whispered, "Take me to bed."

We walked into the house, hand in hand, and I shut the door. Our clothes came off as we moved down to my bedroom, and I was on her the second her back hit the bed.

Our mouths were on each other's, and our tongues tangled together. As her tongue brushed back and forth on my lower lip, I was sent into a numbing ecstasy. My mouth moved almost involuntarily down to her neck, where I planted kisses on every inch of her soft and delicious skin. Her breath caught in her throat as my mouth found her left nipple, and I sucked on it, enjoying how hard it became in my mouth. My left hand found her already wet sex and massaged her clit. Her moans and wetness informed me that all worries about her ex-husband had drifted away, and she was mine right now—all mine.

Before I had another thought, though, Monica said, "Matt, just come here and make love to me. Slowly."

I instantly understood. This was not going to be a ferocious porno-style fuck fest. This was going to be me on top of her, kissing her, staring into her eyes as we made love. As we came together as a couple, I felt this was the moment I had been waiting for. I knew that her feelings for me were now as strong as mine. We were one.

I pulled us down gently to the bed and moved my mouth back to hers. Our lips locked together in a passionate kiss as I slid between her legs, feeling her spread them open for me, and I slid my erection deep inside her. Again, her warmth and tightness were unimaginable pleasures. I pumped in and out of her in a steady but slow rhythm. We enjoyed each sensation of pleasure as we continued to kiss. We stayed like that, lips locked, our bodies pressed together for the longest time until I couldn't take it anymore. I raised my chest off of Monica, pushing myself up, arms straight, and repositioned my hips to pump more furiously inside her. The rhythm picked up, as did her moans and my breath. We still felt like one entity moving together, breathing, and moaning together.

"Oh, my god, Matt, please don't stop. That feels so good. Come with me!" Monica screamed out.

I continued like that until, involuntarily, I pushed up into a plank position, my orgasm so close and my legs very stiff. I gave about five more thrusts until Monica's pussy spasmed and clamped around me. I gave one last pump and came with a shout as I emptied myself deep inside her, my eyes clenching shut as I climaxed.

I shuddered as my body relaxed from my orgasm and collapsed next to Monica, holding her, our sweaty and pleasantly exhausted bodies pressed close together again. It all felt so comfortable, so perfect, and so right. I was so happy. And a little sex drunk because what happened next was completely unexpected.

"I love you," I said.

"What?" asked Monica.

Her question wasn't from anger or shock at me saying that, but it certainly wasn't the "ditto" response I sought. She seemed to be asking for clarification while hinting that I better not pick this time for some revelation about how I wanted a life with her. I knew I had to backtrack.

"I just love being with you," I said. "I love this; whatever we have right now, I love it."

"Oh, yes," Monica said. "Me, too."

This all seemed to be smoothed over, but I sensed I had been wrong about her feelings earlier. I was in love with her, but now I sensed she wasn't reciprocating. She liked me a lot and knew we were good together, but the slow game still needed to continue. My excitement about going ahead with our relationship wasn't the correct vibe right now. But where we had gotten to felt so good. I wasn't about to lose that. We drifted off to sleep, holding each other, and after this crazy up-and-down day of emotions, conflict, talking, and sex, we were on a great path. Nothing could ruin my happiness now!

Unfortunately, the morning would prove that idea very wrong.

Chapter 15

We woke the next morning to the buzz of a text on Monica's phone. She sleepily picked it up, read it, shot up in bed, and shouted, "My fucking piece of shit ex-husband!"

"What?" I asked, both in alarm and through my morning grogginess.

She didn't even look at me. Almost like she was on autopilot, she read the text on her phone out loud, saying, "Good morning, Monica. Hope your evening with your *friend* went well. I know why you were so agreeable to moving out and not involving the kids during this time. Couldn't have your fuck fest interrupted by the bother of parenting? I'll let the courts know this when they settle our proceedings. I hope you enjoy your *friend* time."

"Wow, he sure doesn't believe what you said last night, and his hypocrisy is off the charts. This would be funny in its stupidity if it weren't so blatantly rude," I said.

"There's nothing funny about it," Monica snapped, still staring at her phone.

"You're right. That was a bad choice of words on my part. But like I said the other night, don't worry about him trashing you. He is just trying to get into your head," I said, trying to calm her down.

"I shouldn't worry? Whose side are you on, Matt? He's trying to take my children away from me!" Monica screamed, now finally looking at me with a look I had never seen on her face before.

"Monica, I don't mean it like that. I mean that he can't do that. The courts will have plenty of evidence of how good a mom and person you are. You have plenty to back up your character here. Lots of people will verify that."

"It isn't that easy, Matt. I have too much to lose here. I have a good reputation, but he could easily destroy that," Monica said, still seething.

Monica clutched her phone like she would break it and marched upstairs. A few minutes later, she returned, dressed, holding a bag, and heading toward the door.

"Where are you going?"

"Somewhere other than here," she snapped.

"Monica, I'm... I'm on your side here. I am telling you that you can't stoop to his level and play this blame game. That will make things messy," I said, trying desperately to reconnect with her.

"They are already messy, Matt. You don't get it. You don't have a wife, and you don't have kids," she said, opened the door, and left.

I stood there, frozen. I couldn't believe how gutted I felt by her last statement. It was as if every bit of joy and love I had felt in the past few weeks had left me in one breath. All of the pain of the last year came flooding back in waves. I just stood there. Tears were running down my face, and anger was coursing through my veins. I couldn't believe what she had said. I had been there for her, and then she just left me like that. I was standing there with all that hurt and suddenly found it difficult to breathe, so I sat on the entryway floor and stared at the door. I had fallen in love with her. I thought she had fallen in love with me. I was wrong, and I felt stupid about it. After a year of swearing to myself that I would not get involved again with a woman, I did just that, and it led me to this. I was sitting in the middle of my entryway floor with tears streaming down my face. The only thought I could muster was of my two children's faces and how much I missed them.

I don't know how long I sat there, but I finally decided I couldn't be inside for one more second. I needed to get out of the house, and there was one coping mechanism that would do it.

I changed into base-layer pants and shirt, put on my old cutoff cargo shorts, and got on my bike. Being on the bike would exercise my body and give my brain time to think. The September weather was cool this morning, but it felt invigorating as I pedaled. My legs were pounding fast, working out my anger, my hurt, my confusion, and my tension. I didn't even know how I had gotten here. It seemed like I had lived a serious and long-term relationship in a few weeks without being in an actual relationship. This fling, which I thought was turning into something where strong feelings were reciprocated, had just blown up in my face. And that was what hurt the most.

That was bullshit, and I knew it.

That was not what hurt the most. Lovers can get into fights. Lovers can make up. How could I judge if my feelings for Monica were reciprocated when we hadn't discussed it? I had said some nice things and told her I liked being with her, but I hadn't been honest. I could be truthful about that.

What hurt the most was her last statement. Did she really think I didn't know what it was like to have your life crumble around you? Did she think that a divorce was the same as having your entire family killed and taken from you in one fell swoop? I couldn't push past that comment. My only thought was what I had been trying to get out of my mind for the past year: I could never be with anyone again because they wouldn't understand. For some reason, I thought that Monica and I had that understanding. That we had *bonded* over that understanding. Instead, I felt as alone as ever. I felt I *needed* to be alone forever. I had tried and failed at this. I needed to pick up the pieces and return to my solitary life. At least then, I could manage the pain of my heartbreak and not have more piled-on top.

In the last few miles of my ride, I set my sights on several things. I would continue coaching the volleyball team until Monica asked me not to. I had made a commitment to those players and didn't want to disappoint them. I also didn't want Monica to explain why I had disappeared after only a few weeks. The other commitment I made to myself was to focus on getting a coaching license. Thinking about how much fun I had coaching the volleyball team made me realize I should have started coaching basketball long ago. That would make me happy and keep me busy. Those were the two best things for me and for the rest of my life.

When I coasted back into my driveway, I felt much better. I was resigned to not having Monica in my life, but I was also aware that she was probably going to leave in a few weeks anyway. This was supposed to be short-term.

I pulled out my phone and texted Monica, saying that I was sorry and that she could always use the spare room she had been renting. I finished by saying I would see her at practice tomorrow. I left it at that. I expected no immediate response but hoped for a delayed response.

I didn't get either.

After working on those online coaching classes for the whole afternoon, I went to bed that night with nothing from Monica. I assumed now that she wasn't coming back, and I was, in fact, alone again.

Chapter 16

The next morning was very quiet. I woke to the alarm clock, showered, had a protein bar, and went to school. Even my classes seemed subdued. Everybody was having a really difficult Monday. I know I was trying not to just go through the motions, but introducing teenagers to basic chemistry principles wasn't the most exciting way to get my mind off Monica. However, by lunchtime, I had settled into a groove and had let myself get distracted. All that changed at lunchtime.

"Hey, Matt. How are you?" Rachel asked.

She realized quickly that I was hiding in my room for lunch and not going to the staff lounge.

"Oh, I don't know," I said. "From the look on your face, I'd guess you have spoken to Monica."

It wasn't a question.

"Yeah, she stayed at our house last night. She was pretty upset with her ex and felt you were more on his side than hers," Rachel said.

"Are you kidding me?" I asked. "After everything—"

I cut myself off. I remembered that yesterday, I had decided that I had gone overboard with my feelings, and it wasn't my place to get into this until Monica wanted to—if she ever decided she wanted to.

I changed course.

"Rachel, Saturday was the weirdest day. It was a roller coaster. Half the time, it went badly, and we didn't feel like a good couple, but everything seemed amazing by Saturday night. It felt like amazing things were happening between us. I thought she was falling in love with me as I had completely fallen for her. But I don't think that was the case. Instead, I think I just overwhelmed her and gave her unrealistic expectations. I was on her side yesterday but didn't convey that well."

"Matt, I think—"

"No, Rachel. We have been friends for a long time, but if she stays with you, you need to be there for her. I did send her an apology text that she didn't respond to. I didn't expect her to, but now she needs space. We both probably do."

"Really, Matt? Do you really want space from her?"

Before I could respond, Rachel went on.

"I certainly don't think she knows how much you feel for her, but she may be responsive to that."

"Rachel, she is going through so much right now. She doesn't need me complicating her life more than it already is," I said dejectedly.

There was silence.

"Besides, she..."

I couldn't finish the sentence. I couldn't tell Rachel that she had said I didn't have a wife and kids, so I didn't know what it was like. That comment still hurt too much.

"She what?" asked Rachel.

"She just... well, the last thing she said before she left hurt me. I don't want to get into it," I replied, looking down at my desk.

"Oh," was all Rachel said.

"Listen, I don't want this to stick you in the middle of weirdness. You take care of Monica, and I'll be fine. She is brand new to this life chaos stuff. I have more than a year of experience with it," I said, still not looking up at Rachel.

"Matt, that's not fair to anyone in this situation. Especially you," Rachel said pointedly.

I finally looked up at her.

"Rachel, It's the truth. Fair or not. Grief and pain cannot be judged on levels. She is going through her own, just like mine is mine. Just be there for her. She needs it."

Rachel paused as I took a bite of my sandwich.

"You know, I don't want to see you hurt," she said.

I smiled at her, but I didn't think it was convincing.

"Too late for that."

There was another pause, and I knew our time was short before the bell rang.

"What will you do about the volleyball team?" she asked.

"What do you mean? I'll keep helping them. They could use the help."

"But Matt, you can't honestly go in there and pretend nothing is going on between you two."

"Sure I can. We hide our personal shit from our students all the time. I'll do whatever I can to help the team and Monica. I said I loved her. I still want her in my life, even if my feelings are stronger than hers. I'm not going to turn my back on her. She can turn her back to me or ask me to leave the team, and I will oblige, but I'm helping with the volleyball team because Monica asked me to."

"I think you are a glutton for punishment."

I dodged the statement by changing gears.

"Oh, speaking of sports teams, I am buckling down on my coaching license work. The idea of coaching basketball appeals to me and is keeping me busy, so thanks for pushing me to get that going."

At that instant, the bell rang.

"You are welcome," she said. "Want to help me with the girls basketball team this season?"

"Oh wow. Definitely," I said.

As students started to shuffle in, Rachel moved toward the door.

"I'll be in touch. Good luck with everything," she called out as she entered the hallway.

I knew that the students didn't catch anything in her voice about the fact that I had been sleeping with the volleyball coach and that we were no longer together, but I caught it. And thoughts of how the practice would go this afternoon consumed my thoughts for the rest of the school day.

Chapter 17

*F*ull disclosure: walking into that gym was nerve-wracking. I assumed Monica wouldn't be there yet because she could never get there that fast from work. Today was no different. Mercedes was there but working with one girl on her serves. The other girls were arriving and were chatting and getting warmed up. I gave them a few minutes, but at 3:15, I called them into the sideline.

"Okay, everyone, I'll save the pre-practice speech for Coach. Let's get three laps around the court, and Kinley will lead the team stretching. Go!"

The girls did their laps and fell into a rough circle around Kinley. As they finished, I realized I hadn't turned around at all. I'd been facing away from the gym doors this whole time and didn't even know if Monica had arrived. As I turned to the team, I caught that Monica was there as the stretching ended. I put my attention back on the team.

"Okay, good. Coach will take it from here," I yelled out.

I backed off and let Monica address the team. I made sure to stay out of her sight, and she didn't glance at me. I wasn't sure if she would for the rest of the night.

As Monica started, Mercedes and I did our normal thing of automatically jumping in where needed. Again, this meant I chased down balls during serving practice or tossed balls over the net for the girls to return. The practice went smoothly, and Monica and I didn't interact, which wasn't outside the norm. We usually didn't interact during practice.

At the end of practice, Mercedes and I cleaned up as Monica addressed the team. We were in the season now, and you could feel a competitive fire in the practice. That was good for the team, Monica, and me because it distracted us.

Monica kept the team a little longer tonight, so Mercedes and I were done before Monica dismissed the girls. That was perfect timing for me to leave the gym almost unnoticed. I'd hoped it would turn out that way. I felt it was better for everyone.

On my way out, I ran into Rachel, and she asked how it had gone.

"Pretty smoothly. Just a normal practice," I said, maybe too cheerfully. I could even hear how fake it sounded.

"Matt, I want you to remember that you have been hurt, not once but multiple times recently. It may not be as easy to turn your feelings on and off as you think. Just take care of yourself."

I tried to form words for a rebuttal, but I couldn't. I knew she was right, and this would not be easy. I didn't want this to get any weirder than it already was. Maybe that was impossible by this point. I didn't know.

"Yeah," was all I could say to Rachel. I turned and walked out of the school.

I wanted to ask whether Monica was staying with her again tonight, but it seemed like prying, and I didn't want to do that. Plus, like I had told Rachel, I didn't want her caught in between. Monica needed her friendship more than I did now, even though I knew that was probably not a good way to think of it. My therapist had told me not to lock myself away and keep people at a distance. The problem was that I was getting pretty good at keeping my distance from people over the past year. Monica had changed all that, but now that was gone, too.

As I got into my car, my phone rang. My mood instantly changed when I saw who was calling.

"David!" I cried out as I answered. "How are you?"

I started my car and headed for home.

David was one of my best friends from high school. I had grown up in the Chicago suburbs, hours away from Waterton, and my best friends were David and Michael. When I met Robyn in college, her career brought us to Waterton. So, with my parents both deceased, I didn't see David or Michael much anymore. The last time I had seen either, other than at my dad's funeral, was right before my dad got sick. Those were the days when a trip back home meant I would feel no guilt about going out and seeing my friends for a while and leaving my dad. After his cancer diagnosis, I made sure to spend every moment at home with him. So, I was excited to hear his voice and catch up.

That is, until he spoke.

"Umm, yeah, hey, Matt," he said.

I could hear the pain and sadness in his voice.

"What's wrong?" I asked.

"Well, Matt, I don't know how to tell you this, but Michael's parents were killed in a car crash this morning."

I had no words. All I could think about was the grief Michael must be going through. I knew that pain all too well.

"What happened?" I asked.

"Oh, it's really sad and just plain stupid," he said. "They were driving early this morning to Michael's sister's house. It was very foggy, and you know how his dad always insisted on taking back roads? They came to a railroad crossing in the country without gates and never saw or heard the train. They drove straight into it."

He paused.

"Matt, they never had a chance. They were killed instantly."

I kept driving, but it was like I was on autopilot. I couldn't focus correctly on what was happening. Right away, I had no words that made any sense. I finally broke the silence by asking about Michael.

"How's Michael? Have you talked to him?"

"I've texted him, but he is busy with arrangements today. He says he has been with his sister all afternoon, getting everything in order. It looks like the funeral and burial will be on Saturday. Are you able to make it?"

"Definitely. I wouldn't miss being there for Michael and his sister. Even though I don't know Nandi very well," I responded.

"Yeah, being six years younger meant she wasn't around us much growing up. She and Michael have been close, though," he trailed off.

There was silence as I waited for him to say something more.

"Anyway, I'll text you the funeral information, and we can catch up this weekend. I still need to call some people tonight."

"David, do you need me to do anything?"

David paused briefly and said, "No, just come home and see us this weekend. Okay?"

"I'll be there on Friday night," I said.

"It will be great to see you. I wish it weren't under these circumstances. Michael will need all the support he can get."

"I understand. See you this weekend."

"Until then," David said, and disconnected.

I drove the rest of the way in silence. Suddenly, everything felt out of place. The emotions I felt just a few minutes earlier with Rachel had seemed so raw and visceral. My current predicament with Monica consumed my thoughts, and nothing could rise above those emotions.

Then, this news.

This brought everything back into perspective. Yes, I'd been so torn up, feeling like I had lost Monica from my life, but it wasn't a loss like I had felt the year before. It wasn't a loss like Michael was feeling right now. It didn't even compare. It felt stupid—all of it. A car hitting a train in the fog, two great people dying, me falling for someone I didn't know and shouldn't get involved with, and me thinking that I could get close to someone again. I just felt stupid and angry. Angry at myself. Angry at the world. Why did I have to experience so much loss? And why the fuck did Monica have to tell me that I didn't understand her feelings because I didn't have a wife and kids? That still hurt me more than anything. It felt like she threw the memory of my family completely under the proverbial bus.

All of this anger was simmering inside me when I got home. I had originally planned to go home and eat something and relax. Instead, I paced around my living room like a crazy person. Replaying every damn word of Monica's anger at me, Rachel's watching out for me, and David's information about Michael's parents.

I couldn't take any more. I put my coat back on and went for a walk.

It was the longest walk I had ever taken.

Chapter 18

I woke up the next morning for work with a bizarre feeling of energy. Last night's walk had finally calmed my nervous and angry energy, and I slept well. Perhaps "collapsed" was the better term for it, but still, it felt strange to feel so good in my body while my emotions still felt depressed. And, as it turned out, if I thought that would be the extent of the day's weirdness, I was in for a rude awakening.

My first-period class took a test that morning, leaving me sitting at the front of the classroom, working on grading papers and watching over the test takers. My phone was on vibrate, but I had it on the table beside me. I wished I had just put it away. The notification on my screen told me a text message had just come in. Normally, if I recognize the sender in class, I don't respond because I want to wait until I am not in front of students. It isn't like I have anything to hide, but it is just professional to do, and it would be a courtesy to the sender if I could give them a focused response. As a teacher, you find that the second you try to do something non-school related is the second you get 20 students with questions, comments, and complaints. So, normally, trying to respond to a message has to be left for breaks in the day.

However, this was an unrecognized number, so I picked up my phone to delete it, assuming it was a junk message. What I read caused my eyes to bug out of my head.

It was a message from Anna Webster, saying Ethan was out of town, and she wanted me to work her back door like I did on Saturday.

I quickly put the phone down and ensured it was back on the lock screen. I had no idea what to say to this. This was an invitation for no-strings-attached sex with a beautiful woman, but coming at a time when my emotional state was about a million miles away from wanting this. I also had no idea where Anna was coming from. *Was* this no strings attached, or was she interested in something more? I wasn't interested in any more drama this week. I can tell you that. Although, that woman had a body for sin and an ass that begged to be worshipped. Oh, who am I kidding with the PG-rated stuff here? She had an ass that begged to be fucked. I did that on Saturday and wasn't opposed to doing it again!

I grabbed my phone to text her back, but when the phone came to life, I saw the time and that the class period was almost over. I quickly changed my mind about responding to her right now and waited for the class to finish the test. When everything had been turned in, and the bell rang, I dismissed the class and immediately pulled out my phone. I quickly texted Anna back that I loved the idea, but my super shitty week didn't have me in the mindset to be "social." I told her I would call her tonight and give her my final answer. Her response was a laughing emoji and a "call me whenever." This let me know she was cool with my lame "I need to consider your offer of sex" response. I appreciated that. I had no clue what the cosmos was throwing at me this week, but I could barely handle it all.

As I put my phone away and started my second-period class, I assumed this would be the only thing on my mind all day, but I was wrong. The weirdness would continue before I even had my lunch.

As the fourth-period bell rang and my students left for the cafeteria, Rachel swung by my classroom. However, she wasn't alone. The athletic director of the school, Curt Hughes, was with her. This was a first-time occurrence. I didn't even know the athletic director left his office during the school day! I had never seen him anywhere else.

"Hello," I said, hoping I didn't sound weirded out by the two of them arriving unannounced in my classroom.

"Hello, Matt," said Curt.

"We have a question for you, Matt," Rachel said.

"Yes, as it turns out, Rachel told me you are working on your coaching license and helping the volleyball team. How is that going?" Curt asked in his low voice.

I couldn't figure out what this was all about. They seemed to want some level of secrecy, or maybe they were trying to gauge something in my response, but I figured it couldn't be anything bad. I hadn't done anything to make a player file a complaint. I felt confident about that. However, it struck me that maybe Monica had complained or put Rachel up to ensure I didn't help her anymore. If that was true, I was going to be pissed at Monica for not just talking to me. I liked this foray into coaching, and I wanted to continue. I wanted to be a head basketball coach!

"Curt, it has been going well. The classes are online and easy. I already have the district background checks and vetting done, so I assume I could start looking for basketball coaching jobs in the spring and assist in some other sports like I am now."

There was a pause, and Curt and Rachel looked at each other. Curt finally spoke.

"Well, Matt, we are here because we wondered if you might want to start looking at basketball coaching jobs now."

"I... I don't understand," I stammered.

"Well, Matt, please keep this information to yourself, but my varsity girls basketball coach quit this morning."

I looked at them both for a second.

"Now I *really* don't understand. Rachel is your varsity girls basketball coach. Who quit?" I asked.

"I did, Matt. I have been applying for head coaching opportunities in the college ranks. Eastern Iowa Technical, in Cedar Rapids, interviewed me, and I got the offer to be their women's head coach last week. I accepted yesterday and told Curt this morning. That's why we want it kept secret. The word isn't out yet, but Curt asked me who I thought would be a good replacement, and I told him you were interested."

I sat there for a second, not believing what I was hearing. I couldn't believe Rachel was leaving. She had been at the school longer than me so I didn't know the school without her. We met on my first day when my NBA T-shirt got her talking to me. Our friendship blossomed from there. I always respected her work with her teams and her special education students. I figured she was a lifer! I guess I was wrong.

"Yes, I am interested, but why me? I mean, I have no experience yet. We don't know if I will be any good."

"I think you will be fine, Matt," Curt said. "Rachel gave you a great recommendation, and she saw you with the volleyball team. She can't believe how quickly you connected with that team, and you don't even know the sport. Monica said great things about you when I spoke to her last week about how the season was going."

At the mention of Monica, I glanced at Rachel, and she gave a subtle grimace.

"Plus," Curt continued, "we may struggle to find someone we can trust on this short notice. I would like you to apply for it, and then we can see. If a better candidate applies, then yes, you may not be the person for the job. Or, if you do it and hate it or think it was a bad fit, we can always have that conversation and re-hire the position next year."

Curt paused and added, "Just with much more notice than September 20th!"

With this, Rachel laughed, and I couldn't help but smile.

"Okay, Matt. We will get out of your hair, but think about it and let me know what you think. If you are enrolled in those classes, we can work with you and the state on your license," Curt said and turned to go.

"I don't have to think about it," I said. "I'm interested and will apply."

"Great!" Curt said. "Let me know if you have any questions."

"I will."

Rachel stayed behind and talked a bit more about her new coaching job. It sounded great, and she and her wife would stay in Waterton now. She also told me I could always ask for advice, and I knew I would be doing plenty of that! Then she asked about how I was doing. After telling her about Michael's parents and the upcoming funeral, I surprised myself by immediately launching into another rant about Monica. How I missed her and how I wished she would talk to me. How I wished I knew what was going on inside her head.

"I think she just needs time and space, Matt. And you are giving her that. I will tell you that she feels bad about how Sunday morning went, but she isn't in a place to discuss it. I think she has conflicted emotions, too."

"Thanks," I said. "That helps. But her final words really hurt me, Rachel. To tell me that I don't understand losing a family when she is simply talking about divorce and financial proceedings, and I *did* lose them all; I mean, they died on the same fucking day. That hurt. I'm not over that."

Rachel paused.

"Wow, Matt. She never said anything about that. I didn't know she said that. I'm sorry," Rachel said quietly.

"Yeah. So am I," I said bitterly.

The end-of-lunch bell rang, interrupting us.

"I've got to go," Rachel said.

As she turned to leave, I called out to her.

"Rachel, congrats. I'm happy for you."

She smiled and disappeared into the hall. And just like that, it was time to teach high school chemistry. This had been a weird morning, and it wasn't about to change as the day went on.

Chapter 19

It had occurred to me that I hadn't reached out to Monica about being gone on Friday for the funeral. We had another match that night for the volleyball team, and although my presence wasn't crucial for game nights, I thought I should let her know. The only problem was that I didn't know how to phrase it. I wanted to be super friendly about it, but that felt all wrong. Instead, I laid out that I would be attending the funeral of one of my best friends' parents. I was straightforward and honest, and the message was businesslike. However, I couldn't resist telling her that I missed her at the end.

I probably shouldn't have told her I missed her, but it was true. I wanted her back in my house to discuss what had happened. I wanted to try to reconcile things at least and not give each other the silent treatment. This felt like one huge lover's quarrel and a little misunderstanding between friends, all at the same time. I was confused and hurt and wanted both to end. Hopefully, her response would break that—at least a little.

There was no response.

So, practice started the same way as it did yesterday. I ran the girls through warm-ups as Mercedes set up and

Monica arrived from work. When the girls were done with warm-ups, I announced that I would be gone on Friday for a funeral and hoped they could somehow find a way to win without me! The girls laughed; Monica didn't.

Practice continued, and I helped as much as possible, following Monica's lead. She still didn't look at me, but I felt like we were hiding the fact that we weren't talking anymore pretty well from the team. Mission accomplished.

Except I was dead wrong.

Mercedes whispered as we cleaned up after practice, "Are you and Monica okay? There seems to be some weirdness between you."

"Well, things got messier with her divorce last week, and I think she is stressed. She has been staying with Rachel instead of me this week. I think she needed a better friend around to talk to."

None of that was a lie, and I hoped that Mercedes would accept it as truth and drop it. I wasn't sure she looked convinced, but Monica called me over before the conversation continued.

"Matt, I am sorry for your loss. I got your text right before practice started. The team will miss you on Friday," was all she said.

I really couldn't believe it. I expected something more, even a look in her eyes, that showed she was sorry for what had happened between us, but there was nothing. Just this cold, professional, and quick conversation. It was like we barely knew each other. It seemed almost purposely cold as if she knew I wanted more and refused to give it. I couldn't stand it.

"Yeah, thanks," I said. "Sadly, I'm getting accustomed to losing the people closest to me lately."

I paused but looked down at the ground.

Then I said, more to myself than Monica, "It has been a lousy year."

"Matt—" she started, but I interrupted.

"Listen, I'm sorry. It has been a lousy time for you, too. I'm going to go home and relax. I'll see you tomorrow at practice."

I turned and walked out of the gym. I was mad and sad, and suddenly, going home felt like the last thing in the world I wanted to do.

I pulled out my phone and called Anna Webster as I got into my car.

"Hello, Matt. What did you decide?" Anna asked without preamble.

"Are you home? I want to come right now," I said.

"I hope you come multiple times!"

That was all I needed. I drove over to Anna's and knocked on the door. Anna opened it immediately and closed the door when I was in.

"I'm glad you are here," she said, as her left hand rubbed up and down on the crotch of my pants.

"I'm glad to be here."

"I can feel how glad you are!" she said, unfastening my pants.

Before I could move, my pants and boxers were at my ankles, and Anna was stroking my erection firmly in her hand.

"Oh, fuck, that feels so good!" I yelled out.

"Oh yeah? How about this?" Anna asked and sank to her knees.

Anna's mouth took one of my balls and sucked it gently while her hand continued to stroke me. Her tongue gently massaged that testicle as my erection seemed to grow even harder. Anna's mouth stayed connected to me, making sure that each testicle received a lengthy oral massage. Her hand never hesitated in her continued stroking, though.

Then, just as that pleasure seemed to do me in, she stopped with her mouth but not her hand, and her tongue licked down my sack and to my asshole. She then licked back up, sucking my entire scrotum into her mouth. Her tongue bounced around my sack, sending spasms of pleasure through my legs. My mind had gone almost numb, and I sagged back against the door, reveling in the pleasure she was giving me.

Her mouth continued its tour of my body as she let go of my scrotum and licked her tongue up my shaft, her hand now stopping its constant stroking. Her tongue made it to my opening, pre-cum dripping out of it, and licked the hole clean. My whole body spasmed with the extreme sensitivity of my cock as she gently teased its head with her tongue and then closed her mouth around it. She was treating my cock's head like a lollipop, sending me into shivers of pleasure. Her mouth was teasing me, alternating in giving and taking, when all I wanted was for her to take me as deep as she could and send me into an orgasmic release.

Anna must have been a mind-reader because, at that instant, instead of pulling off me, her hands gripped tightly on my ass, and she slid her mouth down my shaft until she couldn't get any further. She didn't have all of me in her mouth, but that was no problem for me as her tongue wagged back and forth on my shaft. My saggy position against the door was over as I stood ramrod straight, my legs flexing and my heels coming off the floor. I let out a loud moan as Anna slid back off me for a quick breath and then buried me inside her mouth again. This time, with another loud moan, my heels sank back on the floor, and my legs tightened even more; I grabbed Anna's head, pulling it even closer to my stomach, and I exploded inside Anna's mouth. Anna coughed and groaned through her nose at my explosion, but she didn't stop her tongue as she swallowed each successive shot I delivered down her throat. I felt like my cock would not stop spasming, but when it finally did, I had no intention of pausing. I pulled my feet out of my pants that were still around my ankles, pulled Anna up off the floor, turned her around so her back was to me, and led her over to one of her bar-height stools in the kitchen.

I quickly pulled her pants down and off, pulled the stool away from the kitchen island, turned it around so it faced us, and had Anna sit on the stool with her chest leaning against the back and her ass sticking out to me. I pulled her hips another inch closer and admired how her absolutely beautiful ass was spread and waiting for me. I wasted no time in sinking to my knees and running my tongue up and down her crack, tasting the wet musk of her pussy and the earthy sweetness of her back door. Anna, pulling one hand from balancing her weight on the island, wasted no time in moving it to her clit, rubbing herself while my tongue teased her up and down, me wanting the savory smorgasbord to last and Anna wanting me to tongue fuck her ass. I wasn't going to rush things. I wanted her to build to orgasm during this foreplay so we would be on equal ground. One orgasm to one. This wasn't a competition. This wasn't about love. This was about lust.

My tongue finally focused in on the target's bullseye and ran circles around the tiny wrinkles of her beautiful, puckered hole. I could feel my saliva soaking her and her moans telling me she wanted more. I just continued to lick her hole, much like she had sucked the head of my cock. The taste of her, the movement of her hand on her clit, and the now muffled moans I could hear with my face buried in her ass were hardening my cock once again. Now was the time.

I slid my tongue just past her anal entrance and rimmed her as she cried out.

"Oh my god, Matt. Yes. Just like that."

I continued this, twirling my tongue in circles inside her, but just barely. After a bit, I decided to probe deeper inside and slid my tongue into her canal, feeling her clit hand pick up in intensity. This caused me to lose my teasing pace, and

I started madly tonguing her anus and listening to her moan. However, I knew she wasn't quite there yet, and my tongue was tiring. It was time to stretch her out and prepare her for the main event.

I pulled my face back from her, stood up, and sucked my pointer and middle finger into my mouth, soaking them with saliva. I inserted the pointer finger where my tongue had just been, burying it as deep as I could. I just left it there and let Anna adjust to the insertion, which she did very quickly. I pulled it out and carefully inserted both fingers into her back door. This time, her anus was a little more resistant to the insertion, so I left the fingers right there, as deep in her as I could be, and let her adjust to the stretch.

Anna had not stopped on her clit, and now she was wiggling her backside around on my fingers, moaning loudly and dripping juices from her pussy onto my other fingers that were not yet inside her. I slowly moved the pointer and middle fingers in and out of her, letting her get comfortable. When I knew she was ready, I pulled the fingers almost out of her ass and then got my ring finger and pinky ready. With one slow push, I buried all four fingers into her. Two in her ass and two in her pussy. Anna yelled out in utter pleasure, and I quickly forgot about anything slow or careful. I pounded her holes with my hand, my fingers pistoning in her, her hand on her clit working madly. Anna built very quickly, and both her holes clamped around me. I stopped pumping my fingers at this instant and just buried them as deep as possible into both of her holes, stroking her insides with all four fingers. She screamed out in an almost feral growl. Her body, still clamped around my hand, started spasming and shaking, and she fell off the stool, pulling my hand down with her. I caught her in my arms before she fell to the floor!

"Oh my god, Matt. Oh my god," she said.

If that was supposed to translate to "I need a minute," I ignored her. I pulled her back up to the stool in the same position as before, ignored the puddle of her orgasm on the seat, got behind her, and buried my rock-hard cock inside her now stretched-out anus. Her cry of pleasure let me know that although she might have thought she wasn't ready a second ago, she was more than ready. I pumped inside her, not vigorously, but at a pace that felt so good. I wanted this to last, and I wanted us to build together. I sank as deep as I could for a moment and pulsated my cock. With each pulse, I could hear Anna's breath catch. Finally, as I reached the moment of not being able to wait any longer, and Anna finally seemed to settle around my pulsing cock, I pulled back and started pumping furiously inside her ass. More furiously than I planned. The whole thing seemed so dirty and had me so turned on, my grunting and Anna's moans mixed with the sound of our bodies slapping together and my balls hitting against her wet pussy. I don't know how on earth I managed that pace and furious tempo for as long as I did, but finally, Anna screamed out and tightened her asshole around me as she came at the exact moment of my orgasm.

However, our simultaneous orgasms still didn't diminish our need for more. Before I could soften, I pulled her into my arms and off the stool. I kissed her and helped her back onto the stool, but now she was sitting on it normally. I pulled her ass to the edge of the cushion, leaning her back against the chair's metal back, spread her legs into the air, and slipped back into her ass. Anna grabbed onto her legs, pulling them practically behind her head. She was not only incredibly hot and sexy, but the woman was like a goddamn contortionist! I now pumped very slowly, letting us both recover and feel that pleasure all over again. I was concerned that Anna would be uncomfortable in that folded-up position, but she started moaning again. My left hand went to her clit, now that her hands were gripping her legs, and I massaged her clit while my cock continued to pump slowly inside of her.

The plan to recover was a gentlemanly thing to consider, and I am not trying to brag, but recovery seemed not to be a concern. Anna's pussy started dripping again, my cock was now rock hard, and Anna's moans started into screams again. I hit a new, furious pace, both with my cock thrusts and my clit hand, and Anna built up quickly to another orgasm.

"Yes, Matt. Fuck me. Pound my ass hard!" she screamed as her pussy exploded around my hand, soaking it.

Anna tightened around me as she had a squirting orgasm, dripping her juices down her slit onto my cock, and I could not hold back even if I tried. I came impossibly hard, especially for a third time in about 30 minutes, and this time, we did collapse. I pulled Anna into what would be best described as a "takedown" in wrestling, and we just sat there in each other's arms, catching our breath.

"Oh my god. That was even more amazing than I dreamed. I am *so* glad I texted you." Anna breathed out.

"Well, I must admit I was surprised by your text, but it was just what I needed."

However, I wasn't sure I quite believed my own words. Anna was very attractive, but holding her in my arms felt false. All I could think about was how badly I wanted Monica to be in my arms instead. I had hoped this would help get Monica off my mind. It didn't seem to work.

"I'm sorry to dash in and run off, but I must get home and prepare for tomorrow's school day. There is no rest for teachers who have to start at 7:00 a.m."

"Oh, don't worry. You gave me exactly what I needed," Anna said.

That made me feel even cheaper. This booty call had seemed like a good idea at the time—something to take my mind off all the shit from the past few days. Instead, as I left,

I felt cheap and, in some ways, even lonelier. I got in my car and caught my reflection in the rearview mirror. Again, as in the bathroom mirror at Deborah's, I wasn't very proud of the man I saw. I drove home, ate a sandwich, and went to bed. Sleep did not come easy.

Chapter 20

The rest of the week passed by in a blur. I couldn't get out of my head. I thought I could move past Monica, but I couldn't. I thought hooking up with Anna would take my mind off the negative things in my life, but now that just added to them. Hooking up with a married woman for a booty call went against everything I had ever stood for. The old me, a husband and father, would have condemned that instantly. Now I was running around, behaving badly, to get my mind off my troubles. I felt immature and lost.

The volleyball practices felt disconnected. Mercedes even asked me if I was okay. I told her things were bugging me about the upcoming funeral, but Mercedes knew this wasn't true. I am sure she caught me staring at Monica and knew something was happening. I thought I was carefully hiding all of these feelings during practices, but I was not fooling Mercedes. I decided that maybe I needed to come clean with her. On Thursday, I left and walked with her to the parking lot.

"You know you were right, don't you?" I asked.

"About what?"

"About Monica and I, when you said you thought we were a couple. We had a… I don't know how to phrase it… a fling. Things were going great, and then they went off the rails last weekend. It was due to her ex-husband being a dick to her, and then I didn't say the right things, and... well, you get the point. It *is* weird between us right now. I hope we can fix it, but she doesn't seem ready to discuss it."

Mercedes paused in the parking lot and looked at me.

"That's a lot!" she said.

For the first time all week, I laughed. I mean, I laughed out loud.

"Oh, you can say that again!"

"Are you okay?" she asked.

"No, but I am trying to get there. I've spent the last year trying to avoid people and relationships. Then, it seemed like I was ready to change that, but it fell apart this week. I don't know where I am now mentally."

I immediately realized that I had just unloaded a lot of my shit on Mercedes without even meaning to. That was not what I intended.

"Shit. Sorry. That was way too much information. I know I have a hard weekend coming up, but hopefully, old friends can help put things into perspective. Seeing people I haven't seen for a long time will be good."

"Well, good luck. I hope you find some healing this weekend."

I looked at her for a second. The term "healing" was a very powerful word at that moment. I was so worried about being there for my friend's family and helping them heal that I hadn't thought about what this trip might do for me. Maybe it would be good to get away and go back to my roots.

"Thanks. Good luck tomorrow at the game and have a good weekend."

As Mercedes got in her car, I turned toward my own. I needed to go home to pack and get ready to go back to my hometown. A place I hadn't been in a year. A place I hadn't been to since my dad died. I wasn't sure I was ready for this.

I got in my car and drove out of the parking lot. As I drove past the gym, I saw Monica come out. She looked tired. I also couldn't get over how beautiful she looked despite that. She was the last person I saw that night and, later, the last image in my mind as I drifted off to sleep at home.

The drive back to my hometown of Lake Forest was uneventful, unfortunately. I wanted to use the drive to get all the thoughts in my head out and focus on something new. Instead, I could only replay the last week in my head. I was bothered by the hurt of my argument with Monica, Michael's parents' accident, Rachel leaving, the fuck-and-flee episode with Anna, and missing the game tonight. It just seemed like a bunch of negativity that I couldn't kick. A bad mood I couldn't escape from.

Plus, I was heading home, but it wasn't home anymore. I had no family there. I wasn't staying at my dad's house. That house had been sold and was now someone else's home. It gave me the feeling of being in a sci-fi movie where the person travels to an alternate reality. The place they are going should feel familiar, but everything is slightly off. I wasn't a stranger in a strange land but a *native* in a strange land if that makes any sense.

My friends were the only thing I had going for me, but that familiarity would feel good. David had asked me to stay with him. He thought it would be cathartic for us all, and I couldn't argue. As crummy as I felt about my life, I figured staying alone in a hotel would worsen it. David's house would bring me something familiar, which would be very welcome. Besides, David and his wife, Alicia, were high school sweethearts who had married while in college. They had their two kids way earlier than Robyn and I did, so they had two teenagers already. Both girls were gone all weekend for an indoor soccer tournament in Indianapolis, so David had plenty of room for me. However, space was never a problem in their mansion.

When I arrived at David's early that afternoon, he and his wife were home. David and Alicia led lives that were much different from mine. David knew he was going to attend law school when he was ten. He was now a very successful corporate lawyer in the Chicago area. Alicia knew she would be a nurse when she was ten. She was wrong. Instead, she became a pediatric surgeon. You won't be surprised to hear they lived in a house on the lake about five times larger than mine in Waterton. I don't know how they did it, but they were still the most down-to-earth couple, despite their wealth. They didn't have a pretentious bone in their bodies.

When I drove up, David opened the gate to their property, and both of them were at the door when I approached with my suit bag and duffle.

"Hey, stranger!" David said. "Good to see you."

"Yeah, I wish it wasn't under these circumstances, but it is good to see you both."

David took my bags and put them in the closet by the front door.

"We can get these later. Let's sit in the sunroom for now and catch up," David said.

They hugged me and led me through their giant foyer into a gorgeous sunroom overlooking Lake Michigan.

"Before we catch up, how's Michael doing?"

"About as good as expected," Alicia said. "He was over last night. I think he needed to escape all of the planning and responsibilities that come with a terrible accident like this."

"Yeah, I understand that all too well," I replied.

David looked at me and said, "Of course you do. I think this is why it is so hard for all of us in our circle. This reminds us so much of your dad, Robyn, and the kids."

It was matter-of-fact, the way David said it. The kind of comment that was meant with sympathy but also the knowledge that they were so close to me that they went through it, too. David could say it, and I understood. It meant a lot to hear it. I started to thank him for saying it, but the instant I did, the similarity in both events came crashing down on me. The only sound that came out of my mouth sounded like an adolescent voice cracking, and my eyes welled with tears. I looked down and tried to regain my composure, but it didn't happen. Alicia popped up and said she would grab some drinks. David just sat and gave me a moment.

Alicia returned with lemonade, but I wasn't sure if that would be a strong enough drink for me. However, it did give me another moment, and by then, I had regained my composure.

"Sorry," I said. "It has been a rough week."

"We get it," David said.

I looked at him and almost told him that he didn't. He had no idea what my week had been like, but I decided to leave it alone. This weekend was for Michael and his family. It wasn't my pity party.

"To get back to Michael, I think he is doing better than expected. I doubt you know this, but his mom has had some health concerns lately, and the family has been doing end-of-life planning and getting affairs in order. You know what a planner Michael is! Thankfully, having a lot of things in place means he hasn't been scrambling, which can make a time like this even worse."

I understood that completely. It had taken me almost a year to get everything in order after Robyn and the kids died.

David continued, "You know, his wife's parents were older than ours, and they went through hell with their health at the end. Cancer, dementia, nursing home costs, and all of that was horrid. Michael said last night that he was glad there was no suffering his parents had to go through."

"Again, I understand that, too!" I said.

I tried to be upbeat about it, but it was pointless. No one expected this conversation to be anything but sad. I decided to move the conversation along.

"How are you guys and the girls doing?"

This was met with enthusiastic stories about their lives and finally brought a more upbeat feeling to the conversation. I was glad for it because I thought I would hold it together better than I did when we sat down. I was getting nervous about the visitation tonight and the funeral tomorrow. I hadn't been in a funeral home since I buried my wife and kids. I didn't know how it would go.

We sat there for another hour, talking about our lives and reminiscing, before David and Alicia asked if I wanted to see what was new in Lake Forest. I couldn't have cared less, but it would be a good way to keep chatting and keep ourselves busy. I agreed, and we all jumped into David's huge and expensive SUV, and they drove me around Lake Forest. Some things had changed, and a lot of things hadn't. It felt familiar, and I realized my previous thoughts had been wrong. It wasn't the town that was a strange land, and I was a native; it was the opposite. This place was familiar, but I was a stranger. I think David and Alicia had thought this little tour would bring me a sense of closeness or fond memories of the town. Instead, it just made me realize how little like home it felt. I wasn't the least bit surprised.

After a wonderful Italian dinner, we returned to the house and changed for the visitation. My expectation of this being emotionally challenging for me was not the case. We arrived, stood in line, greeted the family, and then hung around talking to people. It was fun to catch up with people I hadn't seen in a long time. I don't know if I was trying to be strong for Michael and his family or whether I had just gotten a lot out of my system during the day with David and Alicia, but I felt a sense of peace at the funeral home. Even the occasional condolences regarding my dad or wife or kids didn't seem to get me down. I liked that these people cared and kept my loved ones in their thoughts.

Of course, Michael was swamped with people at the visitation, so we only spoke briefly in the receiving line. After an hour, David, Alicia, and I decided to leave. I briefly pulled Michael away from the line and told him he should try to come over to David's tonight if he could. He nodded, and we took off.

Back in David's SUV, I had only one remark.

"Not to be rude, but can we get a fucking drink now?"

David and Alicia laughed, and David drove us home. Once we were in the house, David took us into his private pub room. I laughed as I entered. Of course, David didn't have a man cave. He turned a room into his version of an English pub! Oh, to have lots and lots of money.

"Let me guess, you still don't drink anything sophisticated. Whiskey-cola for you?" David asked.

He knew me well. I wasn't much of a drinker, and when I did drink, I wasn't doing it for the sake of the quality of the beverage.

As the three of us sat there drinking and reminiscing about stupid things we did in high school, Michael called and said he was on his way. I was very glad to hear from him. I had hoped we would get to see him at David's tonight. It would be a good way to end the night.

As it turned out, it wasn't the only person I would hear from before the night was done.

Chapter 21

Michael was in much better spirits than I expected when he arrived. He explained that it was so good, in so many ways, to have the visitation over. He felt a flood of sympathy, condolences, and relief. This was one area where I didn't know what he was going through. I felt so dead inside when Robyn and the kids died. I registered only anger and bitterness.

That's why I eventually ended up seeing a therapist!

I talked to Michael briefly about the subject, but he soon ended the conversation.

"I want to hear about you, Matt," he said.

"Oh, there's not much to tell. I teach and bike," I replied calmly.

"Bullshit!" said Michael.

"Yeah, what about this coaching you have been doing?" asked David.

"Oh, well, that's just to help out a friend," I said.

My nonchalance was not working, and I was practically giving away the idea that there was much more to it. However, I stood my ground.

Michael was having none of it.

"I want the whole story, because I know you. You aren't telling us something."

"Like, why are you coaching volleyball and not basketball?" Alicia asked.

"Oh, well, I will be coaching basketball, but a friend asked me to help with volleyball for now," I said, this time knowing I sounded deliberately evasive.

"Must be a hell of a friend to get you involved in a sport you know nothing about," David said with a hint of sarcasm.

"Well, Monica and I—"

"Oh, this friend is a woman! Now it makes sense," Michael interrupted.

I shot him a look, and he didn't budge.

Alicia spoke gently to me. "Matt, tell us the whole story. You are among friends here."

She meant to put me at ease and let me know they knew I had something to share and would be supportive. The problem was that I hadn't felt that at ease in a year, except with Monica. I tried to say something to evade again, but when I looked up from my drink and saw the faces of my best friends, I completely choked up. It just hit me out of nowhere. I wasn't sobbing, but I couldn't find the words. I took another drink from my glass, took a deep breath, and suddenly the words came spilling out.

I started at the beginning.

I don't mean Monica moving in with me; I went back to right after Robyn and the kids died. That was the last time I had sat in the same room with these people. They knew where I was coming from, so I told them about my dark times, not wanting anyone in my life, my therapy, Monica, Rachel's upcoming departure, and my crossroads with what I wanted to do with my life and relationships. I left out the sex party and the hook-up with Anna.

"You just said that Monica made you feel alive again, Matt. That has to be more than just some teen-like crush.

I know she is going through a lot, but I think you need to be clear with her, whatever you decide your relationship is," Alicia said.

"I know. I know," I said. "But it feels like my attempt to be on her side backfired terribly."

"Matt, from what you said, it sounded like you were being on her side, but it still backfired. I don't think she was in the headspace to have you be on her side or not. She was angry and lashing out at that moment, but please realize it doesn't have to be permanent. You are giving her time, and that may be exactly what she needs. Don't give up on people. You are too good a guy," Michael said.

I had never heard him sound so serious in his life. It wasn't rocket science he was speaking, but it made sense. He told me that I was being too hard on Monica and myself. I needed to be there for her if she would let me.

"We want to see you happy again, Matt," Alicia said.

"Thanks, Alicia. Thanks to all of you. I never realized how much I missed you until right now. You are the best."

Michael finished his first drink and announced it would also be his last. He had to get back and make sure everything was ready for tomorrow. We understood. I was tired, both physically and mentally. I could only imagine how Michael felt.

After Michael left, and David, Alicia, and I had another drink, I excused myself and went to my room. I grabbed my bags from the foyer closet and headed upstairs. As I walked up the stairs, my phone buzzed with a text message. My hands were full, and I couldn't check it immediately. Besides, I was tired and preoccupied with my thoughts from the conversation with my friends.

I unpacked my stuff for the night, brushed my teeth, stripped to my boxers, and grabbed my phone off the bed to charge it. Then, I saw that the text message notification on my phone had Monica's name on it. The text was simple.

It told me that they won the match, the team missed me, and she missed me in her life.

I called her immediately.

"Hi," Monica answered.

"Hi. I got your message, and I'm glad the team won."

An awkward silence hung between us.

Finally, Monica asked, "How are things there?"

"They are good. The situation is sad but seeing people I know and love is good. The time with my friends has been very cathartic and I have been given some good advice to pull my head out of my ass and talk to you about things. About *us*, I should clarify. I really miss you."

"Matt, tonight in the locker room after the match, the girls were happy but said they missed you. It made me realize how much I miss you, too—and not just on the bench. I talked to Rachel, and she shared what she has heard from you. I think this week has just been … well, stupid. I want to see you when you return and talk about things, too."

At that moment, I knew I was leaving after the funeral and going home, not staying here. I needed to see Monica and let her know exactly how I felt.

"That sounds great. It is late now, anyway. Let's get some sleep, and we can talk on Sunday. I should be back late tomorrow, after the funeral."

"Perfect. I can't wait to see you," she said.

"Me too. I will see you on Sunday."

"Good night."

I responded with the same and hung up. I was suddenly very happy and very tired. I fell asleep surprisingly quickly!

Chapter 22

I woke to thoughts of Monica. I wanted this talk to happen as fast as possible, to be with her, to make it all right again, and to hold her in my arms.

But I slammed the brakes on that and rubbed my face as I lay in bed to bring myself back to reality. I had a funeral today. I had friends who needed me. I had other priorities right now. I also needed to make sure I didn't fuck things up with Monica even worse.

It would be a mistake to immediately run to her, yelling, "I need you, I want you, I'm in love with you, and now that I've said it, it's all better now, right?"

I also needed to listen to her and find out what she wanted. Those lines of communication had been pretty damn good up until that Sunday morning. I hoped we could get that back.

I got up and went downstairs to the kitchen. Alicia made excellent pancakes and eggs, and the coffee was good and strong. I needed that to help clear my head of all the thoughts running through it.

"Alicia, you didn't need to cook for me," I said as I ate.

"Give me a break! I'm a mom, not a cook. I had these in the freezer. The girls are usually too busy for me to cook a lot, so I make meals ahead of time and freeze them."

"Well, everything is fantastic. Thank you."

"It is good to have you here. Speaking of that, are you staying tonight, too?"

"Actually, no. I had planned to, but I want to get back tonight."

I didn't quite know how to say that I wanted to get back to Monica without being crass about the funeral, but I decided just to be honest.

"Actually, I heard from Monica last night, just before I went to bed. She said she misses me and wants to talk. I want to get back tonight so I can see her tomorrow," I admitted.

Alicia looked at me and smiled.

"She seems important to you."

I paused. Alicia's use of the word "important" was not what I had expected. I had been thinking about more mundane words to describe how I felt about her, but Alicia was right on.

"Yeah, she is. Maybe more important than anyone else I have ever met, Alicia. And, without probing too deep into that confession, I can't explain it. She is like everything I had with Robyn, but more."

I paused.

"Actually, Alicia, that's not true. Monica is like everything Robyn wasn't. Yes, we connect on a deep level like Robyn and I did, but she is so much more energetic and fun. Maybe it is just the excitement of being in that first-love stage, but she seems perfect for me."

Alicia said nothing.

"Was that too much? Too cliché?" I asked.

"No, Matt. I'm just glad to hear you talk like that. I think it is time you open yourself to these feelings, and you have found someone. Go for that, and don't run away from it."

I looked at her and nodded.

She broke off the relationship talk and told me that David was working out in their home gym and then would be in for breakfast. We waited for him to arrive, teased him about how bad he smelled, and sat in the kitchen talking as he ate. We all needed to get ready soon for the funeral, so I excused myself and went upstairs to shower, dress, and pack my things. When I came downstairs, I saw no one else was around, so I returned to the sunroom and looked at the lake. I always took the lake for granted when I was growing up here. Right now, it looked beautiful, and it somehow grounded me. I sensed a feeling of home, but now I also felt ready to move on confidently and start living again for the first time in a long time.

I felt happy.

I heard Alicia and David come downstairs, and they turned as I walked out of the sunroom.

"Wait!" cried Alicia. "Stay there. Come here, David."

Alicia brought David into the sunroom and pulled out her phone.

"When we walk outside, our moods will change because we are going to a funeral. Before that, let's take a selfie and remember the fun of getting together again. Let's make sure we capture some of the happiness this weekend!" Alicia said.

We stood together as Alicia snapped the pic. It felt good to be with these friends and to feel that happiness!

The drive home felt like I was moving at a snail's pace. I left the funeral luncheon at around two o'clock. It was a good day of memorials, laughing, crying, and reminiscing. I was glad I went. The weekend had been good for Michael's family, but it had been good for me, too. I finally felt like my head was screwed on straight. I knew what I wanted. I wanted to do more with my life. I wanted to achieve things I had thought about but hadn't done. I wanted to live again and stop hiding in the shadows of my gloom and grief.

I wanted to be with Monica.

The thought of her never really left me all day. I texted her before leaving the church parking lot, where the funeral and luncheon were. It was a quick exchange detailing how the funeral went and that I would be home around dinner time that evening. I couldn't wait to see her tomorrow!

I put my phone down and drove out of the parking lot. I turned on an audiobook and headed for home. I had a three-and-a-half-hour drive and couldn't wait to be there. I had been surprised by how motivating this weekend had been, and then it occurred to me that maybe it was because I was around good people who knew me and wouldn't let me wallow in my bullshit. Monica had been like that with me, and I loved her for it. I thought that was what I probably needed to tell her tomorrow. Unlike anyone else I had met, especially in the last year, she was the one person I wanted around, and I was better for it. She had pushed me outside my comfort zone, which I liked. That was what I wanted to say to her tomorrow. Instead of some line fresh from a sixth-grade hallway, I would tell her that she made me a better person and I wanted her in my life. I had never met someone I seemed so compatible with but pushed me to do things I normally wouldn't do. That seemed fair.

It also felt like I shouldn't spend the next three hours overthinking this! So, I settled in for the trip and focused on the audiobook. I would need all the distractions I could get before I saw Monica tomorrow!

Chapter 23

could forget about tomorrow. Monica's car was in the driveway when I got home. She still had the key and could come over whenever. I just thought she didn't want to come over right away. I was not going to push her at this time.

My stomach was doing flips as I walked from my car into the house. I didn't know how to start this conversation. What should I say? Should I play it casual or get down to business?

None of that mattered. As it turned out, no words were necessary.

When I walked in, she came out of the kitchen and straight into my arms. We said nothing but just held each other. Three minutes ago, I was worried about the words coming from my mouth. Speaking was not what Monica wanted to do with our mouths.

She started kissing me, and I felt she meant it as a romantic and sweet gesture, but it only stayed that way for a moment. As I kissed her back, our passion for each other and the longing we had been experiencing the past week exploded as our mouths pressed even harder together. The taste of her, the feel of her tongue tangling with mine, and the pulse of electricity that flowed through me when she bit down on my lower lip reminded me even more why I loved this woman. Being with her made me feel alive like nothing else.

As we moved down to my bedroom, our mouths didn't separate. I have no idea how we even managed to walk down the stairs like that, but we did. We were a single entity moving together, locked together at our mouths. Only my lifting of her shirt over her head broke our kiss. Almost telepathically, we quickly got out of our clothes, and I was on top of her on the bed, our lips locked together again. This was not about foreplay or taking it slow. We wanted each other. No, we *needed* each other! I broke the kiss, raised, rubbed my incredibly hard erection up and down her slit, and easily sunk deep inside her.

Her gasp as I entered her told me that she wanted me as much as I wanted her. It wasn't a gasp of surprise. It was a gasp of satisfaction. She had gotten exactly what she wanted.

So had I.

My lips returned to hers as I made love to her. Monica's warmth drove me wild with ecstasy. She felt so good back in my bed. In my arms.

We made love like that for a long time until I could take no more slow and steady. I rose and started pounding into her. Both of our moans exploded out of our mouths as we started to build to orgasm. It was as if we were synchronized. We built together, moaned together, and came together as she tightened around me, and I exploded into her, both of us convulsing and falling into each other's arms again.

But I didn't pull out. I went back to slowly pulsing my cock inside her and let us both prepare for session number two. My cock barely lost any hardness, and after a bit, was rock hard and ready to go again. Usually, at this point, I would try to plan something erotic or creative, but my mind was on autopilot right now. I flipped Monica over to her knees and entered her from behind.

Monica yelled out, "Oh my god!"

I instantly knew those three little words translated to "pound me as hard as you can." And that is what I did. I pumped so furiously into her that I didn't even recognize myself. This was like something out of a porno film. Monica's screams of ecstasy also did nothing to eradicate the porno analogy. This was unreal. It was ferocious passion and animalistic fucking!

I even yelled out, "Oh fuck, you feel so fucking good. Fuck I missed you!"

This spurred her on, and I continued giving her what she wanted.

But it didn't last long.

Her walls tightened around me again, and I came hard again! Monica shuddered and came around me as I yelled out my orgasm. I instantly pulled out and collapsed beside her on the bed. I held her tight, and we didn't say a word. I just laid there holding her. I never wanted to let her go.

Except, soon, without really realizing it, I had let go a little. My left hand was now caressing her back, and Monica gave a little hum that told me she enjoyed the massage. I started focusing on massaging her back and giving her a different kind of pleasure than what we had just experienced. And that plan was a good one. Until I moved my hand down to her lower back and brushed against the top of her ass; that very little brush, feeling her butt crack with my palm, sent me right back into a sexual passion.

I moved my hand to her ass and rubbed the incredible firmness this woman had in her glutes. She responded by turning completely on her stomach as I continued to massage her cheeks. After a few seconds, I straddled her legs and started using both hands to knead the muscles in her ass. I ran my eyes up and down this woman's unbelievably sexy body. Even the curve of her lower back turned me on. Every inch of her was sexy and turned me on so completely that I wasn't sure we would ever leave this bed.

My hands spread her ass cheeks apart, and I dipped my tongue down to her crack. I licked up and down, knowing she liked that teasing. I alternated this with kisses on her cheeks as my hands reached up to continue rubbing her back. I planned to continue this message and tease for a while. Monica had other plans.

Monica moved, putting her head down on the bed and raising her ass in the air, exposing her beautiful back door to me. The teasing was over. Monica was telling me exactly where she wanted my tongue.

I obliged.

With one more lick, starting at her wet pussy and ending at her tailbone, I pulled my tongue off her for a second and then stuck my tongue straight into her backdoor.

"Fuck, yes!" she breathed out.

Again, it was more like a sigh of satisfaction and less of a cry of surprise. She wanted every inch of my tongue inside her, and she knew I would be there for her. I probed her with my tongue, felt her fingers brush against my chin as she rubbed her clit, and could hear her moans increase in volume and tempo. My tongue seemed to synchronize with the tempo of her moans, and soon, I pulled out and replaced my tongue with two fingers. Monica gave a little cry as I entered her, and she stopped massaging her clit. She then took a huge breath and settled against the stretch I was giving her. I kept my fingers frozen in place, deep inside her, as she found that rhythm on her clit again. I then started probing, massaging, and fingering her slowly. I knew that she was slowly building in pleasure, but I also knew this was not going to be what put her over the edge. She wanted me to fuck that backdoor hard, and I was ready for it. I just wanted to make sure that she was ready, too!

That moment arrived pretty quickly. Her hole was stretched out nicely, properly wet from my tongue and her natural wetness, and I removed my fingers and positioned my erection directly at her entrance. I didn't tease. I didn't hesitate. I just pushed slowly and steadily into her anal cavity, burying myself deep inside her.

"Oh my god, Matt, that feels so good. Just stay there for a second."

I did just that. I stayed there, buried deep in her ass, and pulsed my cock so she could feel the head engorge inside her. I remained in that position for a while, just listening to her breathe and moan. Her breaths still seemed ragged, and her hand was moving frantically on her clit. Her hand reached back a couple of times to play with my balls. I was in no fear of losing my erection, but her hand on my balls made sure I was as hard as possible. This distraction was nice, but Monica was ready for me.

"Enough, slow stuff. Fuck me hard!" she said.

I started pumping slowly to make sure she was ready. She immediately told me she needed it harder, and I picked up the pace. I was initially worried that she wasn't ready for me to pound her, and I didn't want her to be uncomfortable. But suddenly, her cries, her moans, her hand on her clit, and her incredibly gorgeous and tight ass turned my brain off. The only thought was pleasure—an animalistic desire for this woman.

I started pounding her ass as hard as I could!

We were both grunting and moaning, loud and out of control. There was no thought about decency now. We were engaged in great sex, and that was the only focus in the world for both of us. There were no words. Just the sound of our bodies slapping together as I pumped in and out of her.

I don't know how long we lasted, but we once again built our orgasms together. Monica clamped her sphincter down on me as both of our bodies trembled and convulsed with orgasms while my seed shot deep into her ass. I stayed inside her for a moment, just holding on to her while my vision cleared from what had been, again, one of the most powerful orgasms of my life.

After a bit, though, I pulled out, and we collapsed on the bed. I held her close to me as we caught our breaths.

"That was amazing. You are amazing!" I said.

Monica turned over so she could look at me.

"I'm really glad to be back here. I'm so sorry I left like I did. I completely freaked out, and it wasn't fair to you."

"Monica, things were moving fast. Probably too fast for what was going on in our lives. We both should be sorry for some things, but I also don't want to focus on that now. Let's focus on us and take this at whatever speed works. I don't want to pressure you, but I want you to know I really want to be with you. My life is so much better now that you are in it."

Monica continued to look at me, but with tears in her eyes. She was silent as she gazed into my eyes as if gazing into my soul.

"You are just so kind and patient with me. And," she paused, "I haven't had that in my life. Even as a kid, I was always expected to put my head down and be good at whatever was asked of me. Don't think about it, do it, and success will be your reward. It was such a grind in school, volleyball, and my marriage, and no one could see me for me."

Monica abruptly stopped talking, and now the tears really came. I said nothing but held her tight and let her cry. I wanted her to feel like she could be whatever she wanted around me. I was just glad to have her back in my arms and life. I now knew that she felt the same way. Maybe not as in love with me as I was with her, but this was an excellent start—or retake—whatever this was.

Her head was still buried in my chest, but she wasn't crying hard anymore. I pulled her face up and kissed her. She responded by putting her hands on my head and pulling me in for an even closer, more intimate kiss.

When we finished, she looked at me and said, "I know this sounds crazy, but I'm so head over heels in love with you!"

I laughed out loud—a loud, raucous belly laugh.

"What?" she asked.

"That's what I have been so scared to tell you! I am so head over heels in love with you, too!"

She laughed right along with me, and then Monica moved on top of me, and we kissed some more. The fact that I was hard again was not lost on me. It also wasn't lost on Monica either as she lifted off of me, positioned my erection at her pussy, and slid down, taking all of me inside her. I moaned loudly and pulled her mouth back down to mine for more kissing.

Actually, we ended up doing a lot more than kissing!

Chapter 24

I had never had sex before in the spooning position. After Monica had ridden me to another orgasm and two more for her, she cuddled into me, and we spooned for a long time. I caressed her back, and we talked about how much we had missed each other over the past week.

"I realized this week that you have changed my life. You are so supportive of me—for example, just the coaching thing. You have involved me and taught me so much. You have made me think about who I am and how to overcome the last year of tragedies. You have made me a better person," I said.

Monica grabbed the hand that was caressing her and squeezed it.

"Plus, you have definitely made me a better lover. I have lost count of the number of orgasms we have had!" I added.

Monica responded by rubbing her ass against my cock.

"How about we add one more," she said dreamily.

I thought she was going to move, but she didn't. I wasn't sure what to do, but then it popped into my head to not move us from our current position. Although we were both on our sides, I could easily hold Monica's leg up to find her entrance. Plus, I couldn't be powerful with my thrusts in this position, which was fine. We had already done the powerful thing. This was more about being together and having a leisurely fuck. I guess, *another* leisurely fuck since we had just done that.

I pumped in and out of her, both of us building very slowly to our orgasms. This time, it was my hand on her clit as I fucked her, and that did the trick. Monica orgasmed once, but I continued to pump in and out of her and massage her sensitive nub. After another few minutes, my orgasm built, and my pumping and clit massaging became more powerful. As my balls tightened, so did my legs, and I gave two more powerful thrusts before burying myself as deep as possible, my seed exploding out of me. My massaging hand had fallen and gripped Monica's hip as I cried out with my climax. Monica took this opportunity to rub herself into another orgasm as my cock twitched inside of her.

As I slipped out of Monica, I was glad we had that brief conversation in bed because after this, our second leisurely fuck, we fell asleep in each other's arms. We spent Saturday night doing nothing but having sex, snuggling, and sleeping.

When we woke up the next morning, we were starving.

"Let's go to the Main Street Cafe and get breakfast," I said.

"Are you saying you are done being in bed with me?" Monica playfully asked.

"Not at all. I need sustenance for my sexual energy to be at peak performance, and then I plan on bringing you right back here."

Monica laughed and said, "That sounds good. I'm hungry."

The Main Street Cafe was almost empty. I was surprised, but realized it was fairly early on a Sunday. People would be flocking in between 8:00 and 11:00. We sat in a back booth, nursing the coffee the hostess had poured for us, and looked over the menu.

"What are you getting?" Monica asked.

"The breakfast burrito. That is my favorite here."

"Oh, I've never had it. I'm more of a pancake and eggs girl."

"Well, now that we have that out of the way, I think we know everything about each other that's important. The relationship is a done deal."

I immediately froze. I hadn't meant anything by it other than to be funny and cute, but my god, had I just undone the good thing we had going on?

"Sorry!" I exclaimed.

The look on my face must have been priceless because Monica laughed.

"Matt, you can talk about us being in a relationship. That's why I came back last night. Did I freak out a week ago when everything felt perfect and settled? Yes. Did I struggle with you saying that I should ignore my husband, that he was trying to get under my skin, and that I was in a fine position, legally, in my divorce? Yes. However, after many conversations with Rachel, Deborah, and my lawyer, I concluded that you were correct. You were the mature adult, and I shit all over you and ran away. I am not proud of it, but, most importantly, I realized I wanted to be in a relationship with you. I was scared that I was just on a rebound fling. I am not. I do have serious feelings for you. Coming off a failed relationship made me panic."

I looked at her for a moment. Then I said what had been digging at me for the past week.

"Monica, I don't know quite how to say this without being a dick about it, but I don't think you are coming off a failed relationship. I don't think that relationship was ever there. I don't want to say that I am better than anybody, but fuck, I think I am a way better partner than John ever could be. I intend to prove that to you as long as we're together."

I had more to say, but this felt like a good place to stop. I had said that I needed to calm down my desire for this woman and take things at a different pace. Maybe talking about being her partner for the long term wasn't keeping with that philosophy. I thought I should at least wait until after she had her pancakes eaten before asking her to marry me!

Monica looked at me, and her face took on a very serious look.

"Matt," she almost whispered, "you are amazing. Compared to anyone."

I smiled and almost reached across the table to hold her hand, but our waitress interrupted us.

"Hey, guys! I was just in the kitchen and didn't see you come in. What can I get you?" Carly asked.

Carly was on the volleyball team and was our team captain. She wasn't the best volleyball player, but she was the team captain because she was the best leader. She was an awesome student, played three sports, and worked at the cafe. I hadn't known about that last one until she approached our table. I was sure she realized Monica and I hadn't gotten together for breakfast so she could give me some volleyball pointers. I knew it would be difficult for Monica and me not to come across as a couple from now on. Ten days ago, that thought would have panicked me, but right now, it felt pretty damn good!

"Hi, Carly," Monica said. "Can I get the pancake and egg special with scrambled eggs?"

"Sure thing! And for you?" Carly asked me.

"Breakfast burrito with sausage and green salsa."

"Perfect. Are you both good with just coffee?"

We both responded in unison, "Yes," and Carly took off to the kitchen.

"I think this," I pointed back and forth between the two of us, "will be the locker room talk tomorrow."

"Matt, she is probably texting the team right now. It will probably be old news by tomorrow. Besides, they asked me about the two of us after your first practice. They aren't stupid." Monica laughed.

I just sat there for a moment, taking it all in.

"Wait. I know Mercedes caught on, but the team did, too?"

"Matt, Rachel teased you about checking out the head volleyball coach too much during practice. You may have been more guilty of that than you knew. Not that I minded it, you understand!"

I was blushing.

"Besides, I'm assuming some of the girls have heard about my divorce from Ashlynn," Monica added.

"Okay, speaking of Ashlynn, I know nothing about your kids. You haven't brought them up much since I met you, and I didn't want to interfere."

I just ended with that. I didn't know if Monica would even want me to ask specific questions, so I figured she could go into it if she wanted. I didn't want her to feel uncomfortable, but she just laughed.

"Yeah, I have kept the kids out of my conversations, but it hasn't been on purpose. I want to protect them, somehow, but I don't think I have to. As I said about the team, my kids aren't stupid either. They saw how bad it had gotten between John and me. I think this is difficult for them, but also a relief. That is why we decided to keep them out of this for now. Let them live their lives at college, and we will figure that out as it happens."

She paused and looked at me. I could tell there was something more.

"What is it?"

"Well," Monica said, "I think there is something else. I think I kept quiet about my kids because of you. I mean, us. I never expected our relationship to happen. I never expected *any* relationship to happen. So, I think that is why John's text last week upset me so much. To a degree, he was right. I ran away into the arms of a new guy and enjoyed the escape from all of my problems. That was why I felt so guilty and upset last week. However, with Rachel's help, I concluded it wasn't just an escape with some random guy. I realized what I felt was way more than that with you. It just came so unexpectedly quickly after things fell apart with John."

I laughed and agreed with her. Things had happened fast, but I told her that it didn't mean it was wrong. She told me she knew that now. I wanted so badly to reach over and grab her hand now, just like before. Carly interrupted again with a coffee refill. This was an acceptable interruption.

"Oh, and speaking of Ashlynn and Rachel, did Rachel tell you that Ashlynn is trying to play volleyball *and* basketball at Pitt? She's there, on scholarship, for volleyball, but she tried out and made the basketball team, so we will see how that goes. We always assumed she would play volleyball at a high level, but she fell in love with basketball in high school. I think it is because of having Rachel as her coach. Rachel showed her how to excel, but more than that, I think Ashlynn was ready for a coach that wasn't her mom. You know, Rachel versus your mom as a coach. It was a no-brainer who she was going to like better! But I haven't told her Rachel is leaving and they need a new basketball coach. She loved Rachel, and I think she will be a little crushed by her leaving."

I took a sip of coffee and looked at Monica.

"So, you haven't heard anything about the new coach they have in mind?" I asked.

"No. What do you mean?"

"Oh, It's not good. They are looking at a former player who has never coached before. Except for helping a volleyball team while ogling the team's head coach!"

"Wait. What? You?"

"I'm sworn to secrecy. I cannot tell a soul!" I answered with a mischievous grin.

"Oh, that would be great for you!"

"The better question is, would it be great for Ashlynn and the current high school girls?"

Monica paused, got a serious look on her face, and thought about it.

"You know, my initial thought was that it might be weird for them to have a man as a coach. But the girls on our team love you, so I think it will be a smooth transition for them. You are wonderful with the girls on our team now. As for Ashlynn, I'm not sure what she would think about her mom's new boyfriend as the coach, but I just told you how well she has been taking everything. She would approve if she knew you like the girls on our team."

I just stared at her with what must have been the dumbest but happiest look on my face.

"What?" Monica asked.

"Her mom's new *boyfriend*? That seems like a pretty official title. One I would accept with pride, but I still want to clarify what I heard."

"Yes, silly. I am calling you my boyfriend. Isn't that why I came back last night?"

"I hoped it wasn't just for the sex!" I whispered.

"Well, that, too!" she whispered back. "Besides, you promised me more after breakfast, so let's eat up and get back there!"

Carly brought our plates right then, and I jokingly started taking super-fast bites to show Monica how dedicated I was to getting her back to my bed!

Chapter 25

It isn't easy to drive safely while your girlfriend is jerking you off during the car ride back to the house. I am not complaining but simply stating a fact.

The second we got back into the car after breakfast, Monica unsnapped my pants, pulled down my zipper, and had my cock out, her hand gripping it tightly. I sat there, the car still idling in park, with my eyes closed, moaning.

"We should get moving," Monica said.

I opened my eyes, put the car in gear, and as soon as the wheels started moving, so did Monica's hand. She slowly started stroking me, and I found it very difficult to concentrate on the road. My cock was so hard in her hand that it almost hurt, but what she was doing felt so good. The drive home was not long, but as I turned onto my street, I thought I might orgasm in the car. I wasn't sure it was even possible for me to do that while doing something else. This had never happened to me. I thought this was warming me up for what would happen when we got inside. Monica had a different idea.

As I pulled the car into my driveway, practically panting with my arousal, Monica pulled her hand off me, spit into it, and then went back to jerking me off. Only now, she wasn't going slowly at all. The warmth of her hand and the lubrication of her spit had me so close. I slammed the car into park, and Monica continued pumping her hand on my cock.

"Oh my god!" was all I could say before I exploded.

I shot three spasms of cum over myself, practically convulsing while doing it. Monica's hand and my clothes were messy, and we needed to get inside. Immediately! She wiped her hand on my T-shirt, and we raced into the house and immediately went down to my bed. The clothes we had thrown on to go to breakfast were cast aside quickly, and Monica, who was naked first, got on the bed, laid on her back, and watched me struggle with my socks. I think she thought that I was going to get on top of her and plant my mouth on hers. I, however, had a much different plan for where my mouth would go!

As I got my last sock off, I was in a bent-over position, so instead of standing up and getting on the bed, I slinked my way up the bed and immediately buried my face in her sex. Flattening my tongue, I explored up, down, and all around. Monica cried out as my tongue entered her and explored as deep as it could reach. I pulled it out again and explored back up to her belly button, kissing her everywhere I could. When I finally focused my tongue on her clit, Monica screamed out like the pleasure was almost too much to take. Almost.

My tongue worked Monica's clit in circles and then flattened itself against her, pushing against her clit and deeper into the sensitive skin around it. I kept that up at a steady tempo, never wavering. I could sense Monica was enjoying this tempo and was building very steadily toward her orgasm. Just as I had that thought, though, Monica started moaning much louder. I knew she was closer than I even thought. I kept my tempo and allowed her pleasure to build organically, not rushing anything. She lasted longer than I guessed she would, but then, just when I started to doubt my skills, her legs tightened around my head, and she pushed me deeper into her crotch. I switched my tongue from the circular pattern and started licking her clit up and down like a lollipop. The musk of her pussy was exquisite, and her juices were already soaking my face. Suddenly, Monica's legs let go of my head, spread wide, and she sat up like she was doing an ab crunch. (I knew this only because I could feel those abs touching the top of my head. My face was too buried in this woman's beautiful pussy to be able to see anything!) She ran her fingers into my hair and then gripped tightly as she pulled my face even more into her wetness. I could barely breathe, but I didn't mind as she screamed out, spasmed her hips into my face, and gushed her warmth into my face and mouth. I swallowed her cum and slowed my tongue but stayed there, letting her body spasm and shake as her body came down from her incredibly powerful orgasm.

She was limp as I pulled my head away from her and snuggled up next to her, my hand playing with her nipple.

"Fuck, no. I can't take it. Way too sensitive right now," she breathed out.

I pulled my hand back down to her side and just snuggled her until her body calmed and her pulse slowed.

"How do you do that?" she whispered.

"Do what?"

"Make me come so hard all the time!"

"I don't know. We always seem in sync, no matter what we are doing. Plus, I am so incredibly attracted to you that it is pretty easy."

"Yeah, but Matt, I mean, I have never squirted before in my life, and you make me do it almost every time. I hope you don't mind," she said sheepishly.

"What?! Monica, how can you think that isn't the hottest thing in the world? Watching you experience an orgasm that powerful is the most amazing thing I've ever seen. Come in my mouth whenever you want!"

This made Monica laugh. But the laugh didn't last long. I rolled on top of her and slipped my erection deep inside her pussy. Monica gasped at the insertion, and I gave her very little time to adjust as I raised and started thrusting inside her. We had both had very recent and powerful orgasms, so we lasted a long time, but I never stopped, and we never switched from that position. We stared into each other's eyes as we made love for what seemed like forever. It was incredibly pleasurable, and we seemed to be linked together as a single entity. It was a very weird experience but also one of the most powerful experiences of my life. When we finally came together, I kissed her, swallowing her orgasmic scream as our bodies spasmed together.

I collapsed next to her, and we tried to catch our breaths. We unconsciously slipped into a snuggled-up spoon position and closed our eyes.

"You know I'm in love with you, right?" I whispered.

"Yeah, I know."

"Does that scare you?"

"Not at all. It's how I feel, too," she said.

"Perfect."

No other words were said as we fell asleep.

Chapter 26

The next week was one of the best of my life. Monica and I continued to be as synchronized as two people who have been friends their whole lives. We made love at night and in the morning, texted each other when we could during the day, and had so much fun at volleyball practices. She was very helpful as I did my coaching licensure work. It was like we couldn't get enough of each other!

Our post-volleyball practice routine was getting something to eat and relaxing on the couch, which wouldn't last long before she was going down on me or I was performing analingus on her. That would, of course, lead to about an hour of sex on the couch until I realized I had school or licensure work to do. I would be a good boy and get that done, and then Monica and I would usually have more sex. It was great. But Thursday, after practice, it was different. I had done a lot of running in practice, and instead of taking off my hoodie like a normal person, I left it on and got sweaty. I felt gross when we got home. I told Monica I needed to shower quickly and would be ready for food afterward.

The shower was quick, but Monica wasn't in the kitchen when I got out. I exited the bathroom wearing only my towel, but she was standing by the bed, wearing nothing at all.

"Aren't you hungry?" I asked.

"Oh, I'm hungry. Just not for food."

"What do you want?"

"You," was all she said, pushing me onto the bed so I could sit.

"Lose the towel," she demanded.

I dropped the towel, and once I had done that, she sank to her knees, her hand now on my balls.

"Lean back so I can move these out of the way," she said.

I didn't quite realize what she was saying, but I leaned back. As I did, she released my balls, pushed my legs up into the air, lifted my scrotum, and licked her tongue up and down my ass crack.

My body shook with pleasure, and I cried out like an over-acting porn star. I didn't mean to, but I had never had this done to me. This was a fantasy I never thought would come true! Monica just continued to lick me up and down. Every time she hit my hole, my body would spasm with pleasure. She could feel it, too. I knew she could. She was teasing me. She knew I wanted that tongue to stay right there on my backdoor, licking and, hopefully, fucking me soon. My wish was granted when her tongue stopped going up and down and just focused on wetting that tight little target. My body couldn't stop twitching with each sensation of her tongue on my hole. I was super sensitive there, like an erogenous zone beyond comprehension. This was pure pleasure and felt so amazing and so taboo at the same time. I had been on the giving end of this many times with Monica, but I never knew how good it was to receive it! It was mind-boggling.

All descriptions were surpassed when the tip of her tongue entered me! My body shuddered with the pleasure and the surprise of this new activity. Monica's tongue sank deeper and started moving around my entrance as I cried out in a combination of ecstasy and shock. Monica was now working me like this was some tongue exercise for her, and I absentmindedly started stroking myself. I knew I was close to coming.

Monica pulled out and said, "No, that's my job. Get on your knees."

I was confused but rolled over in the bed and got on my knees. Monica pulled on my hips so my ass stuck out to her even more, and she re-buried her tongue in me and grabbed my cock with her hand. Her tongue and hand moved in a furious rhythm, eating my ass and jerking my cock. As it turned out, I was right. I had been very close to coming. My hips bucked as I shot my load all over the bed sheets. With each buck of my hips forward, I would move away from Monica's tongue but then slam back with the recoil, driving her tongue deeper. Those sensations seemed to prolong the orgasmic feeling, even as I finished spraying my seed on my bed.

Monica continued to gently lick me as my body stopped shaking from my orgasm and my pulse slowed. However, as I recovered, Monica also made sure that my dick didn't. Her tongue continued working my hole while she gently massaged my balls. I had never had such a powerful and explosive orgasm and not even softened after it. I believe the sex scientists refer to this time between erections as the "refractory period," and right now, mine was zero. Monica was unrelenting, and I was here for it!

"Switch me places!" Monica said.

I couldn't quite react to what she said. I was in too much of a sex haze to realize what she wanted. Monica laughed and gently pushed me to the side and assumed the same ass-in-the-air position that I had just been in. I figured out what she wanted when I saw that beautiful ass shaking itself playfully in front of me. But I changed my mind as my face moved in to reciprocate the favor.

I went over to my bedside table and took out some warming lube I had recently bought but hadn't used yet. Instead of my tongue finding her, I licked my index finger and inserted it into her tightest hole. Her surprised cry told me I had caught her off guard, but she liked it. I pulled that finger out, licked my middle finger, and inserted them both, keeping them deep inside her ass but not moving. When I felt Monica had adjusted to this intrusion, I fumbled open the lube bottle with my left hand and squirted a liberal amount onto my erection. I closed the bottle, dropped it on the bed, stroked the lube onto my length, and pulled my fingers out of Monica quickly. Her gasp at my fingers leaving her ass was interrupted by a louder gasp as my cock substituted for the job my fingers had been doing. Monica screamed out as my cock, which was much thicker and longer than my two fingers, slid deep into her backdoor canal. Only staying there a moment, I then started pumping in and out of her very gently, letting the lube do its job and preparing Monica for the ass fucking she was going to get in a minute.

We hadn't done anal for a few days, and she seemed so incredibly tight and warm. I mean, the lube helped with the warmth, but still, it was like her ass was sheathing me perfectly. It felt so good that I hadn't even realized I had sped up my tempo considerably. I reached around her hip with my left hand and found her clit unattended. I worked her clit and fucked her ass and just listened to her moans and breaths increase in speed and volume.

"Fuck me, Matt. That feels so good. I'm going to come all over this bed like you did." she screamed out.

Well, that changed things. Her dirty talk always drove me over the edge. I couldn't continue with this pleasure exercise anymore. I needed to fuck her hard!

I pulled out, which elicited a groan of displeasure from Monica, stood on the bed for a much better angle at her ass, plunged back inside her now gaping hole, and pounded her as hard as I could. This lasted a longer time than I thought possible (props to our stamina!), but finally, her body spasmed and clamped onto me as we both exploded together.

Exhausted, we collapsed to the bed, not caring about how wet and gross the sheets were. I don't know if there is a world record for the number of amazing orgasms in one night, but it felt like the two of us could compete for it!

Everything was perfect between us now, and nothing could challenge that. However, life still had a couple of curve balls to throw our way.

Chapter 27

As the next week progressed, Monica and I fell into a routine. Morning sex, work, volleyball practice, dinner (or maybe sex first), relaxing or preparing for the next day, lots more sex, and then sleep. If that sounds boring, it wasn't. Not for one second! A lot was going on in our lives. First, I was almost done with my coaching license work, and the girls varsity basketball job would be posted soon. If all went well, I would be very busy preparing for my first head coaching experience. Almost equally as joyous was that Monica's ex-husband had calmed down, and it looked like their divorce would be settled quickly. That made Monica so much happier and calmer.

What didn't make her calmer was the volleyball team. But in a good way. We had started the season with low expectations from the media. We weren't even expected to win our conference. However, the volleyball team was now undefeated, highly ranked, and considered a state championship contender. Exceeding all expectations is good, but the team also felt the pressure of being highly ranked. Through it all, Monica was great at keeping the girls focused, but at home, she confessed that she felt overwhelmed about leading them to the playoffs and maybe the state tournament. I found that I was good at keeping the team loose in practice, and also, sometimes, even Monica would crack up at my stupid shit. We kept it very professional, but we knew that Mercedes and the girls had figured out we were more than friends. It didn't seem to matter. It might have gelled the team a little. I don't want to sound cliché, but it started feeling like a family on the court. We hoped it would stay that way for the rest of the season!

So, things were going great when I received a text at lunch on Thursday. It was from Anna Webster. I hadn't even thought of Anna since Monica returned and we got serious as a couple. All of a sudden, I felt a pang of guilt. Well, two. One for forgetting about her and one for not being open with Monica about that night during our "breakup." I felt so guilty about even doing it; I think I had blocked it from my mind. It had felt cheap and not intimate at all. Besides, it felt like I had done it behind Monica's back, which I hated. Monica was the only one that mattered to me, so why had I done it? That was my first time doing something like that, and I hoped it would be my last. Now I was worried Anna wanted more.

However, Anna didn't want more. She thought Ethan would be cool with her "exploring" without him, but that was wrong. He was fine with the swinging parties they attended together, but not one-on-one hookups. She wanted me to forget it had happened.

I laughed and texted her that although it was fun, it might not have been the most mature decision. I added that Monica and I were now a couple and that I would be glad to pretend nothing happened!

Anna agreed, and we said we would move on from it. She did add that she hoped we would be back at another Small-Town Swingers Club party. I told her that we would await our invitation. That was the end of our texting, but

I wasn't sure if there would be another swinging party for Monica and me. That was something we hadn't discussed.

So, I felt better about putting the incident with Anna out of my mind, but I still didn't feel good about keeping it from Monica. I thought at first that she didn't need to know what had gone on that week. It wasn't like we were officially dating or anything at that time. We were both single, and we could do what we wanted. However, I had gone against my better judgment that night, and although it was in the past, it still didn't seem right to me that Monica didn't know. I didn't want to blurt it out, but I didn't want Monica to learn it from Anna. I hoped there would be a good time to get it off my chest. I didn't know when that would be.

And then, as we got home that night from practice, Monica caught me completely off guard.

"Deborah talked to me today. She wants to have another swinger party in a few weeks. Do you want to go?"

"Oh, I..." I stammered and couldn't think of anything else to say.

"What's wrong? Do you not want to go?"

All of the stuff with Anna jumped into my mind, leaving me at a loss for words.

"No, I have been in 'exclusive' mode with you the past couple of weeks. I hadn't thought about it. Do you want to go?"

"Yeah. I had a lot of fun at the last one."

"I remember that you did. It was fun for me but also weird. But to be honest, I think it will be much easier for me to get into it a second time, especially if you want to go. Besides, I think last time, I was very much stuck in my head about being with you and only you. I was unsure where things were going, but I am much more comfortable now, so let's do it!" I said and kissed her.

For some reason, this didn't seem like the time or place to bring up the Anna situation.

"Excellent! I'll tell Deborah that we are in. Now, I think you need to kiss me more."

"Oh, I plan on doing more than that!" I answered as I took her down to my bedroom.

The next two weeks were spent with the volleyball and basketball teams. The volleyball team was still undefeated, and we were now looking at preparing for regionals and then the state tournament. The Waterton volleyball team had never made the state tournament before. At the start of the season, Monica had told me that she thought the team would be good, but to be undefeated and highly ranked in the first week of October was crazy. So, Monica was busy trying to push the girls but not overdo it, either. Monica told me that was a mistake she had learned from her college coach. You can push your players too hard at the end of the season, hoping for success, and then find you have a team that is too fried to compete well. So, our routine at night had become very thrown off as Monica spent more time with volleyball than me.

Of course, I wasn't any better. The basketball season practices would start in a month, and although I wasn't officially hired, I was acting as if I was. I met with Rachel periodically to review what she had done with her teams. It was more than just coming up with drills and plays to run. Rachel ran through a lot of the pitfalls of coaching. She told me that drills are good, but you can't bore them to death with two hours of drills a night. I understood that from Monica's practices. Her practices were always intense but had a sense of fun to them, as well. Yeah, the girls would have to run and do other things they didn't like, but I understood that if the team knew this was making them better, they could get behind the idea.

So, that was what our October was going to be. Work, lots more high school girls sports, and a lot less sex. That last one was unfortunate. But through it all, Monica and I remained committed to improving our relationship. The night before our last regular-season match, Monica came home well after me. She had to meet with her lawyer after practice and then return to her office to do some things for work. She came home to find me stressed out over grading papers and preparing my season for the basketball team. Monica, the one who had work, a divorce, and a team she was leading to a hopeful state championship to worry about, asked me what was wrong. As I opened the refrigerator to put food away, I told her how stressed I was and immediately felt silly complaining to this amazing woman who had way more on her plate than I did. This was something Robyn never would have let pass when we were married. She would have told me that others had it worse, and I should get over myself. (Robyn also would have given me crap for my current outfit—basketball shorts, and nothing else.) However, Monica handled it differently.

Monica approached me, closed the refrigerator door, and said, "Let me see if I can help relax you."

I thought she was being cute and would give me a kiss or something. Hell, I expected her to tell me I had nothing to complain about and to get my head out of my ass. Instead, she sank to her knees right in front of the refrigerator, pulling my shorts and boxer briefs down with her. Her mouth took my flaccid member into her mouth, and she bobbed her head up and down, instantly eliminating the flaccid description. It had been a few days since we had anything but a morning quickie, and Monica's mouth reminded me how long it had been.

Her tongue folded around me as her head bobbed up and down, and I leaned back against the refrigerator, not bothered in the least by the cold metal on my back. The warmth of Monica's mouth and the quickening of my pulse kept me warm.

Monica's mouth continued to bob up and down on my shaft a few more times before she pulled off and started sucking my balls. I went rigid with pleasure as my erection seemed to grow even harder. Monica moved back and forth, pleasuring each of my balls until I was moaning so loudly it seemed to reverberate off the refrigerator. Monica switched it up again and licked up and down the bottom of my shaft, each time stopping at the top and licking pre-cum from my cock's opening. After multiple licks up and down my shaft, Monica placed her lips around the head of my cock and twirled her tongue around and around, up and down, on just the very sensitive glans. This would make me come very soon, and I let Monica know about it. She immediately went back to bobbing her tightened mouth up and down my shaft, looking up into my eyes, sucking me hard, and pressing her tongue into my penis, making the suction around me unbelievably tight and pleasurable. Her eye contact drove me crazy because I could see the lust and enjoyment in her eyes. She knew exactly what she was doing to me and loved it!

At that moment, my legs tightened, my moans became yells, and my cock started pulsing in her mouth. Monica knew I was seconds away from blowing my load and responded with the unthinkable. She slid her mouth all the way down me, took me into the back of her throat, milked me with her throat muscles, and then froze, with her nose touching my belly button, as I exploded into her throat. My legs shook as my hips spasmed with each shot of my load. My moans had been building for what seemed like forever, and I finally exploded out in a scream as my cock exploded into Monica's mouth. Monica didn't move but let my seed go down her throat. When my hips finally stopped bucking, Monica pulled up off of me, took a deep breath, smiled up at me, and licked my shaft clean. My legs had stopped shaking; they were only trembling now, and I slid down the refrigerator to join Monica on the floor. I kissed her gently.

"Are you okay?" I asked.

"Oh, yeah. Why wouldn't I be?"

"Well, you… you took me deep in your throat, and I came hard in your mouth." I said sheepishly. "I just hope you are good with that."

Monica laughed.

"Matt, I love giving pleasure as well as receiving. I wouldn't have done it if it wasn't good for me, too."

After kissing me quickly, she said, "You know, for someone so good in bed, you can be a prude sometimes."

I laughed at that.

"Yeah, I know. Let's say I have never had a sex life like I have with you. It is amazing. *You* are amazing!"

This earned me much more kissing right there on my kitchen floor.

"Feeling more relaxed?" Monica asked.

"Oh, yeah. So relaxed I can't move."

"Well, that's too bad because I want you to take me to the bedroom now," Monica said with a shit-eating grin.

"Oh, yeah? Then forget what I just said. I am more than ready to move. Ready, willing, and able, my love!" I joked.

Then, a thought hit me.

"Wait, don't you need dinner?"

"Nope. I ate on my way to the office. Right now, the only thing I need is you," she said in a sexy voice; I thought I would melt.

With that, I easily found the power to take Monica to the bedroom. My body had recovered nicely, and I *was* ready, willing, and able!

Chapter 28

I wasn't sure how we found any stamina after that long day and after what had happened in front of my refrigerator, but we made love for a long time. We couldn't get enough of each other.

I led Monica by the hand to the bedroom and laid her down on the bed, me on top of her. Our lips found each other, and we kissed deeply, passionately, our tongues tangled together, her teeth biting my lower lip. I was hard as a rock again, and instead of any foreplay, I guided my hardness up and down her slit. Her pussy was already incredibly wet, and I slipped inside with no other warning. Monica's gasp told me this was a good decision, and her teeth bit down on my lip even harder.

I pumped into her slowly because, one, I wanted to, and two, I was still lying on top of her and kissing her. I couldn't get a great angle in that position. However, right now, it didn't matter. This was a passionate moment, and the closeness of our bodies and our intertwined mouths made for pure ecstasy. I could hear Monica's moans get louder as I continued to slide back and forth in her wetness. The feel of her pussy tightening around me and the taste of her mouth had me right where I wanted to be.

Suddenly, Monica tore her mouth away from mine and let out a louder moan. I seized the opportunity to move my mouth down to her neck, kissing every inch I could. I nibbled gently on her earlobe, and when her moans became louder, and her breaths became more ragged, I knew I had her on the precipice of pleasure.

"Oh my god, yes!" she exclaimed.

I moved down to the base of her neck, near her collarbone, and intended to kiss her. However, Monica's moans triggered a more passionate frenzy, and I bit into the skin here, sucking it. I knew this would leave a mark, but I also knew she was marking me with the way her fingernails were scratching into my back.

I raised off her, being able to take no more, and I started pounding her hard. The frenzy now had us both in its grasp. Monica screamed out as my hips bucked into her as hard as they could. I kept that furious pace for a long time, amazingly, and then, as I sensed Monica's body tense with her orgasm, I raised into a push-up position, my body rigid, and I sunk as deep into her as I could with a few powerful thrusts. It was only a few because she soon clamped her vaginal walls around me, and her body started spasming.

"Come with me!" she shouted.

As her orgasm built to that tipping point, I felt my hips buck one last time before my body spasmed, and I shot yet another load into Monica. Her body spasmed, seemingly as she felt my seed inside her, in rhythm with mine as she came on my cock. My body seemed to have a few more convulsions before I sank back on top of her and returned my mouth to hers. We stayed like that, with me still inside her, kissing and realizing that we still wanted more. I made sure not to pull out of her, and as my cock regained its hardness and pulsed inside her, I realized Monica's moans were already back. This time, I pushed up off of her again and started pumping more gently than before. I wanted this to go slow and build much more gradually than we had done a minute before. I then lowered my head down to her left breast. I sucked on that nipple, feeling it harden in my mouth. Monica's moans became louder, and I switched my mouth over to her other nipple, making sure that one was just as hard. Monica's moans started to drive me insane, and I rose back up, feeling my head fall backward in ecstasy.

Monica was feeling a little bit more ecstasy than me because I soon realized that she was going to beat me to the punch. She orgasmed while I was still pumping away, my orgasm feeling very far away. However, any fear that her orgasm had her in a mood to quit was unfounded. Monica seemingly had that orgasm and fell right back into the building for another one. She was insatiable, and I loved that about her!

I continued to pump in and out of Monica but suddenly needed her in a new position.

"Get on your knees!" I almost shouted.

I pulled out and guided Monica to a doggie-style position. I slid into her from behind, pulled her even closer to me so I was as deep as possible, and threw the idea of slow and gentle out the window. I pounded Monica at a frantic pace, both of us on our knees. This time, I could feel my orgasm build quickly.

"Yes, Monica. Yes! I'm going to come. Come again with me!" I shouted.

She needed no instructions. I gripped her hips and, with one final thrust, buried myself deep inside her as my body shook and my cock erupted. We both screamed out, came powerfully, and shuddered as our bodies stayed pressed together for a few seconds. After that, we collapsed to the bed, me still holding her in my arms. We were so pleasantly exhausted and out of breath! We just lay there together, not moving, not talking, feeling each other's body thrumming with pleasure. We were both not going anywhere for a while!

"You are so amazing in bed," she said, "for a prude!"

I laughed at that and held her close.

"Well, maybe you just bring out the depraved sex addict I never knew about."

Monica laughed big at this. She turned in my arms so she could face me, and then she kissed me.

"Are you sure you are okay with Deborah's swinging parties?" she asked.

I paused at this. I thought about giving her a politically correct answer, but then I realized that if this relationship was going to work, I needed to be honest.

"When we went to the last one, I wasn't. I felt like I wanted you and only you. Then, when I was with the other women there, I felt like I was somehow cheating on you. It confused me. But now, I view it as a party we are going to. It is just fun, and then I will come home with you. It doesn't freak me out at all now."

I then added before she could respond, "Besides, I might learn some things to bring home to our sexual escapades!"

Monica laughed and responded with, "Good to all of those responses. I never had fun in my marriage. I mean, outside of my kids. My husband was boring and didn't seem to like me very much. I want to have fun now. Yes, I am totally into our relationship, and I don't want to ruin that, but I don't want to be boring, either. I still want to party, I guess."

"I can understand that. Plus, I probably could use a little excitement to come out of my shell, so to speak. The most important thing is that you are into our relationship. I am so happy to hear that!"

We kissed, and Monica got a funny look on her face.

"What?" I asked.

"You know when you asked me about dinner, and I said I already ate?"

"Yes," I said, drawing out the word.

"Well, it wasn't much, and I'm hungry. Can we go get street tacos at Bonilla's?"

"Definitely! We have worked up an appetite."

As we got out of bed and dressed, I thought about how lucky I was. This woman still gave me butterflies in my stomach, but now they were because of excitement, not nervousness.

My life felt amazing and carefree. However, that would be the last carefree moment for a while!

Chapter 29

Curt Hughes stopped by my classroom before school started. I assumed he would let me know when he needed me to interview for the basketball position in the upcoming week. That wasn't quite the timeline he had in mind.

"Matt, I want to finalize this open coaching position. Can you stop by my office at lunch and talk to me? That will serve as your interview."

"Wait, what? Today?" was all I could stammer.

"Yeah. Don't worry about it. You are the only candidate because the other person who applied has no Iowa license. So, we will talk quickly and probably announce your hire at the end of the week."

"Wow. That's great. Rachel told me she usually starts promoting the upcoming season around this time, so I could get that started next week!"

Curt agreed and left after telling me he would see me at lunch. Things felt very real. We had our last regular-season volleyball match tonight, and then we would prepare for a state championship push. However, I would organize the girls basketball team while helping with the volleyball team.

Life had changed a lot since the summer. Things were moving quickly. I probably should have been more freaked out than I was, but I felt a sense of calm. For some reason, this all felt right. I don't know if Monica moving in with me was serendipitous, but she had certainly changed my life for the better. I didn't think I could be this happy again after I lost Robyn and the kids, but it had happened. Now, I just needed to figure out how to be a basketball head coach!

The morning flew by as I taught, and before I knew it, I was in Curt's office having my ten-minute interview. I gave my credentials and my plan for the season. This plan had been stolen from Rachel. She had been nice enough to give me that help, especially since she had left almost immediately to start her new coaching job. Eastern Iowa Technical College had not had a good women's basketball program for a while, and I felt that Rachel could change that. She had the basketball knowledge and the coaching experience, but everything came down to the talent she would have now and could recruit in the future. Her help had been invaluable in allowing me to believe I could do this well in the first year. Curt knew all this and was very happy to have me on board. He would make everything official soon.

So, with Rachel's plan and what Monica had taught me, I had a good idea of how I wanted this season to go. However, as is the problem with most things, I didn't know where to start. I was lucky with the volleyball team. The team already had their rapport, and Monica had already built the culture within the team. Now, I had to figure out how to do that myself. I thought back to my coaches and what they had done. My high school coach utilized screaming and being a prick. That wasn't my style. My college coach was more of a practice teacher and a game tactician. That seemed to suit me better. Teaching was what I did. We might be successful if I could get the team to learn about the game, how to play together, and how to implement the skills we learned. Talent would be a hell of a help, too.

After my afternoon teaching, I went home to grab food and change for the game. I arrived to find Monica at home, in the shower. We had not planned this, so I took advantage of the surprise. I stripped down and walked into the bathroom. She was rinsing her hair, and I knew she had no clue I was there. I slid the shower door slowly and silently, with a magical plan of her melting into me with an orgasmic sigh as I wrapped her in my arms. It was a scene of pure pleasure and romance as I joined her in the shower.

There was no orgasmic sigh. The second I touched her, she screamed in horror, and her body tensed in a fighting response as she turned to see me.

"Fuck. Sorry. It was supposed to be a pleasant surprise, not a heart attack!"

To this, Monica completely relaxed, laughed, and playfully slapped my chest.

"You scared the shit out of me! But now that you're here, I'm glad for the surprise."

The orgasmic sound now came from me as she wrapped her hand around my ridiculously hard cock. Her mouth went to the pulse point on my neck while my hand found her belly button and slid slowly down through her soft pubic hair until my fingers found the hard nub of her clit.

We stood there, our mouths and hands exploring each other, the spray and steam of the shower adding to the heat of the moment.

Monica's hand, which had been slowly stroking me, picked up its tempo. The moisture in the shower seemed to act as a warming lubricant as her tight grip pumped at me. This increase in tempo led my fingers to probe open her lips, and when I found her opening, I slipped two fingers into her pussy. We stood there, moaning, getting each other off, until I could take no more. I spun her around, backed us into the shower spray, and gently bent Monica over. She found a perch for her hands on the tile bench at the back of the shower as I entered her. Monica's gasp was so loud and feral that it drove me wild with lust. I wasted no time pumping in and out of her, the only goal being for us to come together in that warm shower spray.

When that happened, when Monica clenched around me, shuddered against my body, and I exploded into her, I caught her as the strength in her arms gave out, and she started falling forward.

I pulled out of her, pulled her back tight to my chest, kissed her neck, and went back to massaging her now even more engorged clitoris.

She needed no recovery time. Her moans had already picked up (if they had even stopped), and I knew she would come again if I were attentive to her body. I kept the same pace, never faltering, constantly urged on by her moans, which kept increasing in volume.

"Oh my god. Don't stop!" she breathed.

And I didn't.

I kept that circular motion under the clitoral hood until I felt her body tense. I knew she was close and wanted to increase the pressure and tempo, but I didn't. I kept her building and building, waiting for her to climax. After a few times of her body tensing and a deep breath, she did. She screamed out as her legs twitched and her head tilted back, allowing my mouth even more access to her neck.

I could tell that most of her weight was in my arms now. Her legs weren't working correctly, and I couldn't have been happier. I held her there for about five more minutes until she whispered, "I want to stay like this forever!"

Hey," I joked, "we've got to shower and get to the school. We've got a match to win!"

And we did win. The Waterton girls volleyball team was now moving on to the postseason as the undefeated number two team in Iowa!

Chapter 30

The next week was incredible. It may sound too simplistic, but it was exciting. After completing an undefeated season, a conference championship, and being ranked second in the state, the hype around the team was huge as we prepared for sectionals. Monica had the team ready for much stiffer competition and focused on moving one match at a time. Although we didn't anticipate much competition in sectionals, losing focus now would not be good.

My position as the varsity girls basketball coach was now official, but the news wouldn't come out until Tuesday. However, Monica surprised me by ending practice on Monday by announcing to the volleyball team that I was the new girls basketball coach. The reaction was tremendous, especially from the few girls who played basketball. They all huddled around me, clapped, and whooped as I turned a shade of red that would be a good color on an Iowa barn.

Embarrassment aside, I was so relieved that the reception all week to my new coaching position was positive. I even held a pre-season meeting at the high school to discuss the upcoming tryouts and the start of practice. I had 62 girls show up, which was a surprise. I had expected about ten! However, I wasn't complaining and didn't have to do so. I was working so hard with teaching, volleyball, and basketball that I barely had time for anything else. Even my bike hadn't been out in a couple of weeks. I needed to get out there on the trails and enjoy the last of the autumn weather before snow buried the trails.

Even Monica and I weren't getting as much time together. And, if we were, we were busy spending it planning practices, traveling for sectionals and state, and teaming up to get me ready for the basketball season. I even had a couple of Zoom meetings with Rachel to get her input. It didn't leave much time for us as a couple. We went to bed every night together, but it was to collapse and sleep!

However, one morning, I woke up early. Monica spooned up against me, my hand draped over her hip, and I realized that my fingertips were touching the little bumps of her shaved pubic hair follicles. Monica had apparently shaved off a lot of her pubic hair, but I hadn't even noticed. We were busy!

My fingers stretched and found a little landing strip of hair, which I greatly enjoyed. That landing strip directed my fingers down to her folds, which were quickly spread apart so I could wake her with a massage of that wonderfully sensitive nub of hers. Monica emitted a little moan, still mostly asleep, while her body recognized what exactly was going on.

I wasn't exactly sure when she woke, but finally, she whispered, "Oh my god."

I quickly slid my body on top of hers, keeping us both under the sheets. We shared a passionate kiss as I eagerly slid into her wetness. We made love slowly, our passionate kissing continuing before we both found our climax together.

After resuming our spooning position, we fell asleep for a few minutes until the rude awakening of our phone alarms signaled the start of the day.

This would be the last day of practice before sectionals. We both felt that the team was firing on all cylinders. The girls were dead serious about going after a state championship but still had a looseness, which was good. Monica said that my presence was the key to that. She had confided to me that she had a coach in high school who had pushed them too hard to get to the state championship. They were so keyed up in sectionals with that pressure that they played terribly and lost, never even making the tournament. This was a mistake Monica didn't want to make herself, so she was glad to have my "good cop" persona when she had to be hard on them.

So, as I walked into the gym after the school day ended, I told myself to stay loose, even though the walk through that door had the butterflies going. The girls didn't seem to have any butterflies, which soon posed a problem. Their carefree attitude carried over into the start of practice, and I could tell they weren't ready. I could also tell Monica was pissed. But like a lightning bolt, I thought of a swerve drill my college coach used in basketball to focus us. Go down the court, pass the ball, and do not dribble or drop passes. Any violations were counted. When you hit ten, you ran.

I quickly interrupted Monica and told her I had an idea.

"Girls, we are starting with a contest today. Split evenly on each side of the net. It is a bumping drill only. No serves, no spikes. You can set it to a teammate if needed, but you get only three touches. You get a point if the ball hits the floor on your side or you hit it out of bounds. The first team to five points will run laps. Got it?"

They nodded, and I split them up. I tossed the ball high into the air, into the nearby court, and they started.

"Just bump it back and forth, but the ball doesn't hit the floor!" I shouted.

Immediately after I said this, Cali and Olivia didn't talk, and they both watched the ball hit the floor.

"Talk about it out there! This team trails zero to one," I shouted.

That did it. Their focus and competitive juices started flowing. The energy went through the roof, and no one reached five. I stopped them after ten minutes.

"Good. Remember that focus. Remember the basics. Remember your communication. Now, listen to the coach," I said, pointing at Monica and giving her the floor.

After smiling with pride at me, Monica took it from there, and she and Mercedes led what turned out to be a great and intense practice. We didn't tire the girls out, but everything seemed smoother and more refined. The next day, I felt very good about sectionals.

Monica, after practice, was feeling good, too. When we were alone in the gym, she confessed that she couldn't have been prouder to have me on the coaching staff when I had improvised at the beginning of practice.

"You are going to be a great coach! Scratch that. You already are a great coach. I can't believe how in love with you I am."

"Wow," I said. "I can't believe how in love I am with you!" I laughed. "Can I take you home and show you how much?"

At this, Monica's face fell.

"I wish. So much! But I have to meet with my lawyer. Everything seems to be going well with the divorce, and I think this may be the last meeting before it is final. I also need to stop at work and get things ready for me to be gone tomorrow for the sectional game. I'm so sorry. I hope you can forgive me."

"Of course! Selfishly and unselfishly, I want this divorce final. I can't wait for that shadow to not be over you and us."

I looked around, saw no one in the gym, and kissed her quickly. She gave me the biggest if-we-weren't-in-the-gym-right-now-we-would-be-having-mind-blowing-sex look and turned to leave.

"Good luck. See you at home," I said.

She turned and returned to me, putting her mouth right by my right ear.

"I'll text you when I am on my way, and you better be naked in bed when I get there," she whispered.

She then turned and left, looking back at me when she reached the double doors, giving me a quick and devilish little grin.

I didn't wait for her text. I drove home, grabbed some quick food, and hurried to the bedroom, where I made sure to be naked and in bed.

Chapter 31

I hoped that sectionals would go well and that we would succeed in the state tournament without too much stress. It was way better than that!

We didn't lose a set in our sectional game or our first two state tournament matches. None of the sets were particularly close. Our serving and net play, which we thought had been good all season, now seemed on a different level than the other schools in the state. We were the most well-rounded team there. But that didn't necessarily mean anything as we looked ahead to the championship. Beaver Creek was our opponent, and they had the Crook sisters.

The Crook sisters were twins. They were both 6'4" and could jump out of the gym. They had former Division One college athletes as parents, and they were both going to Wisconsin next year as top ten national recruits. They led the state in kills and blocks and seemed like they could win matches by themselves. They outclassed us at the net. It was the best duo versus the most complete team. This match was going to be different!

Monica texted me the morning of the championship because we were in separate rooms. Monica and Mercedes shared a room, the girls were four to a room, and the only man, me, had a room all to himself. Monica and I had agreed not to do any sneaking around during the tournament. Our only flirting was by text. This text was more than just flirtatious, however. Monica told me that her divorce paperwork was in the final stages. She would soon be free.

I asked her if she would start dating or if she was already seeing someone. Her response was priceless. She said that she was already seeing someone with a big dick who made her orgasm over and over.

I told her that I was happy for her and loved her. She replied with three red heart emojis.

This information assured me that Monica would not only be in a good mood today but could also relax and focus better on our match. After breakfast, we had a practice and needed to return to the arena by about 4:30 that afternoon. Monica had decided to use our practice more as a walk-through and discussion of strategy for the Crook sisters. She didn't want to mess with a good thing.

So, that's exactly what happened. We discussed hitting away from or over the top of their net defense. We talked about how important digging would be against those sisters trying to power every ball into our side of the floor. It went well, and the girls were focused. It was just going to be a long day of waiting.

In anticipation, Monica gathered the team downstairs in our hotel's conference room at 3:30. She ran the girls through warm-ups and stretching, keeping the mood light. I joined them in the stretches and purposely did mine badly, with many old man grunts and groans. (I hadn't been biking, so those grunts and groans were more real than I wanted to let on!)

Finally, we grabbed our stuff and left for the arena. Monica asked the girls to change into their uniforms before we left the hotel. She knew I wasn't going in that locker room, and she wanted us all, coaches and players, to be together as much as possible after we boarded the bus for the arena. Team unity and focus was the ultimate goal.

We boarded the bus, and as we pulled out of the hotel drive, the girls hit play on their favorite song and sang in noisy unison to it. This had become a season tradition when we traveled, and we knew they were pumped up and ready to go!

Pregame warm-ups went well. Monica's pregame speech was great, and we went out, took the court ... and proceeded to lose the first set. Badly.

During the break before the second set, Monica told the girls they weren't playing their game. They were sloppy and just a tiny step slow.

"Our defense is digging everything out, but we aren't doing anything with it! We have to get that ball away from the sisters!" Monica yelled.

At that moment, Bailey spoke to Cali and Olivia down the bench, saying, "Hey, we will dig everything out; you just send that ball back to them. You've got this."

I don't know if that was all it took, but I saw the proverbial light bulb go on for Cali and Olivia. Monica and I had discussed that these two juniors were our best athletes and just needed to put it all together. If they could go to the next level, they would be unstoppable.

They got off that bench, and when play resumed, they *were* next level and unstoppable. They both were jumping higher and hitting with more power and accuracy than anyone had ever seen them do before.

We easily won the second and third sets. We needed one more set, and the state championship would be ours. I guessed both teams were now tired and feeling the pressure, and nothing would come easy.

I was correct.

The score in that fourth set just see-sawed back and forth, but after an awesome block by one of the Crook sisters to put them up by a point, we scored the next two and were serving for the set, the match, and the state championship.

Bailey sent a twisting serve deep into Beaver Creek's court. Beaver Creek didn't get a good bump on the ball, and the set at the net was not good. One Crook sister jumped for what looked like a spike, but it was a fake. The other sister tapped the ball, hoping the soft shot would confuse us. It didn't. Cali bumped the ball to Olivia, who performed the secret weapon play we had planned. Instead of setting it back to Cali for a typical third touch, Olivia sent a soft shot, almost a rainbow, over the Crook sisters, right by the sideline. Beaver Creek never saw it coming. The ball fell to the floor, and our bench exploded! The girls went crazy in a huddle on the court as we coaches all took a moment to celebrate and then got the girls back to the net for a handshake line. After that, the celebration started. Our fans were going wild in the stands, and the girls all smiled as they accepted the championship trophy. Mercedes, Monica, and I tried our best to be professional, but we were grinning ear to ear. It had been such a magical season, and the girls deserved this.

As we all moved to the locker room to have one final huddle, now as champions, I joined them all, something I usually didn't do. My strict rule of never being in the girls' locker room could be ignored this time because we were in a big arena, and the tunnel to the locker room gave us enough privacy as a team. I stopped the girls and asked them all to meet outside the locker room so I could be part of the celebration this time. This had also started to feel like my team in the past few days. I didn't feel like an outsider who was helping out. I felt like a coach, and I liked that feeling.

In the tunnel, Monica gathered the team and gave the last speech of the season.

"Hey, all of you, this trophy is a team success. Don't ever forget this moment. You all worked hard this season and won as a team. No one put themselves above the team, and everyone went out and gave their all for every match. I am so proud of you all, and you deserve this trophy! You beat a great team. Today, you are the best in the state!" Monica yelled.

The team cheered as Monica tried to get their attention back.

"Okay, the season is over, but the celebration is only beginning. Olivia, break us down one last time. Although, this time, let's do 'champions' on three."

The team huddled together, and Olivia put her hand in the middle. The team and coaches all reached in, all hands touching, as Olivia screamed, "One, two, three," and the team responded, "CHAMPIONS!"

The girls all hugged each other and gave high-fives to the coaches. Suddenly, Bailey interrupted the proceedings.

"Hey, everyone. Quiet down for a second. I have a request," Bailey shouted.

Monica looked at her and asked what the request was.

Bailey said, "Well, Coach, now that the season is done and we are champions, will you please just kiss Matt and stop pretending you two aren't dating? You know you want to!"

Monica blushed so red that the team burst out in giggles. She turned to me, and I pulled her into my arms. Before she could react, I gave her a passionate but quick kiss and then pulled away. (The girls did their teenage oohing, ahhing, and clapping, and we were both fully embarrassed!) I pointed to her and yelled, "Your state championship coach!"

The girls and Mercedes exploded in applause and laughter, and they all turned and entered the locker room. That was my cue to leave. I turned to Monica and whispered, "Great game, Coach. I'll see you on the bus."

That was the happiest school bus ride of my life. Monica and I sat together; we were the happiest we had been in a long time!

Chapter 32

"Are you sure you are ready for this?" Monica asked.

"Oh yeah!" I said. "My life is on cloud nine! My girlfriend and I just coached a state championship on Thursday. We are going to a swinger party now, and I start my first-ever head coaching job on Monday. I'm just living the dream as the luckiest guy in the world! Why?"

Monica laughed at my comment and then continued.

"Well, you told me you weren't into this at the last one."

"Yes, but I think that was because I… was stuck in my head. I wanted you and didn't know where we stood. Today, I feel like this will be fun. I can relax because I get to go have great sex all day and then take the most beautiful one home for more!" I said, and kissed Monica on the cheek as she drove to Deborah and Lane's.

"Well, I'm glad you are more relaxed. I certainly want to go home with you, but I also want to have fun. Does that make sense?"

I laughed out loud.

"It does now! It probably didn't a few weeks ago, but I get you and us much better now. I love our relationship, and I love you, to be honest."

I left it at that. Monica smiled and kept driving.

"What, no response to that?"

"Nope. I'm just driving," she said, and I knew she was messing with me.

"Oh, okay, fine. You don't love me. It is all one-sided. I get it. I guess we'll go to the sex party, and I'll have to win you over there!" I said sarcastically.

Monica still didn't say anything. She was enjoying watching me squirm. I turned and looked at her.

"How exactly does a man win over his woman at a sex party?" I asked, my tone dripping with mock naivete.

"Umm, I think with your amazing dick, Matt!"

I guffawed and couldn't stop laughing for a long time. This cracked up Monica, and as she parked outside Deborah and Lane's house, she leaned over and kissed me on the cheek.

"I do love you, and you already won me over with your dick."

I turned and took her lips with mine. We shared that passionate kiss and hopped out of the car to walk to the house. We had been told to walk in. If you knocked, you hadn't been invited, and someone needed to answer the door with clothes on!

I don't know why I expected this party to be any different than before, but it was. Very different. I hadn't even asked Monica about it. I was in such a good place with Monica that I hadn't put much into this party. We would have fun with the same people and then come home. It wouldn't be anything surprising.

However, just before Monica opened the door, she said, "I hope you are ready for this!"

She opened the door before I could question her and led me inside. It was everyone I expected and more! Deborah and Lane were getting everyone their drinks. Anna and Ethan Webster raised their drinks to Monica and me as we entered the kitchen, as did Kasey and Rob McHenry. Two more couples entered the front door as we walked over to talk to the Websters and McHenrys. I did not know these couples, but they were considerably younger than we were. We were all close to 40, but these people appeared to be ten years younger, if not more.

"This is Kristy Anderson for everyone who wasn't at the first STSC party. She is our neighbor and is introducing her new boyfriend, Marcus Peterson, to our festivities!" Deborah said.

Kristy and Marcus were a couple that worked out. You could tell that by looking at them. They both had athletic builds, and both were tall. Marcus was the only guy here that was taller than me. He also looked to be the strongest by a large margin. You could tell he and Kristy were a new couple, but they seemed very excited about today. Not nervous at all. However, that was an understatement for the other woman. She seemed like she couldn't wait to start!

"This is Lainey Lanigan and Brady Geary, everyone. Lainey and Kristy work together, and in a not-at-all-appropriate work conversation, Kristy let her know about our parties. Lainey was more than agreeable to attending today with her boyfriend," Deborah stated.

We all said hello, but I found myself quiet as I took in Lainey. Listen, we were all adults, trying to keep ourselves in great shape and pretend we could do what we did in our twenties. I don't want to say that our stamina was ever questioned, but we weren't 20 anymore! Lainey looked to be the opposite. She had to be in her twenties, and she looked like she could fuck forever. She exuded a party-girl personality, was funny, loud, and brash, and you knew she was always ready to have a good time. She was incredibly attractive, and her blond curls seemed to bounce on her shoulders with her endless energy. She was also the smallest woman here, except for her breasts. How she could be so tiny and so curvy at the same time was mind-boggling. Plus, the way those blond curls framed her beautiful face and gorgeous smile caught me almost off guard. I was in a room full of attractive women, but Lainey was in another league. And please don't misunderstand, she wasn't going to make me forget about Monica. Monica had my heart. Monica was the person I wanted to be with every second of every day. But Lainey? She was, what a teammate in college used to call, "fucking hot as shit!"

"Is this everyone?" I asked.

"No, Sarah and Logan should be here any—"

Before Deborah could finish, Sarah and Logan West walked in. Immediately, I was reminded of our 69 from last time and how wonderful her pussy tasted as we improvised that blowjob line.

"Hi, guys," Deborah said. "We are glad you are here, but not as glad as Matt. He seems ready to go!"

"Huh?" I asked.

"Well, you came in, got a drink, and immediately asked if everyone was here. You seemed a little impatient," Deborah said, laughing.

"Well, shit, Deborah! Have you seen how gorgeous the women are here? Let's get this party started!" I said a bit too enthusiastically.

Everyone laughed at this and agreed that we should hurry up with our drinks and get to it.

Deborah spoke up with instructions.

"Today, I want to do something a little different. I read about this idea on an internet site about a round-robin partner party. We will all be in the living room. Thankfully, it is a big room, but you can move into the kitchen if needed. The women will position themselves around the room and stay in that area. The men will draw a starting position and be with that partner for 20 minutes. Then, the men rotate to the next partner. We do that until every man has been with every woman. After that, if anyone has anything left, we can improvise, like usual."

Deborah numbered the women, starting with herself. The women then lined up in a circle around the living room. Deborah, Anna, Monica, Kasey, Lainey, Sarah, and Kristy stood there as Deborah pulled names to find the men's order. Brady was starting with Deborah. Lane's name was next, which meant he was starting with Anna. It then continued with Ethan getting Monica, Logan with Kasey, myself with Lainey, Marcus with Sarah, and Rob with Kristy.

"Perfect," said Deborah. "No one ended up with the person they came with, and I got a young man to start. Those are my favorites."

"Hey," all of us, except Brady, yelled in mock disgust.

"Sorry guys, I just have to be honest about my desires," Deborah said while removing her clothes.

We all chuckled, but seeing Deborah strip down quickly changed our attitudes. We got down to business, stripped, and joined our starting partners.

I walked over to Lainey and introduced myself.

"Hi, I'm Matt, and you are gorgeous," I said with a hopefully disarming grin.

"Hi Matt, I'm Lainey, and you have a really big dick," Lainey said as she grabbed hold of said dick and stroked it.

I was hard as a rock in her hand, and her grip on me rolled my eyes back into my head. However, no one would have known that because my eyes were clenched shut in pure ecstasy. We weren't going to wait for Deborah to start us!

Lainey went to her knees immediately and sucked the head of my cock into her mouth. She clamped down with her lips and started running her tongue around me, already turning my legs into Jell-O. My cock pulsed inside her mouth as her tongue explored every inch it could reach on my shaft. Lainey continued sliding her tongue back and forth on the underside of my hardness as she slowly slid her lips down my length. This movement was either to tease me as more and more of me disappeared into her mouth, or it was for her to get used to my size, but whatever the reason, I couldn't wait for her to take all of me. And after a few moments, she did. I felt my length slide down into her throat. I had spent my adult life believing deep-throating was simply a construct of porno movie fantasy, but the last few weeks had shown me that it was very much a reality. I couldn't believe the ease with which Lainey worked her throat, mouth, and tongue around me.

Lainey slid off me to catch her breath, and I immediately pulled her up off the floor and onto the couch. I leaned her back, and she automatically opened her legs for me, showing me her completely shaved pussy.

"We don't have much time, and I desperately want to taste you, too!" I said.

Leaving no time for a response, I dropped to my knees and licked up and down Lainey's slit, gently and slowly. I wanted to make sure she was wet enough before I fucked her, but that wasn't an issue. She was already very wet, and her entire pussy glistened in the light of the living room. After a few times of this licking, I honed my lips in on her clit, sucking it into my mouth. Her gasp told me she was enjoying what I was doing, but I decided I wanted to hear a bigger gasp from her. So, I stood up, pulled Lainey back up to me, turned us, laid us out on the couch, and quickly slid inside her in a classic missionary position. This gasp was more of a howl as I buried myself deep inside her, letting her adjust to the insertion. Just as she caught her breath, I started pumping inside her, trying to start slowly and build as we went. However, that would have taken control, which was probably impossible to ask for. Lainey felt so tight, so wet, so amazing that I found myself pumping furiously almost right away. My eyes took in the bouncing of her huge tits and then moved up to see her eyes glass over in pure pleasure, and then suddenly pinch shut, as I felt her clench around my cock even tighter as she came. Her body spasmed, and her breath caught, but she didn't stop moaning as I continued pumping inside her.

"Oh my god, don't stop. I'm already close to coming again!" she breathed.

This put me over the edge. I could feel my orgasm building in my stomach and balls, and my cock was rock hard and pulsating. I moaned loudly, and just as I approached the tipping point, Lainey surprised me.

"Pull out and come on my tits!" she exclaimed.

I was practically beyond thinking at this moment. I had never done that before and was about three seconds away from coming. I blindly followed her directions and pulled out, but my focus on her beautiful breasts distracted my aim. My first shot exploded out of me and hit her in the chin and neck. My second wasn't as powerful and hit her chest, right between her breasts. I still had more inside me, that more dribbled than shot, onto her stomach and where her pubic hair would be if not all shaved off.

Lainey reached forward and stroked me as my legs stopped shaking, and my breath came back to me.

"Wow, you came all over me. That was fucking hot!" she said.

"Yeah, but I missed your target."

"Well, maybe you can practice your aim next time."

I looked at the clock while Lainey continued to stroke me.

"We still have nine minutes on the timer," I said, pulling out of her hand and slipping back inside.

She moaned so beautifully as I started fucking her again. I wasn't thinking about the fact that we probably wouldn't come again in such a short time, but her moans turned into one statement that changed all of that.

"God, Matt, you have the most amazing cock. It feels *so* good. Fuck, I'm going to come again!"

That put us over the edge again. I just pumped inside of her, both of us feeling immense pleasure all over again. Lainey's pussy squeezed around me again, her warmth, tightness, and wetness drawing my second orgasm out of me. I had much better control this time, and as my cock erupted, I pulled out, slid up to her chest, and, with a roar, jerked myself off onto both of her breasts as Lainey held them tight together. I just stayed there, on my knees, in that awkward position, captivated by my cum glistening all over her large breasts, but Lainey grabbed my butt cheeks and pulled me closer to her mouth, where she cleaned my cock with her mouth and tongue before I shuddered and pulled away.

"Fuck, I'm way too sensitive for that!" I gasped as I stood up on the floor next to her.

"Time!" Deborah shouted.

Lainey and I turned to face the room and noticed everyone staring at us.

"What?" I asked.

"Talk about coming in under the buzzer, guys. Literally!" Monica laughed.

"Yeah," Kasey said, "we all finished and waited for the timer. You got greedy!"

"Hey," I said, "I just like to maximize my time. I can't help it that I am better at time management than you all!"

This elicited a laugh from everyone, and Deborah had us all trade partners. I turned and looked at Sarah, my new partner, as she sat in a recliner next to the couch I had just fucked Lainey on. She was sitting back in the recliner with her legs spread and her completely shaved pussy glistening with wetness. My cock twitched erect instantly, and any thought of verbal greeting left me as my body immediately stepped forward, knelt, and my face sunk into that wetness, my mouth sucking her already engorged clit between my lips. Sarah elicited a sound that wasn't quite a moan of surprise pleasure but more of a moan of satisfaction. She seemed to be telling me, "It's about time!" with that simple sound. I figured this was also a clue that she would want more than this, but suddenly, as I started swirling my tongue around her clit and flicking it up and down, her hips raised off the chair, and her breath caught. For a second, I wasn't sure if this was a good or bad thing, but when her hand gripped the hair on the back of my head, pulled me even tighter to her sex, and then moaned very loudly, I knew I would be here a while. And I was more than ready for it.

I sucked her clit some more, eliciting more staggered breaths and moans, and then gave her slit some serious up-and-down licking, stopping in the middle to bury my tongue as deep in her pussy as I could. Sarah was now writhing in my mouth, her abs crunching and her hips rising off the chair in a rhythm. I pulled my tongue out of her wet hole, sucked her clit back into my mouth, and Sarah shoved my head into her as hard as she could take. My lips and tongue took turns working her clit, while my upper body contorted to match the bucking of her hips. Sarah's body then went taught, her breath caught, I bit down gently, and Sarah screamed out, shoving her hips up into my face even more. I caught her backside with both hands and kept her there, biting down on her clit while her body spasmed with her orgasm and soaked my face.

I gently lowered her down to the chair again, and before she could realize what I was doing, I buried my cock in that same wet hole.

"Oh my fucking god!" she screamed out.

I loved hearing that and started summarily pounding her. I didn't know what had come over me. I had done this group sex thing once and found it to be not my thing. Today, I was feeling like I couldn't get enough. These beautiful women were ready, willing, and able, and I was here for it. Especially this moment when Sarah started clenching her muscles around my cock as she came again. I was so close, but suddenly, I was aware of Lainey screaming next to me. I looked over to see Logan pounding away at Lainey, doggy style, with Lainey's face only a couple of feet away from me. Lainey watched me pound Sarah, and suddenly, our eyes sensed each other. Lainey looked into my eyes like she was staring into my soul as we fucked other people. I stared back at her, never breaking the contact until Lainey's eyes pinched shut, and she screamed out again, her body now spasming with another orgasm.

Fuck, she is so fucking hot, especially when she comes, I thought. And that thought overwhelmed me. I lost control of myself, drove deep into Sarah, and, with a roar, shot a surprisingly powerful load deep into her. I stood there, shaking, my dick pulsating, my eyes glancing over at Lainey. I felt bad thinking more about Lainey, but I also couldn't believe how hard I came with Sarah after what I had just done with Lainey. I collapsed half onto the chair and half onto Sarah as we checked out the clock. We had only a minute left.

Sarah looked at me and laughed. "I soaked your face, didn't I?"

"Oh my god, yes!" I replied. "It was amazing."

Sarah whispered, "Lainey's right, your cock is amazing, but your tongue might even be better."

"That's not fair," I said. "It makes me want to eat you out again, and we don't have enough time."

"Well, next time, then." She smiled.

"I hope that's a promise."

Sarah laughed and stuck out her pinky. I laughed at her adolescent gesture in an adult conversation and linked my pinky finger with hers.

"Time's up!" Deborah called.

I exited the chair, said goodbye to Sarah, and walked over to Kristy. I was in order behind Marcus, so Kristy had just been with her boyfriend. I wasn't sure if she would feel sheepish about having me come over right after she had been with him. However, seeing her eyes light up and watching her lick her lips when she saw my erection, I knew she was more than okay with this.

"Holy shit, you're big." she gasped.

"You know, I keep hearing that today, but I don't think it's that big, right?" I asked.

"Biggest one I've ever seen!" Kristy whispered, hoping her boyfriend wasn't hearing her.

"Well, I will take the compliment and make sure you get to enjoy it!"

Kristy, who had been on the living room rug this whole time, stood, grabbed my member, and stroked it. I had had my back to the room with Sarah and Lainey, but now I could see the rest of the people. I stood there, Kristy's stroking hand keeping me hard as a rock, as I watched Deborah suck Marcus's cock. I saw Anna already getting fucked by Rob (Jesus, they didn't waste any time with foreplay!) and Monica on the floor, her legs behind her head, and Brady with his tongue in her pussy. I suddenly got jealous. Monica looked amazing like that. Oh, who was I kidding? She looked amazing 24/7. I couldn't wait to be back with her, alone, at home. We would have our own sex marathon. But maybe tomorrow. I might be a little spent tonight.

"Hmm, seems a little dry," Kristy said, snapping me back to the moment.

Kristy put a big puddle of spit in her hand and then resumed stroking me. The spit was nasty, in a good way, and lubed her hand up perfectly. She definitely had my attention again. Her stroking continued as she moved to her knees, but she did something I didn't expect. She took my balls into her mouth and sucked them. Hard. This sensation seemed to drive even more blood up from the base of my cock to the top. I felt like I had a penis of iron. She continued this for a while but then broke off and slid her tongue up my shaft and to the head of my cock. I saw her mouth open and anticipated the warmth of her mouth, but I didn't get that. Her tongue flicked out to the head of my penis and licked, very carefully, the bead of pre-cum that had formed at the hole. But that wasn't it. She continued to lick, just the hole, in an action I had never experienced before. I didn't know a urethral opening rim job was a thing, but I was an immediate fan. That tongue action, mixed with a still-stroking hand, and the other hand now massaging my balls, surprised me in many ways. The first, of course, was how pleasurable this new act was. The other surprise is that my orgasm built so fast I didn't get any sense of control over it. I had no warning for Kristy as I erupted onto her tongue. Luckily, I had already come so many times that I didn't have a huge load spurt all over her face.

Kristy didn't flinch at this, though. She licked me clean, swallowed, stood up, and whispered in my ear while still stroking me, "Fuck me now!"

I didn't waste any time. I took her in my arms, lowered her to the ground, and did exactly that. Missionary on the living room floor, like we were teenagers left alone in a house for a night. I will admit that we both seemed a little tired by this point. I managed to stay hard for this, but we seemed to be going through the motions a bit. Thanks to Kristy, however, she brought me back to the moment. I don't know if there was any acting involved, but she half whispered, "Oh my god, Matt, that big cock feels so good. Fuck me harder."

That got my mood back, and I proceeded to pump more vigorously into her. Kristy started moaning in a way that told me she wasn't acting, and those moans soon turned to yells and grunts as I pounded her hard. Kristy finally tipped over the edge, and as her body tightened, mine did too. I had almost nothing left, but Kristy seemed to come hard.

I held her body close to mine as she came down from her orgasm, and her pinched-shut eyes reopened. She looked at me.

"Holy shit, your dick is crazy. That big thing hits all the right places."

"Good," I said, "I want it to be so my partners can come as hard as you did. That was beautiful to watch."

"Yeah, my legs are still numb from it," Kristy said.

"Time's up on round three!" Deborah called.

"How about a break, Deb?" Lane called.

"Good idea. Let's all move to the kitchen for another drink and snack," Deborah said.

"A drink?" I called out. "Shit, I need electrolytes, and a protein shake after that workout!"

Everyone laughed and agreed that we would take a 30-minute break. Then, it would be on to rounds four through seven. I couldn't wait!

Chapter 33

*T*hirty minutes passed awfully fast as we all had fallen into conversations and small talk in the kitchen. Please understand the weirdness of this situation; it wasn't completely lost on me. It was your typical party of adults, standing or sitting in this kitchen, chatting about things and enjoying snacks and drinks. The weird part was that everyone was completely nude, and nobody had cleaned themselves up. You could see that someone had shot cum into Kasey's hair, and it was still there. I don't think she had noticed it. The whole thing was just so bizarre and arousing at the same time. I have to admit, I was having fun. I was also getting to know the people I hadn't met before.

Toward the end of our break, I asked Lainey and Brady about themselves. I had to confess, as we drank, that I didn't know them even though they had spent most of their lives here.

"Umm, Matt, you do, though," Lainey said.

"What do you mean?"

"You do know me," she said.

"I do? How?"

I instantly regretted this conversation because, at that moment, I knew exactly what she would say. I hadn't considered how young she was and how she grew up here. I put my head in my hands before she could speak.

"Because you were my freshman-year earth science teacher," she said sheepishly.

The room went quiet as everyone had heard this exchange.

"I just had sex with a former student?" I asked, both in dismay and fake agony. We were both consenting adults now, so it wasn't taboo, just awkward.

"Yes," she said, "but for a teacher, you can really fuck!"

She meant it as a compliment—a way to break the tension. Instead, the roar of laughter from everyone in that kitchen made me turn dark red. Monica hugged me and kissed my neck.

"Way to go, old man!" she teased.

I had no words. Deborah saved me by calling an end to the break, and we resumed in the living room. Deborah ensured everyone was partnered up correctly, started the clock, and told us to go. I was right there with her because it was my turn with Deborah. She turned toward me and took a step closer.

"Nope!" I said and stopped her. "I've eaten and fucked a lot of pussy today. I need a break from that. Get on your knees on the floor and stick that ass out for me. I want to see how far I can stick my tongue in your ass."

Now, Deborah is the mastermind behind the Small-Town Swingers Club. Other women, even some at this party, may have balked or at least blushed at my crude language. Not Deborah. The woman turned back around, got on her knees, stuck her ass out, shook it at me, and started working her clit with her right hand. She wasted no time, and neither did I. My tongue licked up and down her ass crack eagerly. The tasty musk of her ass and the smell of her already fucked pussy, now wet again as my probing tongue discovered, was more than enough to have me hard again! I licked and licked her crack until I finally settled on her tight little back door.

The wrinkles of her anus were even perfect. I don't know if people discuss beautiful anuses, but this woman had it. I mean, Deborah had it all. She was unbelievably attractive, always horny, and remarkably insatiable.

As my tongue circled her hole and the hand on her clit picked up speed, I started probing inside Deborah, slowly loosening her up. The intrusion made Deborah moan, and that, in turn, made me probe even further. By now, my tongue was alternating between plunging inside her anus and licking circles around the rim, driving Deborah crazy. Her moans were increasing in volume, and her hand was rubbing wildly on her clit.

I came up for air, but I substituted a finger for my tongue while I did. Hearing her gasp of pleasure, and feeling her sphincter relax, as I buried the finger as deep in her anal canal as possible, I stayed like that and let her get used to the plugged feeling. As her breathing relaxed just a bit, I pulled the finger out, gave her anus a good dollop of saliva, and inserted my index and third fingers back into her anal cavity. This time, when I reached the maximum depth, I started massaging inside of her, feeling the ring of her second sphincter, searching for her A-spot through the vaginal wall. Although I couldn't be sure I was hitting it exactly, I knew Deborah liked what I was doing!

I didn't want her to come quite yet, however. Knowing how stretched she was, I pulled my fingers out quickly, eliciting Deborah's surprise gasp. I then immediately buried my tongue back in her gaping hole, probing and circling as aggressively as possible. Deborah gave another gasp of surprise and moan of pleasure as I did this, but I couldn't tease her much longer. Hell, I couldn't take it much longer. I was so turned on by her acceptance of this back door action that I quickly pulled my face out of her ass, spit on my hand, and sank my index and third finger back into her ass while my ring and pinky disappeared into her soaking wet pussy. My fingers in her ass went searching again for the A-spot, and I hoped the fingers in her pussy were hitting her G-spot. I was super intent on listening to Deborah's moans to find out how I was doing, but after the initial moan, well actually, yell is more like it, of pleasure that escaped out of her, she went almost quiet. I was concerned things weren't going well, but just as suddenly, Deborah gasped, as she had been holding her breath. Whatever cries came from her next, whether screams, roars, or some combination of the two, were unlike anything I had ever heard. Deborah's body started heaving, her noises became even louder, and then, her body went taught; she went silent as she closed her eyes and held her breath for a second, and then her body released. She screamed as the most powerful orgasm I have ever witnessed racked her body. Her body shook with spasms, both holes clamped down on my fingers, and her pussy released a warm fluid down my fingers and her legs. Deborah's breaths were still ragged, and normally, I would have given her time to calm down, but this was not about patience or sweetness or romance; this was hardcore fucking her and making her come as much as possible.

As she knelt there, her face buried in the corner of the living room rug she was on, still shaking and trying to catch her breath, I pulled my fingers out of her. She gasped as they left her but screamed out again as I quickly got behind her and pulled her gaping hole back onto my already weeping erection. I buried myself into her rectum, grabbed onto her gorgeous tits, and then started slamming inside of her.

"Fuck, fuck, fuck!" Deborah screamed.

I continued pumping inside her, letting her screams fuel my desire even more.

"Matt! Jesus, I'm coming again! Fuck!" she screamed again.

As Deborah's anus tightened around me, it hit me right at my climax point. I came so hard that I fell forward onto Deborah's back as if I had just tackled her. With my hands on her breasts, I had no way to break my fall. Neither of us could move except to awkwardly fall over onto our sides, my cock slipping out of her as we did.

Deborah just lay there with me as we both caught our breath.

"Jesus, Matt. That was amazing. I mean, amazing!" she said. "That first orgasm spasmed all of my abs. It made my stomach hurt, but in the best way possible. I've never come like that. Never."

"Good. You deserve it. Plus, it is very easy to get horny for you, so the pleasure was all mine!"

Deborah smiled and looked up at the clock.

"Oh, we only have a couple of minutes. I need to get up and stop the timer," she said.

So Deborah, who only had to get up to her knees to reach the timer above my head on the coffee table, surprised me by straddling my face as she did so, sinking her wet pussy right into my mouth. My hands gripped her butt cheeks as I ate her out for the two minutes we had left.

When Deborah called out that time was up, she stood off me and left me there, dazed and trying to catch my breath.

"Come on, Matt, time to change partners!" she said.

"That was not fair."

"Yeah, you're right, but I certainly didn't mind," Deborah said, and smiled.

I got up and moved to the couch on the opposite side of the room from Lainey. Anna Webster was already on the couch, smiling at me.

"Come on, Matt. Come eat this pussy now."

"Hey, who am I to argue with that invitation?"

Chapter 34

I hadn't seen Anna since our last rendezvous at her house. I hadn't thought much about that night since we said we would forget it. I hadn't worried about it but seeing her now made me realize that getting together that night was stupid. I had acted rashly in response to Monica walking out on me, and I wasn't proud of myself for thinking completely with my dick that night. I also wasn't proud that I hadn't been honest with Monica about it. However, now it seemed like something Monica wouldn't care about in the least. She had been upfront about her sexual escapades and wanting them to continue, at least with this swinging club we had going now. I started smiling to myself that I was having worried thoughts about my previous sex with Anna when I was sitting next to her, now getting ready to have more sex with her. Right next to Monica! What the hell was I worried about? Besides, looking at Anna with my member fully erect was evidence that I was thinking about Anna with my dick again anyway.

After a struggle with the timer, Deborah called for this fifth round to start. Anna had already told me to eat her pussy, so I pulled her up off the couch, laid down, and told her to 69 with me. Anna's smile told me she was just fine with that. However, and I wish I could blame this on great stamina, it took us the whole 20 minutes for both of us to have a small orgasm. The reality was that we were tired. Our bodies had spent the last couple of hours orgasming over and over, and we were spent. When I finally shot my tiny load into Anna's mouth, and she had pulled up off of me, she turned herself around and came up to snuggle with me.

"Oh, hi!" I said in surprise.

She laughed.

"Oh Jesus, Matt, I'm not cuddling. I'm just too damn tired to sit up yet. Plus, I wanted you to be able to breathe."

"Oh, I was just fine with your pussy in my face. Never worry about that!" I joked.

Anna laughed and then jumped slightly when Deborah said the round was over.

We managed to get ourselves off the couch, and I went over to Monica and kissed her.

"Hmm, you taste like pussy," she said after the kiss.

I laughed out loud at this statement. Monica could make me laugh like no one else.

"Is that a good thing?" I asked.

"Probably for you."

"True," I said.

"Hey, I could use a break. Do you want to save our round for tomorrow? I will give you way over 20 minutes!" she said, eyeing me devilishly.

"That sounds great," I said, laying on the exhausted tone a little thick.

We went back to the kitchen, which, of course, was only a few feet from the living room. We had a drink, talked, and listened to the sounds of the orgy in the background.

"You seem to be having more fun today," Monica said.

"Yeah, I was really into it for some reason. I guess I was feeling really dirty today. Although, I am still mostly focused on having a sex marathon with you tomorrow!"

"Good. I'll put it on my calendar," she said. "Who's the best so far?"

"Ha," I laughed, "That is hard to say."

I thought for a second and then said, "You know, I am sure people might guess, of the six people here not named Monica, that the young ones would be the answer, but I think it has to go to the ringleader. I would say Deborah is the best, but damn, Lainey is a very close second. They are both natural-born talents, but even at her age, Deborah seems more insatiable than Lainey. I like to think we are insatiable, but she is on a different level. It is unbelievable."

Monica didn't seem surprised at this at all.

"Matt, Deborah usually has these parties planned out for months. She creates these fantasies in her head and then brings them to life. I don't know if you know this, but this whole thing started when her son's best friend helped her one week when he was home from college. Deborah was home alone that week, and her son's friend spent the whole week helping her around the house and fucking her. He was 20 years younger, and she kept up with him just fine. She has no slowdown!"

"After getting to know her, that doesn't surprise me. Do you know what she is planning for the next party?"

"Yes, and you won't be invited," she said.

"Oh? Why not?"

"Girls only party!" Monica replied. "We are trying to get Rachel and her wife to attend."

"Oh wow. What about Mercedes?" I asked.

"Her too. She can be my date."

"Wait, you are doing it?"

"Oh yeah. I think it sounds like fun. I've never been with a woman before. Well, there was a one-time thing in college, but that was because my boyfriend wanted my best friend and me to—" she broke off.

"Keep going," I said.

"Well, he wanted a threesome to happen, and he wanted to have me and my friend 69, but it was an awkward disaster. That boyfriend was a fuckwad. Come to think of it, John was my next boyfriend, and he turned out to be the ultimate fuckwad."

"Well, speaking as the next boyfriend in line, I have often thought that threesomes would be typically better in theory than in practice. It seems like there would be an odd person out during the proceedings."

Monica smiled at me and said, "Yes, my new boyfriend is definitely not a fuckwad! But to your point about threesomes, that is my experience. You need to think things through more than just trying to jump in and keep everyone happy."

"Plan it out, like Deborah does here?"

"Exactly!" she replied.

Our attention was drawn back to the living room as the sounds of sex were becoming louder. Everyone was close to reaching their climax, and Monica and I watched the proceedings. It was odd to watch everyone else. I know some people like to watch others have sex, but this wasn't the case for me. I guess I figured I wanted to participate or not be there. It was one or the other for me. I turned back to Monica, knowing about ten minutes were left in this round.

"Hey, who has been your favorite today?" I asked.

"You know, I don't know. I understand what you said about Deborah, but Lane isn't on her level. I think maybe Marcus will get my vote. The problem is, nobody compares to you. You are the biggest and the best, honestly."

"Wow. I'm taking that compliment and will try not to let the pressure get to me!" I laughed.

"Good! Okay, finish that drink. We have one round left."

"Sounds good!" I said and downed my drink.

As we walked over to the living room, hand in hand, the timer went off, and Deborah called the penultimate round over. It was time for us to switch, and I quickly pulled

Monica in for a kiss and let her hand go. Before I could even turn toward Kasey, my final partner of the day, I felt a hand grab my balls and start squeezing in the best way possible.

"You know, last time we did this, you came all over my face, and I loved it. Let's make sure to do that again," Kasey whispered in my ear.

"Well, you keep rubbing my balls like that, and I can easily comply," I whispered back.

Kasey moved in front of me and just stood there for a moment, staring into my eyes and continuing to massage my balls.

"Close your eyes and let me take care of that big dick of yours," she whispered.

I did exactly that. I closed my eyes and just relaxed into her amazing touch. Her other hand started stroking me, and soon, I was hard as a rock. I understood I was not a teenager anymore, but I could still rise to the occasion quickly and stay that way. However, I was glad that Monica and I took that break!

Kasey had started kissing my neck and then moved her mouth slowly down my chest, sucking on my nipples for a bit, and then, stopping her hand, continuing down to my belly button as she moved to her knees. Her mouth replaced her hand as my scrotum massager as she sucked each ball separately. I cried out in ecstasy as the sensation was both wonderful and gave a little bit of pain as she sucked harder and harder. Her right hand returned to my cock as she jerked me off, and soon I felt that it was too much. I was afraid I was going to come and come too fast. I pulled back from her, grabbed her under the arms, and spun her around.

"I need you now!" I said. "Put your left leg up on the arm of that chair and keep standing."

I helped guide her leg up to the chair and entered her pussy from behind as she stood there doing a one-legged split. I pounded into her, which felt amazing, but Kasey was not as tall as me, and my back couldn't take the hunch I was in to make this work. But I had an idea that would work, especially if she wanted me to come on her face!

I pulled out and guided her to the floor, where I laid her down on her back. I folded her legs up to her head and pulled her low back up against the chair.

"Have you ever done the piledriver?" I asked.

"No," Kasey said.

"Oh, good. Neither have I. Let's try it," I said as I crouched down to enter deep into her pussy.

Kasey gave the most guttural moan I could imagine as I slowly inserted myself into her. The slowness had nothing to do with pleasure; I just wanted to be sure that my balance was good. I tried a few slow pumps of my legs to see if my hamstrings and quads could handle this workout routine. It worked pretty well. I couldn't go fast, but each thrust seemed to sink deep into Kasey, and she urged me on.

"Oh god, Matt. That is so deep and feels so good. Your cock really *is* amazing," she exclaimed.

"You feel and look amazing," I said in a raspy voice, as the ecstasy was both messing with my breathing and voice.

I was gazing down at her face, which was contorted in pleasure. I watched her eyes close tighter each time I bottomed out inside her. I couldn't tell if she was close to coming, but I knew I was. I didn't want to end the day without experiencing all that Kasey had to offer.

"Since this works so well for both of us, I think I should test this position on your other hole," I breathed.

I slowly pulled out of her pussy and pressed the head of my cock into her ass. Gravity and the natural lubrication her pussy had given my cock enabled me to slide easily and deeply into her. She wasn't expecting this because she screamed out incomprehensible noises as I slid into her.

Finally, as I just froze there with my cock buried in her ass, did she form words.

"Oh, shit. Oh, shit. Oh my god. That is so big and so deep. Please don't move. Just leave it right there."

I thought she meant she needed time to get used to the sensation, but that wasn't the case. As I stayed there frozen, except for the pulses I was giving my cock inside her, Kasey built up to an orgasm and came hard. I took in the view of her glistening pink pussy, her tits, her contorting face, and the cum that was still in her hair as her body shook with pleasure. Her feet, which had been relaxed onto my shoulders, spread apart as her legs fell, spread-eagle onto my thighs. I let her relax, but this new spread-eagle position made this all that much hotter, so I also started pumping my legs up and down, so my cock pumped gently into her ass. Kasey started moaning immediately, and her breath, which had just calmed, started to get fast and heavy again. It seemed like her pleasure grew with each pump, and another orgasm was building back up. I couldn't believe how amazing this position worked for us both. I worried that Kasey would be too uncomfortable in this folded-up position, but her face and moans told me that was wrong; she was in pure sexual ecstasy.

My pumping started increasing in power and speed, my cock slamming in her ass and my balls slapping against her butt. Kasey's screams were encouraging me to keep up as furious a pace as I could despite my leg muscles screaming at me to stop. But I couldn't stop. The pleasure sensations everywhere else in my body were overriding the pain in my legs. I knew I would come, and it would happen soon.

The tightening of Kasey's body signaled that she was close, too. Her moans turned to wonderful grunts, and with one huge breath, her body went taught; she squeezed around my cock and came fabulously hard! Before she could loosen her grip on me totally, I pulled out and pointed my cock down at her face below me and shot a nice rope of cum right on her nose and forehead, totally missing her eyes.

I fell backward onto the chair, my legs absolutely fried. I looked down at Kasey and noticed she had rolled over on her side, too exhausted and numb to move.

"How was that?" I asked with a smile.

"Amazing. Absolutely amazing," she breathed out.

"Okay, time's up!" Deborah called out.

I looked around and saw that everyone else was done and looked completely orgasmed out!

"Anyone want any more?" Deborah asked.

We all looked at her and laughed.

"Deborah, we all aren't superhuman like you. I think we are done!" I said with a laugh.

"Well, that's too bad," Deborah said. "I guess we'll have to pick it up next time."

Lainey perked up at that.

"Oh, I can't wait. And I think I know a couple more couples who can join us!"

"Hey, I thought Monica said it was a girls-only party next time," I said.

Deborah looked at me and said, "Matt, you certainly seem interested in that idea, but you cannot come and watch. Besides, I haven't decided yet what the next party will be. I like to be flexible. Although, seeing you pound Kasey in anal piledriver certainly shows that flexibility is a talent of yours."

"Hey, I will take the compliment and think of some scheme to watch your all-female party somehow! Besides, maybe I should temper my excitement about Lainey's friends because they all might be former students!"

This elicited a laugh from the room, but the truth of my statement sobered me up.

I suddenly wished I didn't have to be so damn introspective all of the time. After all of my doubts leading up to this party, I thought I had reached a place where I embraced today and was fully into swinging parties and non-monogamy.

Although today had been great, now I wasn't sure, again, if this was my thing. I had gone into this with the thought that I could be the horny guy who has fun and doesn't look back. I thought that maybe Monica and I could have that open relationship. But now, I started to feel a little like I did after hooking up with Anna right before Michael's parents' funeral. I started feeling like I wanted to go home with Monica and be with her. Coach with her, talk with her, go on trips, and live my new life with her. I wouldn't regret today's party, but I also thought it was time to determine what I wanted. Monica and I had expressed our love for each other. Maybe it was time to see exactly what she felt about the future. I wanted to be completely open to her now. No secrets.

I had no idea what she would say.

Chapter 35

To the outside observer, the drive home from a sex party might be assumed to have a "what happens at the sex party, stays at the sex party" vibe, but it doesn't. You have to compare notes! Monica admitted she was a bit jealous to overhear all of the comments about how I had an amazing cock, but she had to admit that it was her first thought the first time she was with me. She also admitted that my stamina and "power," as she put it, were on par with the three younger guys.

"Although Brady didn't seem all that great, I think he was just really nervous," she added.

"He better be great in bed if he wants to keep up with Lainey," I said.

Monica laughed at this, as did I.

When we got back to my house, I was in good spirits. The party was fun, and my girlfriend told me that she and all the women thought I was a good lover. I was riding high and thought nothing could crash my mood. Then, Monica asked me to give my review of the party as we sat down on the couch to relax.

"Well, I was really into it today, for whatever reason. I loved how dirty it all felt. That surprised me. The other thing that surprised me is how sexual everyone is. You know? I mean, people think sex is over at 30 years old, but these people are really into it, even those who are 40, like us! So, I liked that aspect. But, I am unsure if I want to stay into it. I still feel guilty when I am not just having sex with my girlfriend!"

"Wait, you feel guilty after?" Monica asked.

"Yeah. I felt jealous after seeing how much fun you had at the last one. I hoped you would be my girlfriend, but I wasn't excited to see how much fun you had with other guys. But afterward, I became confident that you did love me as I loved you, and I started understanding where you were at with it. So, when you walked out that Sunday, I didn't know what to think. I was super hurt, and I missed you so much. But, as that week progressed, I got more upset and thought you weren't coming back, so I took her up on it when Anna Webster reached out for a booty call. Immediately after, I felt so guilty, so slutty, and I just wanted you back. So, there's my honesty. I love having this relationship with you, and as we move forward with that relationship, I am glad I understand you and what you want."

Monica stared at me. She didn't say anything for a second and then just exploded into laughter.

"Matt, oh my god, you are so cute. You hooked up with Anna? That's awesome and out of your comfort zone. I'm proud of you!" she said with a laugh.

"Yeah, she texted me to say Ethan was out of town. I thought he knew, but later, she texted me and said she didn't tell him we hooked up. She said she thought he would be okay with it, but when she asked him about one-on-one hookups, Ethan freaked out. He didn't mind the parties, but one-on-one hookups weren't cool. So, Anna and I decided not to discuss it anymore."

"That's weird, that group sex is fine, but one-on-one isn't, but whatever. I wouldn't differentiate between the two, but you shouldn't feel guilty. Matt, we are having fun here, and although I do love what we have, it's not like I'm looking for any monogamy here. I've been there, done that. Not for me," she said matter-of-factly.

"Oh, you mean, you… wait. Let me get this straight. You love me and want to be my girlfriend but have no interest in being exclusive?" I asked, a little stunned.

"Jeez, Matt, you make it sound terrible when you say it like that. Yes, I love you. Yes, I want to be with you more than anyone else. Yes, I want to be your girlfriend. But, with your permission, I still want to have fun. I don't want to fuck guys behind your back, but I guess I do want to be polyamorous."

"Oh," was all I said.

I was in a state of confusion with myself. I had been telling Monica I agreed with this and knew this was where we were, but I think I subconsciously wanted her to tell me that she wanted me and only me. I wasn't hurt or surprised by this, but I was confused about what I wanted.

Could I handle a relationship on these terms?

I realized I had been telling myself that Monica being polyamorous was fine, until she said she wanted it. I was not fine with Monica being polyamorous. Now, my hypocrisy was evident. What exactly did I want for my relationship with Monica and my life?

Everything had been moving fast the past few months, and every time I thought I had clarity, it seemed like life had other ideas. Plus, starting my basketball coaching career in about 48 hours threw another curveball into my life. No wonder I had about a million things going through my head.

"Matt? You there, Matt?" Monica asked, breaking me from my thoughts.

"Yeah, sorry. I just was thinking about a lot."

"Are you okay? Are you okay with us?"

"Yes, to the second one. I want to be in a relationship with you. However, to your first question, I think things have been moving really fast for me. I lived a really slow year after my dad, wife, and kids died. Now, I am making changes left and right. I think those are good changes, but it just has me living in my head too much. And to you talking about not being monogamous, I think that is fine. I think it might be good for me to re-think how relationships work. I have always thought of myself as open-minded, but in actuality, I lived my life on that Puritan ideal of marriage and monogamy. These past few months have opened my eyes to a different way to live, and I like it. It just overwhelms me sometimes."

I had said those last sentences more to the ground than to Monica. When I looked back up, I saw that she had tears in her eyes. I asked if she was okay.

"Yes … and no," she said. "It is amazing how you can say precisely what I am thinking. You did it that day when I first met you, and I just fell for you immediately. Since then, I have just kept falling harder and harder."

I turned her head toward me and kissed her deeply and passionately, but not in a sexual way. This kiss said no matter what happened, we could get through it together.

"Hey, let's get cleaned up and go out for dinner. What are you in the mood for?" I asked.

"A shower and then a place I don't have to dress up for!"

"That sounds like Bonilla's, Pizza Pit, or House of Dragon."

"Pizza Pit," she declared.

"Sounds good. Do you want the first shower?"

"Aren't you going to join me?" she asked suggestively.

"We can share a shower, but if I try to have any more sex today, I think my dick might fall off!"

Monica laughed at this and admitted that she was a little sore herself. She decided to take the first shower and got up off the couch. I watched her tight ass as she disappeared down the steps to my bedroom's adjoining bathroom. She was so beautiful, and I was so lucky. I leaned back against the couch and shut my eyes in a state of relaxation and contentment. The thoughts had calmed somewhat in my head, and I ignored the stress of starting practice on Monday. I had tonight and tomorrow with Monica, and that was enough.

The next thing I knew, my eyes flew open as Monica said my name. I could see that she was dressed and ready to eat.

"Shit, did I fall asleep?"

"Yes. I showered and called out to you to let you know I was done, but you didn't respond. I got ready and found you here, asleep."

"Jeez. Too much sex, I guess! Let me take a quick shower, and we will go."

I went downstairs, showered, dressed, put on a baseball cap, and drove us to Ryan's Pizza Pit. Pizza Pit was your typical pizza and wings place, with cheap bottles of beer and only one TV in their small bar area. It was cheap, and the food was good enough for them to stay in business, but it was one of those places that could only exist in a small town. It had been in town forever, and the place looked like it. Maybe one day they would remodel, but I doubted it.

Monica suddenly got serious as we discussed this and that over cold beers.

"I have a question for you," she said.

"Sure, what is it?"

"Well, I don't want to add to everything going around in your head, but what are your Thanksgiving plans?"

"Oh. I don't have any. Last year, I just couldn't bring myself to go anywhere. Lots of people invited me and told me not to be alone on the holidays, but I couldn't go somewhere and explain to someone's uncle that I was there because all of my family had died recently and their family had taken pity on me, you know?"

"Exactly what has been happening to me! Everyone thinks I need to be with them this year for the holidays, but I have other plans. That's what I wanted to ask you about," she said and paused.

"Sure. Ask away."

"Okay, here goes. I am planning on going to Pittsburgh because Ashlynn can't leave. Volleyball and basketball are both happening right now. Nick is free to leave South Bend because he is a baseball player, and they are not in season right now. So, he is going to meet us there. My question is, do you want to tag along?" she asked and paused again.

I swear she was almost wincing, expecting me to freak out and scream at her that there was no way I would do it.

"Are you kidding? I would love that!"

"You would?"

"Yeah. Monica, I want to be a part of your life, which means not being afraid to be part of your life. I would love to meet your kids. I was planning on having practice for my team on Tuesday night and then giving them the rest of the week and weekend off, so I'll be free. It sounds like a good getaway."

"Oh, good. I was afraid I was putting too much on your plate right now."

"No, I think the meeting of the kids has to happen at some point. You know, I have never thought about that. We are supposed to be nervous about meeting the parents, but at our age, it is more about meeting the kids. Are your parents still alive?" I asked.

"Yes," she laughed, "they are still kicking around. They live in Florida now. I grew up in Wisconsin and went to college in Iowa. That's where I met my ex. Now, here I am in Waterton," she said with resignation.

"You don't like it here?"

"No, it's fine. But now that I am divorced, I guess I am not tied to Waterton. My kids aren't here, and my job could transfer pretty easily. But, there are good friends here, *and* there is someone here I am kind of crazy about," she said, and smiled.

"If that someone is me, then the feeling is reciprocal. And I look forward to going to Pittsburgh with you for Thanksgiving."

"Good! Now, what do you want me to tell my kids about you?"

"What do you mean?"

"Well, they have only really heard about you as the owner of the house I'm staying in. They know we have become friends, but I haven't told them about us, you know—" She broke off.

"That we are fucking all the time?"

This got her laughing so hard that people in the Pizza Pit turned and looked at us.

"Yes. Maybe not quite in those words, but yes," she said, still laughing.

"Would you be comfortable telling them we are seeing each other?" I asked, this time being serious.

"Honestly, Matt, I don't think they would care. They are adults and knew things were bad with their dad. I think my happiness would make them happy."

"Good. I think that is a healthy relationship. Go ahead and tell them the truth. I think they deserve it."

She reached across the table, and I thought she would say something, but she grabbed my hand and squeezed. When I looked up from her hand touching mine, I could see that her eyes were wet with emotion about her life, her divorce, and her kids, and she was trying not to cry in public.

I looked at her and said, "I meant to tell them the truth about us seeing each other, not the part about us fucking all the time!"

This brought a smile and was the thing she needed to get her emotions back under control. Well, the pizza being delivered to our table just then was a big help, too. We devoured the food, drove home, and collapsed in bed. It had been quite the day.

Chapter 36

I woke the next morning fairly early and felt wide awake. I was almost revitalized, in a weird way. It felt like yesterday's craziness had been resolved, and I could move forward. I knew that was probably naive, but still, for whatever reason, I felt good. I looked over at Monica, but she was still dead asleep. I checked my phone and saw it was already 50 degrees on an early November day. I wouldn't miss this opportunity to get out on my bike.

My bike had been my escape when Robyn and I had kids. It was the one thing I could get out and do for physical fitness that also cleared my mind. I bought a discount store bike when we were married, and I pedaled around with the kids in tow, but I also found that unhooking the kids' bike trailer and going for long rides when I could was great for my physical and mental health. So, after the accident, I splurged and bought a road bike with a carbon fiber body and dropped handlebars and spent a lot of time on it. I called it my therapy bike. Hey, it was better than drinking!

I hadn't been riding as much since I had been so busy with coaching and my relationship with Monica. But I wasn't complaining. That would probably be good if I were now spending more time with a beautiful woman over a bike. But this morning, I wanted to let that beautiful woman sleep while I got some exercise.

The day was beyond gorgeous; it felt more like a summer morning. Before I knew it, I had completed my favorite 15-mile loop and returned home to find Monica sitting in bed, texting on her phone.

"There you are!" she said. "Were you out on your bike?"

"Yeah, it is a gorgeous day. We should do something outside today."

"I was thinking about that recently, and I had an idea. I know you like to bike, and I wouldn't mind adding more exercise to my life. I mean, outside of the bedroom!"

"So?"

"So, I texted Rachel, and her bike is still here in Waterton, but she isn't using it, so I thought I might use it and ride with you."

"I would love that! Robyn never did shit like that with me."

That last comment had slipped out and sounded like a dig against Robyn. I stopped in my tracks mid-conversation. I suddenly had a wave of guilt about speaking badly about my deceased wife, but it raised a question in my mind—a question I didn't want to consider right now.

"Matt, are you okay?" Monica asked.

"Yeah, I am just thinking about how much more you and I are on the same page than anyone I've ever met. It makes me happy."

"Good, I like to make you happy," she said, raising her eyebrows.

"You are too much. On second thought, you are perfect," I said, leaning over the side of the bed and kissing her.

She returned the kiss very passionately, and I felt myself get hard in my spandex bike shorts.

"Okay, that's too much, and I'm too sweaty and smelly. Let me shower quick, and then I'll be back!" I said and excused myself to the bathroom.

As I stood at the toilet, trying my best to pee with a rock-hard erection, I couldn't help but smile at how Monica wanted to ride with me. But again, that smile disappeared as I thought of how Robyn would never have done something like that. This was something I had never really thought about before. Had I taken for granted that Monica and I seemed to have had more fun in a few months than Robyn and I ever had? Was Robyn even that supportive of my desires? She never would have wanted me coaching and being gone way more during the school year. Were Robyn and I good for each other or just on a married-life autopilot?

I stood there, erection gone, waiting for the shower to warm up, lost in my head. I was so lost in my thoughts that I didn't even realize Monica had entered the bathroom until her arms wrapped around me and her hands went up to my chest. She didn't do anything else but hold me like that.

"Can I join you?" she asked.

"Please!"

We got into the shower together. I turned around, let the water hit my back, and kissed her again—this time, with the same passion she had on the bed a few minutes ago. We stayed like that for what seemed like forever, our mouths exploring each other, our lips locked together, and pleasure radiating through our bodies. This was not a dirty or crude sexual pleasure, though. This was passion, love, and warmth. These two people didn't want to be anywhere else or with anyone else.

Finally, I spun us around, grabbed the tea tree shampoo Monica used, and let her soak her hair. When she was ready, she turned back around, and I lathered her hair with shampoo, massaging her scalp and dropping my hands to massage her shoulders when I was done with her hair. I then grabbed the soap and lathered her entire body, keeping her facing the water the whole time. Her nipples hardened as I spent a little extra time there. My hands then found her ankles, and I lathered her legs going all the way up until I touched the folds of her sex. Her breath caught, but I didn't linger. I made sure she was clean and massaged. I wanted her to feel pampered and turned on, but I wanted this to be slow and drawn out.

Monica seemed to get the point because she rinsed herself and then turned toward me to rinse her hair. When she was done, she opened her eyes and smiled at me.

"Your turn in the water."

We switched places, and the water felt so good because I hadn't been in its warmth for a few minutes. Monica did to me what I did to her, but when her soapy hands rubbed my scrotum, my dick shot to attention instantly. Her soapy hands then slid up and down my hard shaft as my breath caught and my eyes pinched shut. Monica didn't linger there, but her touch turned me on.

"Okay, rinse off, and let's get back in bed," she said as she stepped out of the shower.

I did as instructed, turned off the water, and stepped out of the shower. Monica had already left the bathroom, so I toweled off quickly and found her in bed, her hair still wet. I walked around the bed to her side and pulled the covers back, exposing her naked body, still glistening from the shower. She looked beautiful, and her hand slowly stroking her clit just enhanced the scene.

"I love that," she said.

"Love what?" I said a little breathlessly.

"I love when your dick goes from soft to rock hard almost instantly," she said, smiling.

"Well, that's what you do to me," I said, and got on top of her and pulled the covers back on top of us.

I know that we had talked about our wild sex marathon today, but I knew that we weren't in that kind of mood. This was going to be slow and passionate. We just wanted to hold each other and express our love. It sounds really cliché, but it was the truth. I wanted to be in this woman's arms forever.

As we kissed, barely even coming up for air, I raised my hips and guided my erection toward her opening. She was plenty wet from her playing with her clit while she waited for me, and I slipped in easily and deeply. Monica's moan of satisfaction seemed to build with every inch I sank deeper, and when I finally inserted all the way, she gasped as her body spasmed with pleasure.

I lowered myself back down on top of her, losing a bit of that depth but pumping very slowly and kissing her. Her teeth found my bottom lip and bit down, sending ecstatic sensations through my whole body. Involuntarily, I rose and started pumping much more enthusiastically, hitting as deep as I could again. The scene had instantly changed from one of slow lovemaking to passionate but furious sex. Our orgasms built quickly, and we came together, our mouths still locked, swallowing each other's climax exclamations. Other than lowering myself back down on top of her, we didn't move. We continued to kiss, and I did not pull out of her while we slowly relaxed from our orgasm.

Finally, I rolled off and lay beside her, holding her in my arms. I was just about to tell her how much she meant to me and how my thoughts earlier were about how much happier I was now than I ever had been, but that never happened. Monica's phone rang beside her.

Monica looked at the phone and answered immediately. "Ashlynn, what's going on?"

I could tell immediately that this was not an expected call and that Ashlynn was upset. Monica glanced at me and gave me one of those sorry-but-this-is-going-to-take-awhile looks. I nodded, grabbed my phone, got up, threw on sweatpants and hoodie, and looked at the time. It was 9:30 on a Sunday morning, and I wanted to discuss my thoughts on

Robyn. I walked up to the kitchen and walked out onto the back deck. I dialed David's number, but Alicia answered.

"Hey, Matt. David is outside, playing goalkeeper against the girls. We have a rare day off from their activities, but I guess they can never stop playing soccer! He must have left his phone in the kitchen by accident. I'll get him.

"Alicia, wait, can I ask you my question first?"

Alicia paused and then said, "Sure. What's up?"

"I don't know how to ease into this, so I'm just going for it. Do you think Robyn was good for me?"

"Wow, Matt. Good morning to you, too. That's pretty heavy for an out-of-nowhere call."

"Yeah, I know, but it is bugging me this morning."

"Well, to be honest, I always thought you guys were a good team as parents," Alicia started, "but I never really cared for how she treated you as an individual. I believe she loved you, but she always seemed to treat you only as a husband, like a means to an end. I think she wanted a husband and a family, and she got that. But I never felt she gave Matt, the individual, much thought. When you were here for the funeral, I was so glad to hear that you were seeing people, doing new things, and getting active in coaching. That felt like the real Matt. I was glad to hear that."

I just paused, thinking about what Alicia had said.

"Is that the way David feels?"

"Yes, honestly, I think he disliked Robyn's treatment of you more than I did. He could tell that she loved you, and he didn't dislike her as a person; he just wanted better for you. I am sorry to say it so bluntly, but I feel like you deserve the truth."

"Alicia, don't bother David. This was all I needed. I just needed reassurance in what I was finally seeing. I did love her, and she loved me. We were great parents together, but I don't know if we were the best couple. I don't mean to speak ill of her, but I want to know what I feel now is right. Does that make sense?"

"Yeah, it does."

There was another quick pause before I said, "Hey, I'm going to go, but thanks so much. This was helpful."

"Matt, are you really happy?" Alicia asked.

"Yes, I am, Alicia. I really am. Monica has invited me to go with her to Pittsburgh for Thanksgiving and to meet her kids. I am excited to go. Plus, I start basketball coaching tomorrow. Things seem to be moving fast, but it feels so good. I feel like I'm alive again."

"Good. Stay happy."

"I hope so! Say hi to your husband for me."

"Will do!" she said.

I ended the call, went inside, and could still hear Monica talking, still naked in my bed, on her phone. I grabbed my laptop from my school bag and reviewed my plans for tomorrow's first day of practice. I felt overwhelmingly happy and confident. With Monica, I felt I could do anything.

A few minutes later, Monica came upstairs wearing one of my T-shirts. The shirt covered her down to her thighs, but it was obvious she wasn't wearing anything else. I liked the look.

"Ah, college drama," she said.

"Everything, okay?"

"In the grand scheme of things, yes, but it feels like the end of the world to Ashlynn. You know. She will be fine, but I am glad I will see her at Thanksgiving. And super, super glad that you are coming along!" she said, coming over and kissing me.

"I'm glad you are glad!"

"What are you doing?" she asked.

"Just looking things over for tomorrow's practice. And trying not to be nervous," I said, and laughed.

"Oh, well, I was hoping I could distract you and get you back in bed. If you're not too busy."

"Nope! All done!" I said, standing up and grabbing her hand.

We walked down to the bedroom, shed those clothes we had put on, and got back under the covers, but they were soon thrown back as we weren't there to snuggle and fall asleep!

Chapter 37

3 WEEKS LATER

Our plane landed in Pittsburgh on Wednesday, the day before Thanksgiving. Monica had found a townhouse rental for the weekend with two bedrooms and a large enough kitchen and dining area for a somewhat traditional Thanksgiving for Monica, Ashlynn, Nick, and me. I say somewhat because Monica and her kids had never had Thanksgiving in a rental with their mom and her boyfriend before!

Monica was super excited to see her kids, and I had shared that excitement for most of the month, but now, sitting in this taxi on our way to the rental, I was feeling nervous. The basketball season kept me so busy that I didn't have time to think about this situation. I was now concerned that this might be worse than meeting the parents. If the kids didn't like me, I might be in trouble. I hoped this would be a good time for everyone and not an awkward disaster.

Monica's phone buzzed with a text. Ashlynn told Monica that we should meet her at the athletic facility. She wanted to show us around before the building closed for the weekend. Monica and I both thought that would be good. We would love the "backstage" tour, and it would let Ashlynn meet me on her turf, where she would be more comfortable. That might be much better than having her show up at a rental house and meet me there.

So, after about a 20-minute ride from the airport, we quickly settled in the rental and then had another 20 minutes of walking to meet Ashlynn. She met us outside the huge Pitt Events Center building. She gave Monica a huge hug, and Monica introduced us. We shook hands and greeted each other, but Ashlynn was too excited to show us around to worry about any other conversation with me. That was probably for the best.

The tour was fun, and the facilities were great, but everyone was trying to get out for the Thanksgiving break. We ended the tour near the coach and administrators' offices, turning to make our way to the restrooms. There, we ran into Ashlynn's basketball coach. Pitt's head women's basketball coach, Coach Tibbets, had been there for many years. Ashlynn introduced us to him and didn't hesitate to introduce me as her mom's boyfriend. For now, it seemed like she was pretty comfortable with this arrangement.

We all stood there making small talk, but then, out of nowhere, Coach Tibbets said, "You look like you have played a lot of basketball."

I laughed. "Not for a long time. I was a good division three player but was absent from the game for a while. As luck would have it, I am just starting a coaching career. I am the new varsity girls coach at Ashlynn's old high school."

"Oh, how's that going?" he asked.

"Amazingly well. I have complete buy-in from the girls and a good roster. I have an awesome young point guard, a couple of good shooters, and a Division One prospect down low, and they play defense for me. The season just started, but we are 2-0, and things are going great. I hope I am not naive about what the season may hold!"

He laughed. "I am jealous. If it continues, I may have to hire you to coach my girls how to play defense! We need it," he said, and laughed again.

"Monica," he continued, "Ashlynn said your volleyball team just won the state title. Congratulations."

"Well, again, we had Matt helping. Maybe you can get the volleyball team to hire him here, too!"

The coach laughed and said, "Hey, great coaches are hard to find. Trust me. I should be going, but it was great to meet you." He looked at me and said, "What was your name again?"

"Matt Vasserheim."

"Right. Thanks again and have a great Thanksgiving. See you at practice, Ashlynn."

We continued on our way out and dropped Ashlynn off at her dorm.

"Are the dorms open over break?" I asked.

"Oh yeah. They only close them for winter break. And summer, obviously."

Monica chimed in.

"Well, good, because we only have one extra room, and Nick will be there."

"Mom, Nick's not going to stay at your rental," Ashlynn said.

"What do you mean?" Monica asked.

"He has a friend here on campus. Some guy he met at a baseball camp a few years ago. He is going to stay with him. He's a baseball player here at Pitt."

I could see Monica open her mouth to protest, but when she caught Ashlynn's look of disapproval, she closed it.

"What time do you want Nick and I to come to your rental tomorrow?" Ashlynn asked.

"We will eat at noon. I'm not doing anything big. I scheduled a grocery delivery tonight, but we aren't doing anything. Do you want to come over and grab dinner?" Monica asked.

"No, a bunch of us are going out tonight. We are going to enjoy a mostly empty campus. Just us athletes stuck here!"

"Oh, okay," Monica said.

I quickly stepped in and kept the conversation moving so Ashlynn could say goodbye.

"It was great to meet you, and thank you for the tour. I will see you tomorrow."

"Yeah, same," Ashlynn said, "I'm going to head off this way to my dorm."

She pointed to the right, and Monica and I realized that we had to go to the left. Monica hugged her and said goodbye, and we went our separate ways. I grabbed Monica's hand and led her off to our rental.

"You put at least two bottles of wine in that grocery order, right?" I asked.

Monica smiled at me and said, "Three, actually."

"Good. Let's go back, find a restaurant that delivers, wait for our deliveries, and enjoy our night alone."

Chapter 38

My expectations for a night alone with Monica in a rental differed greatly from what happened. When we returned to our rental and ordered food, Monica felt nauseous. Our grocery delivery came, and as we put those items away for tomorrow, Monica started suffering a headache. We wondered if food would improve her headache, but it didn't. When our Thai food came for dinner, we sat down at the little kitchen island to eat, but Monica just pushed her food around on her plate for a few minutes, then turned a sickly greenish color, and disappeared into the bathroom. Quickly.

The small rental only had one bathroom, and there wasn't a lot of sound insulation to hide the noise of her retching. I felt terrible for her as I sat there in the kitchen, already done with my dinner, waiting for her to, well, finish vomiting. The cessation of retching, followed by brief silence, was punctuated with the sound of the toilet flushing. This signaled what I hoped, for her sake, was the end of it all.

When Monica emerged from the bathroom, she wordlessly and purposefully went into the bedroom, and I followed. I found her next to the bed, and as she stripped down to her panties, I put my hand on the small of her back and steadied her as a precaution.

As she got into bed, she apologized, and I laughed, saying, "Monica, you have nothing to apologize for. I hope you feel better in the morning. Get some rest, and I will handle all the food tonight and tomorrow."

"You are the best. Thanks," she muttered.

"You are pretty damn awesome, yourself," I said and kissed her forehead and tucked the covers up around her even more.

I left, turning out the light, and she may have been asleep before I shut the door. I wasn't sure if I could pull off a Thanksgiving meal and impress my girlfriend's kids, but I would give it my best shot. Hopefully, Monica would feel better in the morning.

She didn't.

She spent a couple more sessions bowing down to the porcelain god in the bathroom in the middle of the night. Eventually, I slipped into bed beside her a couple of hours after she did, but my sleep wasn't good either. I was worried about Monica and woke every time she got up to go to the bathroom. Plus, I was worried about the next day. I needed to get up early and make this Thanksgiving dinner for Monica's two kids. I didn't even know if Monica could join us. She might be in bed the whole time, and I would have to get to know her kids. This made me nervous about this event all over again!

I woke at 5:50 and gave up trying to get more sleep. I also noted that Monica seemed to be sleeping comfortably now. This made me hope she was getting over whatever this illness was. I took that hope with me to the bathroom, as I decided to clean the bathroom first thing. If Monica needed to be sick again, so be it, but if she were on the road to recovery, this would make everyone feel better. That probably wouldn't be a good way to introduce myself to Monica's son.

"Welcome, nice to meet you. If you want to use the bathroom, avoid all the puke germs in there!"

This was not the start of the holiday I was looking for!

After scrubbing the bathroom and showering, I dressed quietly and left my sleeping girlfriend in the bedroom. I closed the door and walked into the kitchen. I wanted to get started with anything I needed to do, especially thawing the turkey. Luckily, we were smart enough to know we wouldn't pull off a completely home-cooked feast. Our menu included frozen turkey breast, boxed stuffing, mashed potatoes, and peas. The pumpkin pie was from the grocery store bakery. This Thanksgiving wasn't about the feast, but Monica being with her kids.

Monica had been talking to me a lot more about her kids recently. Being away at college during Monica's divorce was good and bad for them. It gave everyone their own space. That was good. Nick and Ashlynn were spared arguments and discussions about finances and new partners—a lot of the messy stuff. However, it also meant that the lines of communication broke down between them. There was an attitude on all sides of not bothering each other while everybody figured things out. Monica hated that and wanted it to change. This trip was a first step in rectifying that. That is why I felt a lot of pressure about the trip and wanted to do my best to step up.

I pulled the turkey breast out of the fridge and felt that the few hours there hadn't done much to thaw it out. So, I threw it into the sink with some cold water and hoped that would do the trick. Thanks to Monica planning this grocery order, we had everything we needed for seasoning and other ingredients. She had asked my opinion on the menu, and other than hearing that there would be no cranberries because nobody liked them, I thought it was fine. (I kept my disappointment of no cranberries and green bean casserole to myself.)

So, with the clock reading only 7:30 and the turkey not needing to go in for another two hours, I peeked in at Monica, who was still asleep, and then sat down to go over things for the basketball season.

At 9:30, I got a text from an unknown number. It was Ashlynn saying that her mom texted in the middle of the night, and she just got it. Monica had asked her to come early to help get the meal ready because she was sick. Ashlynn wanted to check in with me, so I decided to call her.

"Hey, Matt. How's Mom?" Ashlynn asked when she answered.

Her relaxed tone with me was a shockingly pleasant surprise. I liked that.

"I think she's better now," I said. "She had a bad night, but she is sleeping hard now. I hope she is feeling better by the time you get here."

Ashlynn said, "I hope it is just an overnight bug. Do you need me to come early?"

"If you want to, but no, I don't need help with the meal. It should be pretty easy."

"Okay. Just text me if you need anything. Otherwise, Nick will pick me up, and we will be there around noon."

"Sounds good!"

The impromptu phone call with my girlfriend's daughter going that well made me feel good. I already felt like Ashlynn had accepted me. After that, the rest of the morning flew by. I got the thawed turkey into the oven around 9:45, and everything else was easy. By 11:30, it looked like things were good, and I was surprised by the opening of the bedroom door. I turned to see Monica standing there, just staring at me.

"It smells really good," she said.

I walked over to her and held her in my arms.

"Are you feeling better?"

"Oh my god, yes! I don't know what that was all about, but it seems to be gone."

"Well, that's good. I talked to Ashlynn this morning, and she and Nick will be here in about 30 minutes, and everything should be ready. You can join us or return to bed—whatever works!" I said and kissed her on the forehead.

After I pulled away from her, Monica looked into my eyes but said nothing.

"What?" I asked.

"I just can't believe I found you. I love you so much."

My response was to move in to kiss her, but she recoiled.

"No, no. I am not kissing you with puke breath! I need to get cleaned up."

I laughed and dramatically gestured with my arm to invite her to use the bathroom. She laughed at this and disappeared through the door. Before she could shut it, though, she stopped.

"Wait, did you clean the bathroom?"

"Yeah, this morning before I showered."

"Okay, I take back what I said. I *really, really* love you!" she said, laughed, and shut the door.

As I finished getting everything ready, Monica and the kids arrived simultaneously—Monica from the bedroom, and the kids, obviously, through the front door. Both kids knew their mom had been sick, so they were pleasantly surprised to see her up and about.

"Geez, Mom, you had us worried that you were going to miss Thanksgiving," Ashlynn said.

"Well, that would mean more food for me, then!" Nick exclaimed and ignored his mother's glare.

"Nick, be nice to me. I've been up all night puking."

"Well, I hope you're not pregnant, Mom," Nick said.

Monica glared at him as I said, "Geez, I need to converse with her if she is. And, if I'm the father, then I need to have a conversation with the guy who did my vasectomy."

"Enough!" Monica said and then laughed. "This is way too much information *and* inappropriate, especially for Thanksgiving. But, to clarify, no, I am not pregnant."

"Thank god for that," I murmured.

Monica ignored me and brought Nick over to meet me.

"Matt, this is my son, Nick."

"Good to meet you, Nick. Sorry about the whole vasectomy comment. I probably should have waited until after I met you to start giving out details on my reproductive status."

Nick laughed, and Monica rolled her eyes.

"Good to meet you too, Matt. I'm glad my mom found someone who makes her happy. But jeez, Mom, you sure didn't waste any time. How exactly did you meet?"

"Well, Rachel, Ashlynn's old basketball coach, knew I was looking for a place to stay until I landed on my feet and the divorce was final. She and Matt talked; I got his number, texted him, came right over, looked at the place, and moved in immediately. But you are right, it was fast. Kind of love at first sight, I guess."

As Monica came over and wrapped her arms around me, I added, "It wasn't 'kind of' for me. It was definitely love at first sight." I smiled and kissed Monica on the top of her head.

"Okay, enough of the lovey-dovey stuff. Matt, are we ready to eat?" Monica asked as she pulled away from me and went into the kitchen.

"Yes, we are!" I said.

We all moved into the kitchen, where everyone helped me dish up food, and we crammed around the small dining table in the rental and ate. Monica did well; her stomach was over whatever hit her last night. The wine and conversation flowed freely, and I suddenly realized I was having a family Thanksgiving dinner. I hadn't had one since the accident, but it felt good. My nervousness had been replaced with feelings of comfort and love with Monica's kids. I found myself hoping that we could spend every Thanksgiving with her kids and be one big happy family.

Shit, I thought to myself, *you are getting way ahead of yourself again, Matt. Monica has talked to you about this, and you need to respect her desire not to be exclusive. Stop marrying her and adopting her kids right here in the dining room.*

"Matt?" Monica asked.

"What?"

"Ashlynn asked about your basketball season, but you seemed to have left us momentarily," Monica said, and laughed.

"Oh, sorry. Yeah, Ashlynn, what did you want to know?"

"How is the basketball season going?"

"Knock on wood, but so far, it is going great! I inherited a good returning team. Plus, Rachel laid everything out for me, and your mom taught me a lot about coaching."

"I hear you have a good freshman point guard," Ashlynn stated.

"Yes, Amanda Stokes. She is talented and a hard worker. That makes my job easy."

Monica added, "But Matt is a really good coach. He knows his technical stuff, but he connects well with the kids. That's what I am jealous of. He is the kind of coach you *want* to play for. He is knowledgeable, but he makes sure you know he believes in you. Plus, he knows how to motivate at the right times. He is one of those annoying coaches who knows exactly what his team needs at a specific moment."

"Well, that is just taking the time to get to know the individual. That's basically what leadership is all about. You can't force a square peg into a round hole. If you know your players, you can more easily motivate and teach them. I am a teacher. That's my job. I take that same mentality to the court. However, and I learned this a long time ago from my college coach, you always need to remember that the players play the game. The preparation, planning, and strategizing sometimes go out of the window. You sometimes have to put your team on the court and let them play."

"Wow, that is cool to hear. I think you would be really good here at Pitt," Ashlynn said. "I would like to play for a coach like you."

"Ha! I don't think any Division One programs are looking for a guy with only one year of experience in high school coaching. But I will keep my eyes open," I said with a laugh.

As dinner was finished, and we dug into pumpkin pie, it felt like the day had been an incredible success. I was even introduced to another family tradition Monica failed to tell me about. There was mention of a traditional holiday movie that needed to be watched. I was expecting some old, sweet, and innocent movie. The movie turned out to be "Die Hard." Many years before, Monica's family had a good-spirited argument about "Die Hard" being a holiday movie at Thanksgiving dinner. This had led to them watching it every year since then on Thanksgiving. It was a fun way to end a wonderful day with Nick and Ashlynn. As they said their goodbyes, and both surprised me with hugs before walking out of our rental, I didn't think this Thanksgiving could get any better.

It turned out that I was very wrong about that, however!

Chapter 39

As soon as the door closed and Monica and I were alone, I felt Monica's hand on my ass. As she kept her hand there, rubbing my ass through my pants, she came up behind me and whispered in my ear, "Take me to the bedroom. We have a lot of time to make up from last night."

I turned toward her and took her mouth with mine. My tongue probed into her mouth as she did the same in mine. I backed her up toward the bedroom, moving slowly, our mouths never ceasing their connection. Passion radiated off Monica's body as we moved through the bedroom doorway, and I pushed her back against the bed. I assumed she would fall back into bed, but instead, she broke our kiss and sat. Her hands went up and underneath my shirt, rubbing up to my pecs and then back down to my abs. The quick move was so sensual that my eyes closed, and my head leaned back. It took me a moment to realize that her hands didn't stop there. Monica undid my pants, pulled them down to my knees, and took my cock, hands-free, into her mouth. She sucked the head of my now incredibly hard cock as her hands moved to my hips. Her tongue started moving on the underside of my shaft while her mouth continued to work the engorged head of my cock. My head was bobbing back and forth as I tried to watch her pleasure me, but I couldn't fight my head rocking back with each pleasurable sensation that would overwhelm me and close my eyes.

After only a few moments, I couldn't take it anymore. I reached down and pulled her up, off my cock, and up to my mouth. We kissed, our tongues tangling again, and then I broke the kiss and said breathlessly, "I want to taste a different part of you!"

I led her down to the bed gently, and she laid back, spreading her legs for me. She knew exactly what I was thinking. I knelt on the bedroom rug and licked up her slit, stopping with my tongue flat and pressing on the nub of her clit. I then worked circles on her clit with my tongue while I grabbed onto her hips, holding on for dear life. My tongue felt like the strongest muscle in my body. It felt like I could do this forever. I felt that I *wanted* to do this forever! Her pussy was so responsive, so wet. Her moans told me that she wanted this and much more. I moved my tongue down to lick her slit a few more times before plunging my tongue inside of her, tasting the wondrous musk of her pussy.

After tongue fucking her, I pulled out, spread her pussy lips, and sucked that hard nub into my mouth. I suckled on it like a nipple, and Monica started practically hyperventilating. Her body started spasming as I continued to suck, rather aggressively, on her clit. Soon, the spasms and breathing hit the wall. Monica sucked in a deep breath, froze for that second, and then her whole body exploded with a scream. Her legs shook as her pussy dripped on my chin. I removed my mouth from her, gave her slit one last lick, savoring the taste of her juices, and then flipped her body so she was lying on her stomach. Monica was still trying to settle her body and catch her breath from her first orgasm, but I had no intention of pausing. Just as she started to catch her breath and quiet herself, I pulled her ass up into the air and pulled that beautifully toned ass back to the edge of the bed and buried my cock in her wetness. Monica's cry of surprise and pleasure barely registered as I wasted no time pumping furiously in and out of her. I knew that I was not going to last long as pre-cum was already obviously dripping off my cock before I even entered her. Monica's screams now came, full focus, into my consciousness, and I thought that she might be already building another orgasm.

My god, I thought, *I know I have something to do with it, but her ability to build so quickly to powerful orgasms, multi-orgasms actually, is just incredible.*

I focused on those screams and the feeling of her body as I continued to pump inside her pussy. My cock was now almost burning with the sensation, the desire, to have a powerful orgasm of my own, but it was like I was linked to Monica's body. I somehow couldn't release it until I made sure she exploded with me. My pumping and her screams seemed to synchronize into one rhythm as our bodies built to orgasm. Her vaginal muscles started contracting around me, and I knew she was close. I somehow found another gear in my body and pumped as hard as I could until finally, Monica let out an incredible scream, her muscles clenched powerfully around me, and I buried myself as deep as possible as I shot rope after rope of thick cum into her. My scream practically matched hers as my whole body shivered, and my cock pulsated endlessly. Again, the power of this orgasm was overwhelming. My balls almost hurt from how drained they were, and the orgasm sensation went into my stomach.

I think any other time in my life, I would have been too spent to do anything but collapse next to my partner, but with Monica, who was seemingly built for endless sex, I always felt invincible and insatiable. That is why, when I pulled out, I immediately but gently slid her off the bed and onto the floor. Monica was still trying to catch her breath but was frozen in that doggy-style position. I had been counting on that, and when I got her turned on the rug so we could both be comfortable, I positioned my face right on her beautiful ass. I focused on her beautiful puckered back door entrance, and my tongue wanted this taste tonight. I couldn't help but notice my cum leaking out of her pussy and forming a trail down her thigh. I started with some kisses on her back and then trailed my tongue down her spine, down her tailbone, into her ass crack, and ended down at her pussy, tasting my juices mixed with hers. I then brought my tongue back up her crack and then continued licking up and down her ass crack as Monica started to moan yet again. I was doing this slowly, not wanting to rush this. I wanted to take my time to ensure we had time to recover and build up again. I also wanted to savor the earthy and musky taste of her. Since I had never done anything close to anal sex with Robyn, I was still fairly new to this activity, and I couldn't believe how much I loved it. I loved the taste, the sounds Monica made, and how she would massage her clit like crazy when I did it, which she had started doing now. That realization brought an end to my gentle licking. I gave her one more lick, starting at her pussy and then ending with my tongue right on her tight hole. My tongue zeroed in on her opening, and my tongue circled and licked her, probing just a little bit now and then. Finally, after teasing Monica with my tongue, I gave in and did what we both wanted. I probed my tongue as deep into her ass as I could, circling her canal and driving her crazy. Her moans and clit massage both picked up in pace, as did the ferocity of my tongue. I was working my tongue so vigorously that I soon lost that invincibility I had before. My tongue was worn out and sore, but my fingers were perfect. I pulled away from Monica's ass, sucked my index finger and middle finger wet, and then slid them slowly inside her, not going deep but slowly pumping those two fingers inside her. This was simply a warm-up, a literal stretch, for what was coming next. However, Monica didn't seem to be feeling it that way. Instead of this being a moment to calm down and let her body adjust, she almost growled, "Yes! Pump those fingers in my ass. Please make me come again!"

So much for a slow warm-up, I thought!

My fingers picked up the pace, and this went from a gentle warm-up to finger-blasting Monica's ass in about two seconds. This sped-up pace did not diminish Monica's dirty talk at all.

"Yes, yes. Finger fuck my ass! I'm going to come again!" she half-growled, half whispered. Her body couldn't focus on making a strong vocal noise. Everything was focused on her orgasm.

And that orgasm came fast. Monica's anus started clenching and releasing around my fingers, almost like those muscles were pulsing with the convulsions that had started again in her legs and back. This time, however, there was no "eye of the storm," no inhalation of breath while her body froze and released in a huge spasm. This time, she skipped that part. Her anus stopped pulsing and just clenched down hard on my fingers, sucking them as deep into her as they could be. Her body shook visibly, and her guttural cries were as staccato and uncontrolled as the spasms in her body.

I left my fingers buried in her as her body finally started to relax. As her clenching muscles allowed me to retract my fingers, I pulled them out very slowly. Her gasp told me this incredibly gorgeous and insatiable woman was still not done. And I knew exactly how to help.

I pulled Monica back up on the bed and flipped her over again, this time on her back. I pushed her legs up toward her head, and she caught her legs under the knees and in her hands. She was now spread-eagle, displaying her soaked and stretched pussy and ass. It was a beautiful sight as I lined my throbbing cock up to her asshole and pushed inside slowly. Her ass took me with ease but also with incredible tightness.

I almost lost control and came right then as I buried myself inside her, and she automatically started working her clit again with her hand. I started pumping moderately, but with her masturbating, moaning, and looking directly into my eyes while I fucked her ass, moderately was soon long gone. This went into an animalistic frenzy. This scene continued for a bit, but as we quickly built together, I knew I was a goner. My legs locked stiff as I grunted out each pulse of my orgasm. Monica joined me with grunts of her own as she seemed to orgasm with me. Yet another orgasm for this woman who made me feel like the luckiest guy in the world.

I pulled out, my cock super sensitive, and the rest of my body spent. I crawled onto the bed awkwardly and rested beside Monica, staring at the ceiling while we tried to catch our breaths.

Finally, Monica said, "That was incredible."

"Which time?"

"Every time."

"Exactly," was all I could say in response.

Nothing more was said as we crawled into bed, and I held her in my arms. We both fell asleep instantly.

Chapter 40

I woke up the next morning, confused. I had been having a weird dream where I was trying desperately to walk through the shopping mall I went to a lot in high school. I had my high school friends with me, and they were giving me shit about being a virgin. The other complication was that the mall was full of people walking the other way. We were trying to fight through the crowds but constantly losing the battle, going the wrong way on this seemingly one-way path.

I couldn't take it anymore in the dream, so I ditched everyone and stepped into a store. It was a boutique women's clothing store, and nobody was in it except the clerk, who turned out to be Monica.

"Good morning," she said, and walked up to me.

I didn't respond.

"I really, really like your big dick."

At this, she, oblivious to the shopping mall that had somehow disappeared behind me, opened my pants, pulled them down to my thighs, and relished watching my erection spring up from my pants. Her tongue rolled slowly, involuntarily, over her lips. Her right hand reached out and grabbed my cock tightly and started in with long strokes up and down my shaft. That was the end of the dream.

So my confusion upon waking was why the dream was over, but the hand job continued. I quickly came to my senses and realized Monica was giving me a wake-up hand job.

Monica realized I was awake now and smiled at me.

"I thought we had enough of a break, so I woke you up to continue last night," she said quietly, but her voice dripped with eroticism.

"Best wake-up call ever!" I whispered back. The haze of sleep and the movement of her hand made it difficult to get the words out.

"Now that you are awake, I need you on your knees. Flip over!" she directed.

I did as she said, not realizing what her plan was. Her hand left me as I changed positions, and I was vaguely aware that she was getting something off the nightstand. The unmistakable clicking sound of a flip-top lid on a bottle had me guessing what she was doing, but before my muddled mind had it figured out, Monica's hand was wrapped around me, back stroking me, with a warming lube now making the sensation unbelievably pleasurable.

"Oh wow, that feels good."

"Oh yeah? How about if I do this?" and her tongue licked my asshole.

I can't begin to describe the shudder of absolute ecstasy that action gave me. I didn't even utter a coherent word. It was simply a gasp, a guttural cry, as her tongue and hand worked in a rhythmic duet of rim and hand job. The sensation was almost too much; no, too *new* is a better description. This was an act I had never done before I met Monica, and when she performed it on me, my brain went into overload. I didn't want to orgasm; I wanted this to go on forever.

However, it didn't. Monica stopped everything and paused. I could tell she was using the lube again, but I couldn't see anything. My ass was up in the air, and my head was buried in the pillow. But, just as suddenly as she stopped, she was back at it. Her hand and tongue returned to their same speed.

Monica never wavered with the hand on my erection, but her tongue gave me a few more circular motions and then stopped.

"Don't stop, please!" I begged in a desperate and horse whisper. But Monica ignored me. Instead of her tongue returning, two lubed fingers entered me slowly. The cry I made now was guttural, and loud. This new sensation, as my body stretched to accommodate her, as every sensitive nerve ending back there fired at 1,000 percent, sent me practically into convulsions. My breath tore out of me as previously unbeknownst sensations and pleasure radiated through my body.

When she had her fingers as deep as possible, Monica kept them unmoving. Her other hand kept moving up and down my shaft, mixing warm lube and warm pre-cum as my body tried to overcome the absolute mindfuck of what was happening to me.

Monica, however, did not let that happen.

Those two fingers started moving inside me, massaging my prostate and making me cry out even louder now. She was massaging my prostate, jerking me off vigorously, and the pinky finger of the hand that was half buried inside me was rubbing against my balls.

I came.

No, that's not a fair description. I don't know how many times I had orgasmed in my life, but each time before this, I had some build and warning that it was going to happen. This was not that at all. Out of nowhere, cum exploded out of me! With the loudest exclamation of my life, my balls tightened and then powerfully shot rope after rope of cum onto the bed, my hips and abs spasming with each release.

Each pulse of orgasm seemed to bring another cry, almost like I was echoing that initial exclamation.

Eventually, while I rested there on my knees, Monica's right hand pulled away from my backside, and her hand stopped milking my softening cock. She slid her mouth up to my ear and whispered, "I always thought you were super quiet during sex, but not after that! I think you liked that!"

She tried to be cute while I caught my breath, and my body returned to normal. However, that was not what was going on at all.

With a frenzy, I suddenly and frantically pulled up, grabbed Monica, got her in the same head-down, ass-up position, grabbed the lube, squeezed some in my hand, and ate her ass out aggressively. I ignored her cute little gasp at my aggression and moved my tongue around as deep inside her as I could get. I was buying time to get hard again, which wasn't long. I stroked that warming lube on my cock and buried myself into Monica's already wet pussy.

There was no slow, no gentle, no lovemaking.

I fucked her. Doggy style. Hard.

After we came and collapsed on the bed, Monica breathed out, "What the fuck was that? What happened to my sweet guy? Where is Matt, and who is this backshot, sex stud in my bed?"

"Very funny," I said, "but the better question is, what orgasm planet are you from? I mean, no human can be that amazing at sex, right?"

Monica laughed and kissed me. "Hey, can I help that we are perfectly compatible and that you seem more than willing to let me corrupt you?"

"Excellent point!" I said, and kissed her again.

"Unfortunately," Monica said, "we have a plane to catch."

"Okay, fine. We will take a break today, but I get you tonight at home!"

Monica got up to go to the bathroom.

"Okay, but jeez, you are a horn dog!" she said, and laughed.

"That's all your fault!" I yelled as she closed the door to the bathroom.

I could hear her laugh through the door.

Chapter 41

The next few months seemed to breeze by in a cloud of ecstasy. My life, in some ways, had never been better. I know how callous that sounds to the life I had before with my wife and kids, but I had a lot to be happy about. The basketball team went undefeated and captured the school's first-ever championship in boys or girls history. I had now been a part of coaching two straight undefeated state championship teams in Waterton. It was an amazing feeling.

Monica and I were fantastic. Our relationship was still as sexual as ever, but that was the least of it. We built a life together, and she quickly became my best friend. We shared so much, and she was my biggest champion when it came to the basketball team. Plus, we were now biking together when the winter weather allowed, and I loved it. We felt like partners in everything, and it seemed like I loved her more every day.

I also realized I had been unfair to my wife's memory over the past few months. Robyn and I were perfect for each other when we married. However, I think we lost a lot of "us" when we became parents. We lost that sense of partnership that Monica and I seemed to have in everything. We became a parenting team and stopped being lovers, which was a mistake. I don't know what our future would have been together if she hadn't been killed. However, the thing I did know was that I needed to come to grips with the fact that I had not focused on the grief I was going through for my kids. Ashlynn and Nick had made me realize how much I missed them. I had spent so much time grieving Robyn and celebrating Monica that I had not focused on them. My therapist and I worked on this, and Monica was overwhelmingly supportive. I felt like everything was perfect!

However, soon after the state championship, Monica took a call from Ashlynn. I could tell it wasn't good, but Monica just blamed homesickness. I let it go for a few days, but then Monica took another call from her, and the process kept repeating itself. I was starting to get worried about things with Ashlynn, but Monica said it wasn't a big deal. I knew it was bothering her, though. This was maybe the first bump in the road we had experienced since our "breakup" back in the volleyball season. I knew she had something to say, but she kept it to herself. That bothered me, but I figured she would come to me when it was time. I wasn't going to push it. However, a phone call I received from Pittsburgh changed everything in one fell swoop.

On a quiet evening in early March, Monica wasn't home from work yet. I had a college basketball game on the television and was checking my Instagram account when my phone rang. It came up as a Pittsburgh number, which made me think of Ashlynn. I was worried that she was in trouble. But the voice that greeted me when I said hello was not Ashlynn's. It was a man's voice.

"Hello, Matt?"

"Yes, this is Matt."

"Hi, Matt, this is Coach Dale Tibbets. We met a few months ago, around Thanksgiving."

"Sure! Yes. How are you?" I questioned while trying not to sound too confused about this call.

"Well, to be honest, I could be better."

Coach Tibbets didn't give me time to respond. He launched right into the issue.

"Matt, our season here is almost over. We will not be going to any postseason tournaments, which isn't a big surprise, granted how young we are. But it is the modern age, and we need to get something built here that is better than what we have. I am an old-school coach and set in my ways. However, I now see that I need to change things around here. I feel that my staff and I are excellent in the strategy and teaching of the game, but we are older and need a better connection to the young players today."

He paused, and I thought I should say something, but I had no idea what this was about. Why was a major college coach calling me and discussing the problems with his program?

I responded with a slightly forced, "What can I do for you?"

"Well, I will tell you that I have been talking to Ashlynn about you and your basketball team for some time this season. I heard you won the state championship in your first year of coaching. Congratulations. That is a tremendous job and points to you being a talented coach and leader. But, I was interested in how much Ashlynn discussed you connecting with your players. She said the players bought in immediately and loved playing for you. That got me thinking about how we didn't have that here."

He paused again and I still wasn't sure what he wanted from me. Maybe he was calling to congratulate me? But this seemed like too much information to share for a congratulatory call. Was he asking for advice? I didn't think any major college coach would call a somewhat random high school basketball coach to ask for advice. That seemed silly and, to be honest, unprofessional.

"Coach, thanks for the congratulations. It was a magical season. I was lucky to have a lot of help, especially our former coach and Ashlynn's mom. I really enjoyed it. I think there was a bit of beginner's luck, too!" I said, and laughed, possibly a bit awkwardly.

I didn't know what else to say other than asking what the hell this phone call was about.

"Well, here's the thing, I think I need a younger voice, like yours, who can connect with players today, in the gym and on the recruiting trail. I don't know what you think about your coaching career, but I have learned this week that I am losing one of my assistants. I am very impressed with what I have seen of your young career and what Ashlynn has told me. We need a more out-of-the-box hire, and I was wondering what you thought about coming to Pitt and being an assistant here under me."

I was dumbfounded. Never in a million years did I think anything like this would happen. Rachel jumped to the college ranks, but that was after years of success at the high school level, and her jump had only been to a small college. Granted, Rachel was a head coach, and I was looking at only an assistant coach position, but it could turn into something else down the line. As "Matt Vasserheim, national head coach of 2040," flashed through my mind, I was also brought down to earth with the reality.

"Wow, Coach Tibbets, that is an incredible offer. I would almost immediately say yes, but I need to consider it. I have been in Waterton for several years and have a good teaching career, and Ashlynn's mom and I are finding our relationship pretty serious. My life has already radically changed in the past year and a half. So maybe your offer is the perfect conclusion to that or," I paused, "it may be too much right now. Can I take some time to think about it?"

"Certainly! No changes will take place until after the conference tournament. I know there is a chance we could win that and get an automatic berth to the postseason, but as I said, that is the only way we will get a postseason invite,"

Tibbets said. "Take some time and see what you think. I will text you the basketball office number after I hang up. You can contact me through them if you have questions."

"Okay. Wow. Again, Coach, thanks for the offer. I will consider it and get back to you. I'm very pleasantly surprised."

"Great! I think you would be a great addition to the team."

With that, he said goodbye and ended the call.

I stood there just staring at my phone. I didn't know what to do or say. Then, the front door opened, and Monica walked in. I swear that my blank look was matched by Monica's. It was like looking in a mirror.

She looked at me and said, "You look like you have seen a ghost. What's going on?"

"Well, I don't know how to start. However, it looks like you have a similar problem. And, if I may be so bold, I think you have had something to say for a while. Do you want to go first?"

"Oh. Well, I don't know how to get into this because I... I have a lot to say. *I* don't know where to start,"

I looked at her and smiled. "Hey, it's me. Just start at the beginning."

Monica stared at the floor, her hand rubbing her mouth as she considered what she would say. Suddenly, her head snapped up, and she looked at me.

"Do you know how in love with you I am?" she asked.

"Yeah, you tell me—"

"No," she interrupted, "I mean to say, I am more in love with you than you know. I didn't want a serious relationship. I didn't want to feel excited by a new man and get butterflies whenever I saw him. I wanted to have fun and see lots of people. But all of that has changed. I want you and *only* you. I get so excited every night to come home to you. I can't wait to be with you every night. You are like the partner and best friend in my life. I didn't think I wanted that, but you are just perfect. And I think we are perfect together."

I smiled and started to speak, but Monica cut me off.

"And don't you dare say, ...in bed!"

This made me laugh, and I kissed her.

"Well, we are perfect ... in bed! But before I tell you that I feel the same way, I feel there is more to it than that."

"Yes, there is," Monica said.

Her face returned to staring at the floor, and I knew something bad was coming. I tipped her head up and made her look into my eyes.

"Just tell me. If we are so perfect together, we can handle this. Together. Whatever it is," I whispered.

"Ashlynn is having a hard time with everything outside of school. The divorce, her distance from me, her social life at Pitt, everything. And even though the school and sports stuff is going well, she wants me closer. So, I have been looking into it, and work can transfer me to Pittsburgh. But... but I don't want to leave *you*," she exclaimed as tears formed in her eyes.

I stepped back, tilted my head to the ceiling, and let loose with the biggest laugh I had experienced since my wife and kids died.

Monica's teary face now expressed confusion.

"What's so funny?" she asked. I think she was a little hurt.

"Well, do you want to hear my news now?" I asked and continued without letting her answer. "Your wonderful daughter has been letting her basketball coach know all about my exploits and successes here as a coach. I just got off the phone with him, and he shocked me by asking me to join his staff as an assistant coach. So, as of ten minutes ago, I am also looking to move to Pittsburgh!"

Monica looked at me in total surprise. Her mouth hung open.

I returned to her, kissed her again, and asked, "So, do you want to move to Pittsburgh with me?"

Her kiss was the only response I needed!

Chapter 42

Saying goodbye to Waterton was much easier than I ever thought. I had never even considered it after Robyn and the kids died. It seemed so difficult to deal with so much change in my life at that time that I didn't want to add it to my mental distress. However, now, my mind was in a place where I was loving all the positive changes in my life over the past ten months. Besides leaving the basketball team after only one year, moving was easy. My remodeled house was move-in-ready for a new buyer. The house was on the market for only four days and sold over the asking price. Monica didn't have a house, and her work transfer was easy. I just needed to finish the school year in May, and we could leave.

Monica and I had no problems moving on. We both felt that our lives were done in Waterton and, more importantly, that our location didn't matter as long as we were together. Things had changed so much that Monica surprised me with a confession the night before we left.

"Matt, I know I have been clear about not wanting anything too serious, but I am rethinking that."

"So, let me get this straight: You love me and want me to move with you to another state and leave my life here behind? Yeah, I assumed you were getting serious about us," I said, and laughed.

Monica returned my laugh. "Yeah, I know you know that, but I am just telling you, when I told you I wanted to have fun, I didn't think I could have so much fun with just one person. But I do with you," she said, and paused. "I never thought I could have such a good life with one person, but I have that with you. I love you so much."

I looked at her with a very puzzled and serious look.

"So, no swinger parties when we get to Pittsburgh? Not even returning for Deborah's planned all-woman party?"

"Oh, hell no. I am still coming back to Waterton for that. Matt, I have to fulfill my commitments."

I laughed and grabbed her hand. "Come here. I need to make love to you one last time in this house."

I pulled her close to me, and she moved in to kiss me, but I dropped to my knees before she could connect and slid her yoga pants and panties down to her ankles in one motion. As I pulled them off her right foot, I buried my face into her musk. She automatically spread her right leg out, opening her legs and offering herself to my mouth. I spread her labia apart and focused the tip of my tongue on her clit, gently licking it up and down and then twirling my tongue around it, tasting the wonderful wetness as Monica responded to the action. However, as Monica moaned her first loud moan, I pulled my tongue back and closed my lips around her clit, sucking it into my mouth. Monica gasped, and I continued to suckle on her clit.

"Oh my god, Matt, please don't stop that. I am going to come so fast!"

I didn't change a thing. I stayed right there, sucking her off, until her hand gripped my hair, pulling my head in tighter. I continued to suck as her pussy juices dripped down my chin, and her legs tightened together, clamping around my head. Monica, with a shudder, screamed out as her orgasm shook her body and, likewise, my head, clamped firmly against her sex, my mouth still sucking.

Suddenly, Monica pulled my head away from her and gasped, "I'm too sensitive. I can't take anymore."

I sucked in a big breath since I hadn't been able to breathe for a bit, but before Monica could move, I grabbed her and led her over to the one plush chair we hadn't sent in the moving truck to Pittsburgh.

"I have an idea," I said.

Monica nodded, still in an orgasm haze, but I wasn't about to give her a break.

"Sit upside down in the chair so your head hangs over the seat a bit," I told her.

Monica was able to do this rather quickly, and I gave her props for it. She now had her back on the seat and her butt and legs against the back of the chair. I brought my cock to her mouth, and she opened it for me. As my cock slid into her warm mouth, I leaned forward and sunk my face into her pussy. Luckily, the chair was sturdy enough for this!

This position was a complete improvisation, and I couldn't believe how well it worked. Unfortunately, it started working too well for me after a few moments. Monica's mouth had me close to coming, and I reared back from her pussy and stood there, slowly pumping my cock in her mouth. Just as my balls tightened, I pumped my cock harder, and I felt it slide back into Monica's throat. This sensation caused me to fuck her mouth hard for about three thrusts until, on my final thrust, I stayed there against the back of her throat and emptied myself into her. My body shook as my cum dribbled back down out of her mouth.

I helped her off the chair and led her to my bedroom and the twin mattress we would try to share tonight.

"Damn, Matt. That was really kinky. Did you make that up on the spot?"

"Yes, I did!"

"If you're going to be that inventive and kinky, maybe we don't need to find swinging parties in Pittsburgh," Monica said, and laughed.

My response was to kiss her and gently push her toward the bed. Her head went down on the mattress, and her ass went up in the air. Automatically, my tongue went straight to her puckered back door. No licking. No teasing. My tongue probed right into her anus, the earthy taste of her fueling my lust. With my tongue fucking her back door and Monica working her clit, I could already feel my balls get heavy and my hard cock starting to form pre-cum. My recovery from the chair was almost superhuman! I knew I needed to move fast before I lost it right here. I pulled my tongue out, grabbed the lube bottle I had remembered *not* to pack away, and slicked my cock up. I slid easily into Monica and matched her exclamation as I groaned loudly. In pure pleasure, as I felt every inch of her anal canal envelope me, I paused briefly, burying myself as deep in her ass as I could. My brain told me to take it easy and not move fast, but my cock wanted to pound her. It was Monica who answered the dilemma before I could decide or move.

"Fuck me, Matt! Fuck my ass *hard*!" she screamed.

I pulled back, again feeling every inch of her, and then slammed back into that hole as deep as possible. My hands gripped Monica's hips as my hips started in at a punishing pace, and Monica and I both fell into an animalistic passion. We were loud, we were sweaty, we were oblivious to anything else.

"I'm gonna come!" I grunted.

Monica screamed out, and her ass clenched around me as I exploded inside her. I dropped my head and body onto her back, hugging her close. My cock was softening, but still in her ass, as we caught our breath.

Eventually, still saying nothing, we both cuddled into the bed sheets, and I continued to spoon her. Finally, as we drifted to sleep, Monica said, "Matt, you know that when I showed up here, I was committed to never marrying again?"

"No, I didn't know that," I said softly.

"Well, I've changed my mind."

"Umm. Do you have anyone in mind?"

"Yeah, the guy holding me right now."

"Good. I don't plan on letting go!"

With that, I pulled her closer, and we fell asleep for the last time at my Waterton house.

It was July, and for once, I was thinking of the anniversary of the day I met Monica and not about the day my dad died or the accident that took my wife and kids from me. I was now living in a new city, in a new state, with a new job and relationship, and I was happier than I ever thought I could be. If you had talked to me 12 months ago, I think you would have seen a man who was defeated and depressed—a man who had given up on love, happiness, and, to some degree, life. Now, I was living a new life and loving every minute. I had hit the ground running with the Pitt women's basketball team, and everything felt right. I felt that my place as assistant coach at this level wasn't that much different from what I had done with Monica's volleyball team almost a year ago. My connection to the athletes was almost more important than my game knowledge. Coach Tibbets had been great in introducing me to the staff, and they immediately accepted me, the novice, into their ranks. The learning curve hit me hardest with the recruiting rules and process. But now that the July recruiting dead period had just ended, Coach Tibbets asked me to be with him on the official visit meetings that had started up. I found that Coach Tibbets and I were on the same page about what we wanted for the team and how these recruits stacked up. We both surprised each other after one recruit left a meeting with us, and we both looked at each other and said, "Nope!" in unison.

Monica's job had gone better than expected, too. Monica had expected her job with the bank to be similar to that in the small branch in Waterton. However, there is much more turnover in a big city, and soon after arriving, they moved her up considerably in the ranks. She is now in the process of interviewing for the chief financial officer position and believes she has a very good chance of getting it. Life has moved very fast for both of us.

That night, at home, we had Ashlynn over for supper, and she had been teasing us about when we would get married. Monica and I deflected well and especially didn't let on that we had been having some preliminary discussions about it. Well, maybe nothing too serious, but we had been throwing out ideas about how we would like to do it. The idea of getting married again did not frighten me one bit. Spending the rest of my life with this woman was a no-brainer.

As Ashlynn left for her apartment after supper, Monica's got a text.

"It's Deborah," Monica said.

"Oh, is she planning the all-female party?"

"No, it is actually about that murder that happened next door to them, but you certainly seem excited for that all-female sex party to happen." She smiled at me and said, "Obsessed much with the all-women orgy?"

"Hey, umm, no! I just... Well, yeah, I kind of am. I want lots of details after!"

Monica laughed. "I don't tend to kiss and tell, so do you think I am going to eat pussy and tell?"

"God damn, I hope so!"

Monica laughed. "The other part of her message is that she is delaying the all-girl party so I can make it back, and she and Lane hosted another one with straight couples. Do you remember that Lainey girl from the last party?

"Of course. How could I forget?"

"Are you referring to the fact that she blew your mind, among other things, or that she was once your student?" Monica asked with a teasing tone in her voice.

"Shit," I breathed out, "both!"

"Well, Lainey brought some friends along this time, and Deborah said getting some new people involved was awesome. She also added that the stamina of 20-somethings is unbelievable."

"Yeah, sorry about us old guys," I said with fake sadness.

"Oh honey," Monica said as she stepped close and started stroking the crotch of my pants, "there is nothing wrong with your stamina."

We kissed and, of course, then moved to the bedroom. It was time to put that stamina to the test.

Book Club Questions

1. Do you think Matt and Monica will get married and live happily ever after?

2. Do you think Matt was fully healed from his trauma, or did he still have things to work out?

3. Did Matt take Monica back too easily after she walked out on him?

4. Do you think that Matt's guilt following his non-Monica hookups showed his dedication to Monica or his lack of healing after the trauma he had gone through?

5. Do you think Matt will continue his success in basketball coaching, or will that be short-lived?

6. Will Monica miss her successful coaching job, or will she enjoy her newfound success in Pittsburgh?

7. What was your favorite scene from this book?

8. Which of the characters in this book would you like a follow-up book written about?

9. How embarrassing would it be to learn at a party that you were with a former student, as Matt did with Lainey?

10. Is a girls sports dynasty starting in Waterton? Were Matt and Monica foolish to leave that behind?

Author Bio

Dixon Ahl-Knight is a small-town Iowa-born author who loves the idea of passion and excitement in fiction *and* reality! Well-versed in the music/audio production industry, DAK decided to enter the book industry and bring the stories and fantasies of his imagination to print. When not working in the media industries, DAK can be found devouring the books of others, running, listening to underground music, and embarrassing his wife and kids with his silly antics and juvenile sense of humor!

Find Dixon online at @DixonAhlKnight on X, Dixon_ahlknight on Instagram, Dixon Ahl-Knight on Facebook, and dixonahlknight on TikTok. Feel free to email Dixon at dixonahlknight@gmail.com.

Discover more at
4HorsemenPublications.com

10% off using HORSEMEN10